WITHOUT

PRECEDENT

WITHOUT PRECEDENT

J.D. TRAFFORD

THOMAS & MERCER

Text copyright © 2019 by J. D. Trafford
All rights reserved.

No part of this book may be reproduced, or stored in a retrieval system, or transmitted in any form or by any means, electronic, mechanical, photocopying, recording, or otherwise, without express written permission of the publisher.

Published by Thomas & Mercer, Seattle

www.apub.com

Amazon, the Amazon logo, and Thomas & Mercer are trademarks of Amazon.com, Inc., or its affiliates.

ISBN-13: 9781542040327
ISBN-10: 1542040329

Cover design by Ray Lundgren

Printed in the United States of America

First edition

For my father, always optimistic even in passing.
"Somebody has to win the lotto, why not me?"
—JDT

WITHOUT PRECEDENT

Adjective. In the law, a case described as "without precedent" presents a new legal issue or original question of law for which there is no binding authority from an appellate court; such a case presents a novel state of facts involving a question of law never before determined by a court or finder of fact.

CHAPTER ONE

Here's a little secret: most lawyers never see the inside of a courtroom. They sit at a desk, making phone calls, reviewing documents, combing through electronic legal databases, and writing memos. On a good day, they get the privilege to walk down the hall and meet a client in a beige conference room. On a *very* good day, they get to eat lunch at a somewhat fancy restaurant after that client meeting.

The restaurant, of course, would be one conducive to professionals with expense accounts. That means it has cloth napkins, a decent chicken Caesar salad, interesting art on the walls, and prices that are high, but not so high that the pencil pusher in accounting balks at the reimbursement request.

I've never been one of those attorneys. I am a litigator. Lesser attorneys might be content spending their days drafting a will for an old lady or negotiating a contract to buy a building. That, however, wasn't for me.

At one time, I was a hired gun. Corporations paid ridiculous amounts of money for me to go to court and do battle. It was a game, and I was very good at playing the game. My confidence was my greatest asset and also, I've come to understand, my greatest weakness. It blinded me to the unwritten principles of the practice of law: first, creativity is neither sought nor valued; second, the appearance of justice is more important than the achievement of justice; and third, never, under any circumstances, become personally and emotionally involved in any one of your cases, because it will destroy you.

My lack of appreciation and violation of each one of these principles is why I am now on my knees, worshipping a porcelain altar in the sixth-floor bathroom at the Saint Louis Courthouse. I wouldn't say that it's nerves. The evidence is in. The jury is about to deliberate. There's nothing more I can do. Slumped against the wall, I'm left to conclude that my body's collapse was simply due to the realization of how fast and how far I'd fallen in such a short period of time.

CHAPTER TWO

Less than a year ago, I stood before Federal Judge Susan M. Platte. The courtroom was familiar, and I knew the technology and the layout, because this wasn't my first time appearing before the judge. It also helped that my firm, Baxter, Speller & Tuft, had built a courtroom replica where we could practice. The firm's office was on the top floor of a Manhattan office tower, a sixty-story glass box pinning down the corner of Water Street and Maiden Lane.

We lovingly referred to our office as the aquarium, because that was what it looked like, especially at night when all the lights were on. People walking past on the street below saw attorneys and paralegals still working inside. The fish were always swimming, twenty-four hours a day, seven days a week.

Here, in the real courtroom, Trenton Page, senior vice president of BioPrint Pharmaceuticals, sat at my table with a notepad and pen. Next to him was a partner at the firm and my mentor, Francis Kirsch. Even though Francis's presence was unnecessary, the old guard wanted to keep an eye on me. Since I'd made partner less than a year earlier, I didn't mind. I liked Francis. He had guided me since I was a summer associate. He had helped me avoid internal firm politics and fed me good projects along the way. I knew he took pride in my work—in what I'd become—and enjoyed watching me perform.

I waited for Judge Platte to grant me permission to proceed, and, when she did, I stood a little straighter, planted my feet, and began. I had notes on the podium in front of me, but I didn't need them. I knew what Judge Platte wanted. She wanted a legitimate basis to dismiss the plaintiff's case and clear it off her docket, because that was what all judges wanted. They had to manage their caseload and keep it at a reasonable level. Every day hundreds of lawsuits and motions were filed, and if judges didn't resolve them quickly, they'd soon be buried so deep that they'd never get out of the hole.

"Your Honor, as you know, at a very basic level, every lawsuit must state a valid claim. The defendant, BioPrint Pharmaceuticals, filed this motion to dismiss because the lawsuit lacks that most fundamental requisite."

Judge Platte was what our law firm's database referred to as an "active judge," meaning that she didn't just sit and listen. She asked questions and challenged attorneys to debate and consider various hypotheticals. It didn't take her long to interrupt.

"But, Mr. Daley"—Judge Platte leaned forward—"the allegation is that thousands of children diagnosed with cancer took your client's drug and died." She shook her head ever so slightly, suggesting sympathy for the plaintiffs and playing to the audience.

Behind me, in the gallery, there was a reporter for the *Wall Street Journal* and another from the *New York Times*. The rest of the seats were filled with lawyers with similar cases, wanting to see how the arguments played out, as well as law clerks, new associates, and courthouse voyeurs simply wanting to see a show.

Judge Platte continued. "That seems like a prima facie basis of negligence to me. Whether the families can ultimately prove it is another thing, but to stand there and say that your client shouldn't even be subjected to discovery or investigation seems like a stretch." Judge Platte folded her arms across her chest and leaned back in her big leather chair, clearly indicating that she was going to be skeptical of any response on behalf of my client.

I didn't become flustered or defensive. I knew what needed to be done: acknowledge the emotion, redirect the court's focus toward dry legal issues, and shift the liability to somebody else. The last step was key, something that most corporate defense counsel forgot. They'd get bogged down in case law and statutory interpretation. They'd act cold and indifferent to the injured, like a technocrat, and ignore the fact that a judge was human.

I understood that it was important for Judge Platte to think, even if it was an illusion, that the victim would be made whole elsewhere. The judge needed to go to bed at night believing that, although she had dismissed the lawsuit, the victim would still be OK because another lawsuit could be filed in a different court, with different claims, and heard before a different judge. She needed to believe that she did no harm. That was an essential element of any good corporate defense.

"Your Honor." I paused, shifting my focus to Harold Cantor, the victim's father. Then I looked at the attorneys on either side of him at the plaintiff's table. They worked on contingency—they wouldn't get paid unless they won. Although they considered themselves to be top-flight litigators and trial attorneys, they were more akin to gamblers. Once the cards turned cold, they would fold and settle for pennies.

As rehearsed, I held their gaze and took in a deep breath. Then I spoke softly and deliberately. "I think what happened to Megan Cantor and the other children was an absolute tragedy." I bowed my head. Like any good actor, I had the ability to make this gesture seem spontaneous and sincere. "She was too young to die, and I can only imagine the pain that her loss has caused Mr. Cantor and the rest of her family. Their sadness is real. Their pain is real. Their anger is real."

With step one, acknowledgment of the emotion, completed, I turned back to Judge Platte and held out my hands. Almost apologetically, I said, "But that doesn't mean we can ignore the law." My argument moved away from the emotion and now focused the judge on the dry legal arguments that favored my client.

"They have filed a class action," I said, "which requires commonality among all the class members. They assert that the commonality shared is that each of the class members took a cancer medication sold by my client, BioPrint, which I do not dispute. I know my client may not like to hear me say that, because most attorneys want to fight everything, but I've always been straight with the court. The children have that in common. Again, I don't dispute that fact. However, when you read my supporting memoranda and the attached case law, it soon becomes very clear that this commonality is not enough to go forward."

I moved to the side of the podium, controlling my pacing as I transitioned into my main legal argument. "There needs to be a breach of duty. And here, my client did not violate any duty. BioPrint developed an effective cancer drug. That drug was rigorously tested over the course of ten years, and it went through all the studies and safeguards required by the Food and Drug Administration before a new drug can be sold to the public. There's no allegation—none—that my client failed its due diligence or hid information from regulators or anybody else. It got approval for that drug to be sold, and it's been very successful in saving the lives of people diagnosed with various forms of cancer throughout the United States and the world. Nobody is alleging that this drug, *when used as approved and prescribed*, is dangerous or ineffective. It works. When tumors are spreading, whether that's in the lungs or other places in the body, BioPrint's drug inhibits the growth of existing tumors and stops more tumors from growing at the cellular level. I think that even the plaintiff's counsel will concede that this drug works."

I stopped, then repeated myself a third time. "It works." Looking down at my notes, I felt all eyes on me. The silence had drawn them in. Now it was time to begin a new attack from a slightly different angle. "In order to have a proper lawsuit, the plaintiffs need to allege a breach of duty, which they have not. There's nothing in the complaint that indicates any fraud or misrepresentation. Nothing. This drug works when it is used as approved and prescribed."

Judge Platte cleared her throat. "Obviously there has been something." She wasn't going to let me go that easily, and I hadn't expected her to. "There are many cases where the causation isn't proven specifically, but liability attaches. For example, a plane falls out of the sky and all the passengers are killed. Everybody knows that planes don't just fall out of the sky. Something happened, and it really doesn't matter whether it was pilot error or engine failure—liability attaches to the owner and operator of the airplane. *Res ipsa loquitur*, the fact speaks for itself. The fact that it occurred—the plane falling out of the sky—presumes negligence. Isn't that the same scenario as what's going on here?"

The judge's question provided a perfect opportunity for step three: shifting the liability and absolving Judge Platte of any guilt she may feel about dismissing a lawsuit against a company that likely caused the death of little Megan Cantor and others. Now I'd offer her a solution, a path toward granting my motion to dismiss and allowing her to sleep soundly knowing that she didn't just screw over the parents of thousands of dead children. That was what good corporate defense lawyers did.

"There is a difference, here, an important distinction, Your Honor. An airline interacts directly with the public, sells tickets, maintains its own planes, and transports its passengers. That isn't how our health care system works, however. Our health care system is much more complex and fragmented. My client had nothing to do with prescribing this medicine. The injury to the plaintiffs was caused not by my client, but rather by the doctors who improperly prescribed the medication. As you know and the plaintiffs concede, this medicine was approved and tested for adults. It was never approved or tested to be used for children. Doctors took it upon themselves to experiment—"

"But that's not unusual," Judge Platte interrupted. "Off-label prescribing has gone on for years, and certainly BioPrint knew that doctors would experiment."

"You are right." I wasn't going to argue the point, because it would simply undermine my credibility. "There are often four or five additional uses for every drug on the market, and there's nothing per se wrong with prescribing a drug for an off-label use, *if* the parents and children know exactly what is happening and give their knowing consent."

I paused, looking down as if the tragedy was weighing on me as well, then continued. "I don't know if the doctors did their jobs or not, but it would be the primary focus of a medical malpractice claim against the oncologists who used my client's product for off-label, nonapproved purposes. Each of these doctors has malpractice insurance, and there are other courts who are in a better position than this one to hear and determine those individual malpractice claims."

I could see that Judge Platte was listening closely. Her demeanor toward me softened.

"By this motion," I said, "I'm not saying that there shouldn't be accountability. The people responsible should be held accountable. This is a very tragic situation. If the doctor misled or failed to properly advise Mr. Cantor or other parents, then that doctor should be held accountable. My client, however, did nothing wrong. We weren't in the examination rooms. We weren't a part of those conversations between the doctors and the children's parents. We don't know what was said, and the plaintiffs allege no specific action that BioPrint took that caused this harm."

I looked back over at the plaintiff's table. "I'm afraid their attorneys are simply seeking the easiest path to the deepest pocket. They're trying to convert individual malpractice claims into a class action, while ignoring the actual doctors that may not have properly disclosed the risk of this medicine to their patients."

I paused once again, using the silence for emphasis. "There are other legal remedies available to these plaintiffs to make them whole. This lawsuit should be dismissed, and the families should feel free to pursue those other legal remedies. Where, I might add, their claims will be heard and decided much quicker than through a national class action, and, frankly, the damages could be much more favorable than the meager payouts that too many victims receive as a result of these large, cumbersome lawsuits."

CHAPTER THREE

It didn't take long for Judge Platte to rule on my motion to dismiss. The order was issued late Friday afternoon, just one week after our arguments. The timing suggested that she wanted to minimize press coverage, knowing that by Friday afternoon the weekend editions of most newspapers had already been set and few reporters wanted to stay late and write something new.

Since the federal courts had gone electronic decades ago, there wasn't an envelope containing a paper copy of the judge's order. Instead I clicked a link at the bottom of an email sent by the clerk of courts. Judge Platte's order opened on my computer, and I scrolled down to the bottom of the first page.

My heart rate quickened, as it always does when reading these, then I saw it: "*Based upon the arguments, memoranda, and file in the above captioned matter, the Court hereby Orders that:* Defendant's motion to dismiss is hereby granted."

I clapped my hands together and spun around in my chair, like a little kid. Then I scanned her supporting memorandum, recognizing the language and cases that the judge had cited. Judge Platte had parroted back my arguments. Then I smiled as I read her final paragraph, where she sympathized with the families and encouraged them to individually evaluate whether a medical malpractice claim was appropriate.

Acknowledge the emotion, redirect the court's focus to dry legal issues, and shift the liability to somebody else. Works every time.

For a moment, I wondered how the plaintiff's attorneys were going to tell all the parents about what had happened. I felt a small twinge of guilt as I pictured Mr. Cantor's reaction when he learned that a lawsuit that began with fanfare and coverage on the national evening news had ended with a whimper. Then my phone rang before I could give it much further thought.

I looked at the caller ID: Francis Kirsch. I smiled as I picked up the receiver, always happy to hear his affirmation. "Did you read it?"

"I did," Francis said. "Another excellent result."

I leaned back and put my feet up on my desk. "This was a tough one." I looked around my corner office. My degrees were hung, but the walls were still mostly bare. Some books were on the shelves, but a few boxes remained untouched in the corner. I'd been so busy since making partner that I hadn't had time to fully unpack. "Judge Platte was giving me a hard time during the hearing. I had some doubt."

"You're a liar." Francis laughed. "Even when you were a baby lawyer, you never doubted yourself."

I played along. "I neither confirm nor deny the accusations now made against me." I looked at my reflection in the window. During my time as a summer associate, I'd acquired the nickname "anchorman" because one of the legal secretaries thought I looked like a young Tom Brokaw. I ran my hand through my hair and thought, *Maybe.*

"I don't think you've ever lost, Matthew," Francis said.

"Well, I'm sure that day will come." I stood up and looked down at the Brooklyn Bridge and the harbor below. "It'll happen," I said, even though I didn't believe it.

"I just wanted to say that the executive committee is taking notice. My guess is that you'll be nicely rewarded come bonus time." Then Francis's tone grew more excited, as if he had a better piece of gossip. "Do you know who else has taken notice?"

"No idea."

"That *Times* reporter, Ashley Morgenthaler," Francis said. "She was at the hearing in front of Judge Platte, and she wants to do a profile piece for the Sunday edition."

"If it was the *Wall Street Journal*, I'd be a little more excited about it," I said. "Can't imagine she's going to paint me in a flattering light."

"Oh, I don't know about that," Francis said. "Tuft seemed excited about it." He was referring to the firm's managing partner, Tobias Tuft. "Even if she makes you seem like an asshole, our clients will probably think that's great. Sort of like that old proverb, *the enemy of my enemy is my friend* sort of thing."

"And you think it'll be OK?"

"Of course." Francis kept up his enthusiasm. "If you can convince Judge Platte to rule in favor of an evil pharmaceutical company accused of killing a couple thousand kids, I'm sure you can convince the *New York Times* that you've got a heart."

"I *do* have a heart."

"Right," Francis said. "Just keep telling yourself that." He laughed, then gave me a victory prize: reservations at Le Canard, a French restaurant in Hell's Kitchen, for me and my fiancée, Tess Garrity.

◆ ◆ ◆

Le Canard was Francis's favorite. He told me to have a wonderful night out with a good woman and an even better bottle of wine to celebrate another win for big pharma. The maître d', Sully, had Francis's credit card information on file, so I was instructed to just tell the server that Francis Kirsch was taking care of the bill. As a partner, I could now afford to eat at Le Canard or anywhere else, but I didn't protest too much.

Tess and I were put near the front window, which was perfect. It gave us a great view of an upscale furniture store across the street. I didn't know what a $5,000 mattress felt like, but, given the number of people going in and out of the store, it must be quite nice.

Tess ordered the duck pasta that had been written up in *Bon Appétit* a few months before, and I had a special that I couldn't pronounce but tasted like heaven. When the meal was done, we caught a cab. Instead of going home, I told the driver to take us to Brooklyn.

Tess was surprised.

"Trust me." I took her hand as we traveled down Eleventh Street and then over the Manhattan Bridge to Garfield Place. The cab slowed, then stopped in front of a turn-of-the-century brownstone in the middle of the block. Tess put her hand on mine and looked at me with wide eyes.

As we got out of the cab, my Realtor opened the brownstone's stately door. It was dark green with solid brass fixtures, including a knocker in the shape of a lion's head. He stepped outside and greeted us. "Welcome."

We walked through the wrought-iron gate and up the steps. Once inside we toured the first, second, and third floors, each tastefully remodeled to provide every comfort while still preserving the home's history. I glanced over at Tess. Her eyes sparkled. She pulled me closer as each room was revealed.

"I've saved the best for last." The Realtor opened the back door and led us out into the garden, and at this point Tess could no longer contain a squeal of delight. It was a large backyard, especially for Park Slope, divided into four different living spaces. Overhead were white twinkle lights strung from one pole to the next. Lit candles along the path led to a small sitting area in the far back.

We walked hand in hand. It was a brisk night in mid-March, but we didn't mind, distracted by the thought of summer. Both of us were fantasizing about all the evenings spent out back sipping wine with friends. When we got to the sitting area, my Realtor presented me with the documents. "The financing is all set, and I know for a fact that the owner is going to accept your offer, since I also represent the owner." He laughed at his own joke in a way that only New York Realtors laughed at conflicts of interest. Then he handed me his pen and pointed to a line at the bottom of the page.

I looked at Tess and smiled.

She looked back at me. "Seriously? You're really doing this?"

"Correction." I lifted her hand and kissed the large diamond engagement ring. "*We're* doing this, and at four point nine million dollars, it's a bargain." I thought of the bonus money coming my way at the end of the year. "It's time for us to get out of that little apartment. We've earned it."

Her eyes sparkled. "It's perfect."

I leaned over and signed the purchase agreement, then handed the Realtor a cashier's check for the earnest money. "When will you know for sure?"

He took the paperwork and check from me. "I'll give you a call tonight."

◆　◆　◆

The phone rang about an hour later. Tess had been in the bathroom brushing her teeth. She popped her head out of the door with a childish grin. This was it. We had arrived. She knew how much I'd earned this brownstone, knew how hard I'd worked to become a partner at the firm. Tess was also an attorney, with her own dreams of making partner at another big law firm across town—she knew what it took.

Making partner was almost like winning the lottery. After years of living off student loans and then climbing up the firm's caste system, one day your life changes: $900,000 base salary, a chauffeured town car, a loose expense account, and a year-end bonus that ranged from $500,000 to $2 million, depending on whether you made it rain.

"Answer the phone." She smiled, barely containing her excitement. "Come on."

"Take it easy." I tried to play it cool, although I was just as excited. I picked up the phone and automatically accepted the call without looking at the caller ID. If I hadn't been hamming it up for Tess, I'd have seen that it wasn't my Realtor. "This is Matthew Daley." I heard a breath, jagged, and my smile disappeared.

"Matty?" The voice broke. "Little Matty, is that you?"

I recognized the voice, even though it had been years. "Yes, Mom." I heard her start to cry. I looked over at Tess, who seemed confused, then I turned away from her. "What's wrong, Mom?" But I already knew the answer. This was about my big sister, Allison. Something bad had finally happened.

◆　◆　◆

"You're leaving?" Tess stood in the doorway, her arms folded across her chest. "Are you sure about that?" She knew the history. More than anybody else, Tess understood the family that I'd left behind. She hadn't met them yet, but she had come from similar stock. She knew that going back to Saint Louis was the last thing that I ever wanted to do, but she spared me a lecture on healthy boundaries.

"It's my big sister." A knot grew in my stomach. "You know it's complicated." I put my suitcase on our bed and unzipped the top. "Mom doesn't know what's going on. My dad is useless, and my older brother is unreliable on a good day." I picked up a pair of socks and shoved them in a corner. "She's really confused. Mom needs me." What I didn't tell Tess was that my mom was also drunk—standard operating procedure in the Daley household—and there was no way that she'd be able to make any medical decisions for Allison.

"Isn't this what she wants? She wants you to get sucked back into the chaos. Isn't that what you told me would happen?"

I gave Tess a look, and she didn't push the argument any further. Then she tacked in a different direction. "What about work?" As a lawyer, she understood. Even as a partner, life in the aquarium continued. The fish needed to swim.

"I can work remotely," I said. "I don't think I'm in any danger of not making my billable-hour requirement." It was meant to be a little joke but fell flat.

"What about the *Times* profile?"

Tess wanted me to slow down. She was trying to protect me from doing something I'd regret.

"I'll just do the interview over the phone." I picked up a few pairs of boxers from my drawer and packed them away next to the socks. "She's my big sister," I said. "She did a lot for me when I was growing up. She shielded me, as best she could, from my dad, and now I need to be there."

"I know you love her." Tess's face tightened. "But the only time you talk to her is when she needs money."

"She's an addict." I thought about the $15,000 I'd put on my credit card just a few weeks earlier. Allison had told me that she wanted to go to treatment, that it was the only way to get her out of jail. She promised, repeatedly, to pay it back someday. That was as likely as me becoming the prime minister of France, but I forked over the money, figuring that I'd just pay it off along with the engagement ring at the end of the year with the bonus check.

"All the more reason to be careful." She shifted from one foot to the other. Our conversation had grown tenser than either of us wanted. "I'm not saying don't *ever* go. I'm just wondering if you shouldn't wait. Let it play out. See what happens in a day or two."

As I looked down at my open suitcase, my thoughts slowed. I was tired. The wine I'd had at dinner caught up to me. Even though I'd almost finished packing, I couldn't remember what was in my suitcase and what I still needed to bring. No matter—I'd buy anything I'd forgotten when I got to Saint Louis.

I looked back up at Tess, resolved. "I have to be there for her, for all of them." I zipped the suitcase closed. "I'll call Francis, and I'll let him know. He'll smooth everything out for me at work and cover my meetings." I pulled the suitcase off the bed. "He'll take care of it."

"Are you sure?"

I walked over to her and held her in my arms. I could smell a subtle combination of lemon and pine. It was Gypsy Water, an expensive perfume she sprayed in her hair every morning. "I'll be fine. Trust me." I kissed her, then I took a step back. "Allison is special to me. I just need to take care of her for a little while, just like she took care of me, but I'll be back."

CHAPTER FOUR

Five hours later I was in a rental car, driving from Lambert International Airport to Barnes-Jewish Hospital in the Central West End neighborhood. The interstate that wrapped around Saint Louis was empty. What would be stop-and-go traffic in the afternoon rush hour took twenty minutes in the middle of the night.

I parked near the emergency room entrance in a spot designated for loading and unloading patients only, but I didn't care.

Inside, my eyes took a moment to adjust to the harsh light. A security guard looked up from a magazine as I approached the screening area. He pulled his large body from the chair and got to his feet. "Evening." The guard looked me over. I was not bleeding or wincing in pain, of course, so it didn't take the man long to place me in the other category of people who arrived at emergency rooms in the middle of the night. "Got family here?"

"My sister," I told him, and he directed me through a metal detector with a grunt and scanned my legs and arms with a wand. It beeped at my belt and watch, but otherwise there were no surprises.

"Just go to the desk." The security guard pointed as he walked back to his chair. "They should get you where you need to be, always do."

A minute later I'd found the waiting room. About twenty people were scattered there, each in different states of emotional or physical discomfort. My mom was in the corner, a cup of coffee in her hand.

Based upon the wrappers on the table next to her, it had taken at least three packets of sugar and some creamer to make the coffee drinkable, even for her.

"Hey, Ma."

She looked up at me. Her eyes were bloodshot. "Little Matty." Her speech was still slurred, but she'd sobered since our phone call. She set her coffee down and stood up, uneasy. "Come here." She wrapped me up in a big hug. Even though I was thirty-one, she was still the momma bear. Her smell hadn't changed, either, a combination of Irish Spring soap, stale cigarettes, and whiskey.

"How is she?"

Mom snorted in disgust. "They don't like talking to me." She sat back down and picked up her coffee. "Them nurses sent me out here. Didn't like me back there with 'em. Now I'm out here." She looked around the room. "Ridiculous."

"I'm sure it'll be fine." I sat next to her. "What'd they say?"

"Says Allison had a seizure for sure, maybe two." She folded her thick hands in her lap and tapped her foot, a nervous habit. "Terrible."

"Is Allison awake? Is she talking?"

My mother started to answer, stopped, and tried again. Her foot tapped a little faster. Her eyes scanned the room as if she was looking for a way out between quick glances, unable to hold eye contact. That's how I knew it was bad.

"I thought she was in treatment." I wasn't going to tell Mom I'd paid for it, but she may have known already.

My mother shook her head. "She ran from there."

◆ ◆ ◆

Allison was in a small examination room. Taped to her index finger was a plastic device that monitored her heart rate and sent a constant stream of information to a black-and-green screen above her head. Oxygen pumped into her body through a tube, and several IVs dripped fluids and medications into her arm.

I stared at her, waiting for her to move and wondering if she'd ever wake up.

As if reading my mind, the doctor spoke. "You must be the brother." He went to Allison and took her temperature. The machine, which was attached to a pole holding bags of fluid, beeped. The doctor looked at the thermometer, and the machine beeped again. He then turned to silence the machine. After pressing a few buttons, whatever had caused the problem appeared to be corrected and the room was quiet again.

"How long has she been using heroin?" There was no emotion in the doctor's voice, no judgment. It was a clinical question.

I looked down at Allison's pale face. She was thirty-six years old but appeared older. The youthful glow that I remembered wasn't there. The funny, quirky older sister was gone. Her hair was dry. Her cheeks were sunken and pale. Her lips were cracked. Large dark circles hung beneath her eyes.

"A few years." I paused, not really sure. "At least a few years, probably more."

The doctor walked over to a computer in the corner of the room, but he stopped halfway and turned. "I'm sorry for my rudeness. It's been a long night, and I never properly introduced myself." He walked back to me and extended his hand. "I'm Doctor Kenneth Fry. And your name?"

"Matthew Daley." We shook, then I looked at Allison. "What's going to happen?"

Dr. Fry removed his glasses, cleaned them with his white lab coat, and put them back on, slowly, as he appeared to be carefully considering his words. "I know that she had a seizure, probably two. I don't know how long she was out before the EMTs got there. One of them had a Narcan kit, and that's what brought her back."

"Narcan?"

"That's the name the marketers give it. The drug is naloxone, and it basically blocks certain receptors in the brain. It reverses an overdose, if a person gets it in time."

"Is she going to be OK?"

"Maybe." Dr. Fry looked down at my sister. "The risk of another overdose is very high once she's discharged from the hospital, so you need to make every effort to get her into inpatient treatment or somewhere safe."

"She was in treatment before this happened." I took Allison's hand. "But I'll get her back in."

"That's good," Dr. Fry said. "But I also need to let you know that right now she's not showing the responsivity that I want or expect. Although every case is different, her eyes should've opened by now. She should be talking at this point." He stood on the other side of Allison's bed. "I'm concerned about her brain function, so I've requested a neurologist to come by and take a look. I'm afraid that if the machines are turned off, she won't be able to breathe on her own. Right now, the machines are doing everything."

I looked down at Allison, then at the pump on a small metal cart at the side of her bed. It clicked every time she took a breath, steady. I hadn't noticed it before. I watched, hoping that a breath would come independent of the machine's robotic tick-tock. I waited, sinking lower each time her movement remained consistent with the pump.

The machine really is doing everything.

I tried to stay rational. "And once the neurologist examines her, then what?"

"Then we all need to go over our options."

CHAPTER FIVE

Our house was just off the corner of Pestalozzi Street and Jefferson, not far from the Anheuser-Busch brewery. It was pure southside Saint Louis, built for shelter, not status. The house was nothing special.

The whole neighborhood was made out of red brick due to an 1849 ordinance that forbade wood construction. Earlier that year, a boat docked along the riverbank had caught fire, a fire that spread and destroyed a third of the city. Local leaders decided that brick was the safest way to prevent another inferno.

It seemed like a commonsense decision, and it also didn't hurt that the new ordinance greatly enriched a nearby clay pit's owners, who had contributed significant amounts of money to local politicians' campaign committees and directly into the pocket of the mayor. So the new ordinance was good for everybody. Within a few years those clay deposits churned out twenty million bricks a year, employed hundreds of German immigrants, and fueled the local economy.

I got out of my car. The smell of wort from the brewery hit me hard. Wort was one of the initial steps in the fermentation process. The odor was strongest in the early morning, as the brewers extracted liquid from massive amounts of malted barley, corn, and wheat to produce Budweiser and its various cousins. After my senses adjusted, the harsh smell became comforting. It was home. This was how it had always been, and if you lived in the Benton Park neighborhood, that was how it would always be. Nothing was going to change.

Benton Park was home to workers straddling the fine edge of survival. Modest housing lined the streets: two-story homes on narrow lots occasionally interrupted by a utilitarian row house or a three-story apartment building. Nothing fancy, almost like a Lego kit built by a kid with no imagination and only one color to work with.

On the wooden edge above the door to my childhood home, there was a matchbox from a nearby fried chicken restaurant called Hodak's. Inside was a key the color of an old penny. I reached up, retrieved the faded matchbox, unlocked the front door, and returned everything to its place.

"Hello?" I took my suitcase inside. "Anybody home?"

"In here." My father, Frank, made no effort to come out and greet me. That wasn't the kind of father he was, and that wasn't the kind of relationship we had.

I left my suitcase in the small entryway and walked to the kitchen. He sat at our family's Formica table circa 1957, reading the *St. Louis Post-Dispatch* and eating the same breakfast he had eaten every day since I was a kid—scrambled eggs, toast, and cheap, precooked sausage he'd heated in the microwave.

I pointed at the plate as I sat down next to him. "That's not good for your heart."

My father glanced up from the newspaper for a moment. He rolled his eyes. "That's what *they* tell me." The abstract "they" was his favorite nemesis, an oblique reference to the myriad of people conspiring to ruin his life. Sometimes the "they" referenced the government, other times intellectuals or immigrants or black people. This time the "they" referred to his doctors, who were trying to keep his blood pressure down and manage his cholesterol. In short, the people trying to save his life were ruining his life.

"Mind if I take this?" I reached over and took one of the sausages and popped it into my mouth. If I was expecting a reaction, I got none.

I waited in silence as my father continued to eat. It was a familiar situation, waiting for him. I knew he'd never be the adoring parent who couldn't stop bragging about his kids, but I always hoped for, at least, acknowledgment of my existence.

I had dropped everything, had traveled through the night. I was operating with minimal sleep, and I was missing work. Yet there was nothing from him. My first time back in Saint Louis in years, and still nothing.

"Mom's at the hospital," I said. "Are you going?"

He took a labored breath before checking his watch. "Got work." He folded up his newspaper and pushed back from the table.

"I'm sure they'd understand if you took a day."

He responded with a shallow snort. "Just 'cause I drive forklift, don't mean they don't need me."

We'd been through this before. My father was always looking for evidence that I thought I was better than him or that I looked down on what he did for a living. "I'm sure they need you, Dad, but Mom needs you too."

He sighed. He picked up his empty plate and walked over to the sink. "Maybe." He ran the plate under the water, then set it aside. "But now you're here to save the day, so I guess it's all good."

"Allison is in rough shape, Pops," I said. "The doctor wants to meet with the family this afternoon if she doesn't get better. We need to decide how long we wait. If we turn off the machines, he's not sure she'll be able to breathe on her own."

"So that would be that." My father turned from the sink. His face was drawn, and there was a tear in his eye. It was difficult not to judge him. I wanted to scream, but I didn't know what my father had or had not done over the years I'd been gone. Addicts break promises. They lie.

They manipulate. They burn the people who love them. My sister was an addict, and there was no doubt that she had done all those things.

My dad looked at me, about to say something, but then started walking out of the kitchen instead. "I can probably make it after work."

◆ ◆ ◆

My basement room hadn't changed. I turned on the lights and put my suitcase in the corner. Then I lay down on the bed and looked up at the cheap white ceiling tiles that had started to turn yellow at the edges.

The room had been hastily built shortly after Allison hit puberty. There was an incident involving Jackson and I parading around the house with her training bras on our heads and pretending to be aliens from the planet Pretty Titty. That evening my mother declared that it was inappropriate for a girl to share a room with two boys, and Jackson and I were soon exiled to the basement. A lock was placed on my sister's bedroom door.

My dad and a work buddy framed the basement room in one weekend. They wired it the next. Cheap wood paneling was slapped up for walls. Shag carpeting was tacked down on the floor, and it was declared done. The Daley boys' space program was terminated.

I rolled over. Jackson's bed was still on the other side of the room. His Def Leppard poster, now faded, was still on the wall. The comforter and pillows were all the same, frozen in time. No changes had been made. It resembled a Smithsonian exhibit, a moment captured in time, of an America before mass school shootings, terrorist attacks, and six-figure student loan balances, when kids ran free and ate copious amounts of sugared cereal.

As I began to fall asleep, I felt my cell phone vibrate. I took it out of my pocket and checked the screen: Francis Kirsch. Hope sis is OK, his text read. I'll take care of things here. Hustle back. Gave reporter your cell. She'll call you.

I set the phone aside, closed my eyes, and drifted off.

◆ ◆ ◆

I woke up at a quarter past two. It took a moment to remember where I was. Through the ceiling, I heard somebody above, walking around in the kitchen. They were heavy footsteps, and I knew there was only one person that big.

I got out of bed, wiped the sleep from my eyes, and went up the stairs. He was bent over a little bit, rummaging through the refrigerator. It took him a few seconds, but he eventually found a Budweiser behind the eggs and milk. I watched my brother remove the can, crack it open, and take an initial sip in one smooth, natural motion as he closed the refrigerator door.

I cleared my throat, and Jackson turned, his eyes opening wide as he stood to his full height, examining me. At six foot four and a solid two twenty, he filled the room. I was always going to be his little brother by any measurement. "Little Matty." Jackson raised an eyebrow. "Been wondering when the golden child was going to wake up."

He came over to me. He gave me a big hug, just like he used to do, lifting me off the ground. To an outsider, it looked like love. To me, it was Jackson keeping me in my place. He was big and strong. I was the nerd.

"Have you been to the hospital?"

Jackson nodded. "Just came from there. The doctor wants to meet with us in an hour or so."

"How's Mom?"

"About the same." He took a drink, thinking, then said, "Dad coming?"

"I don't think so," I said.

"What an asshole." He walked to the table and sat down. "Tell me what's going on." He rubbed his nose. "What's life like in the big city?"

I felt my phone vibrate. "Hang on." I checked the number, and I was sure it was the reporter. "I have to take this."

Jackson rolled his eyes. "Of course you do." Then he continued to drink his beer as I walked into the living room for some privacy.

◆ ◆ ◆

As we drove to the hospital, Jackson's pickup truck growled and spat black exhaust into the air.

"I thought you were a radical environmentalist?" I said.

"I am." Jackson laughed. "But new trucks are expensive, man."

"You should try getting a job."

Jackson's right hand came off the steering wheel before the words had fully come out of my mouth. He whacked me hard in the chest. "Ha. Ha." Jackson signaled a turn and got onto the highway. "Maybe I was just hoping you'd buy me a new truck, little brother."

"That's not going to happen," I said. "Especially if you keep hitting me."

"Whatever." He accelerated into the left lane, sending a large plume of black exhaust into the air. Cars moved out of the way.

We didn't say another word after that. As we got closer to the hospital, reality set in. Decisions were going to be made. I thought about whether I should call Tess, but I decided against it. I wasn't going to call her until I had a better idea of when I was going back to New York, back to my life.

I replayed my conversation with the reporter in my head. When she had asked, "Is this a bad time?" I should've said yes. I should've rescheduled and then only talked to her once I had a plan, a message. Instead our conversation had been scattered. I tried too hard. That's never good.

◆ ◆ ◆

Allison wasn't in her room when we arrived. My mother wasn't around either. I stopped a nurse in the hallway, but she wasn't any help. "Just started my shift." She pointed toward a cluster of people about fifty feet behind her. "Go to the nurses' station."

Three nurses stood chatting by a large whiteboard scrawled with initials and room numbers. They ignored me and Jackson as we approached. The tall one was in the midst of a story about a man who came into the ER with his penis stuck in a water bottle. It was clear that she didn't want to break her rhythm before the punch line, so I walked over to a nurse at the other end of the long counter.

"Excuse me," I said. "My sister was on this floor, but it looks like she isn't here anymore."

The nurse stopped typing. "I'm sorry, honey, what was your name?"

"Matthew Daley," I said. "This is my brother, Jackson, and my sister is Allison Daley."

She looked over at her coworkers gathered nearby just as the tall nurse completed her story regarding unauthorized water bottle usage and the other two laughed. Then she shook her head, annoyed with being the only one working, looked up my sister's new room number, and sent us on our way.

When we eventually got to Allison's room on the third floor, I entered first and saw a short, muscular man holding my sister's hand and whispering into her ear. He had a lipstick-kiss tattoo on his neck.

I knocked on the doorframe to announce myself and, hopefully, get him out of the room. "Excuse me."

The man jerked away from Allison, then sized me up. Even though he was short, he was wiry and strong, like a wrestler. An odd bulge in the middle of his nose suggested he could take a punch. "I'm having some private time with my—"

From the hall, Jackson moved past me and into the room. Lipstick Kiss's eyes widened when he saw him. They knew each other. Before he could move or finish his sentence, Jackson was on him. "I told you to stay away from her, Perry." Jackson's grip tightened. "I thought I made that clear."

"Well," Perry said, "she didn't want to stay away from me." His mouth bent into a smile, revealing a few missing teeth.

"And now she's almost dead." Jackson swung Perry around and pushed him toward the door. "Visiting hours are over. Family only."

Perry looked past us at Allison, unconscious in the bed. "She loves me, and I love her."

"She loves the drugs, Perry. That's it. That's all. It's never been more than that." Jackson stepped forward, and Perry backed out of the room. As Jackson pulled the door closed, he said, "Don't come back here."

Perry started to respond, but the door was shut before he was finished. Jackson waited a moment to make sure that Perry wouldn't try to come back. His body tensed. His hands balled into fists, ready to fight. Then his shoulders relaxed, and he cracked his neck. "I can deal with that guy later."

"Was he—"

Jackson nodded. "I'm sure he was there, and I'm sure he ran the moment Allison overdosed," he said. "Perry is a coward."

I didn't ask any questions, although I had many. We needed to stay focused. I went over to my sister's bed and looked at her, unchanged from the first time that I saw her, then told Jackson that we needed to find our mother.

❖ ❖ ❖

We met with Dr. Fry, the neurologist, and a nurse practitioner in a conference room just off the family waiting area. This section of the hospital was different than the ER where Allison and my mother had been the night before. The furniture was nicer, the television was bigger, the rooms were cleaner—all indicators that this would be a more pleasant and relaxing place. Anxiety, however, had absorbed into the walls and ceilings. The false sheen of normalcy was unsettling, and I'd have preferred the grit of the emergency room.

Dr. Fry took the lead, repeating all the things he had told me when we had first met. The neurologist described the tests that measured Allison's brain function, which showed no signs of life. Finally the nurse practitioner outlined our options.

"Allison did not have a health care directive, but you knew her best," she said. "You'd know better than anyone the life that she'd like to live and the steps that she would want us to take in order to preserve that life. Based on what the doctors have said, we'd like to remove the breathing tube now, but Allison can remain intubated for up to two weeks. There's not a rush, but every day that she is immobile in a hospital bed, her recovery becomes that much more difficult. Once the breathing tube is removed, we'll get a better sense of her strength, and then there will have to be decisions made about her feeding tube."

Jackson looked at me, and, probably for the first time in my life, he let his little brother take the lead. I asked, "What are the chances that she breathes on her own?"

Dr. Fry held up his hand. "I can't say that."

I knew he actually could, because I had doctors testify in court all the time about the odds of survival and the chances of success. I switched into lawyer mode. "Dr. Fry, this isn't your first patient in this situation. Does Allison have more than a fifty percent chance of recovery, or less? From your statements it sounds like less, but I want to be sure."

"I'm not going to answer that." Doctors hated being pinned down. "It's unknown. Every patient is different."

Growing frustrated, I pressed him harder. "I know there's nothing guaranteed, and I know that there are people who beat the odds, but we can't make an informed decision without understanding the risks and the likelihood of success."

"And I said that I'm not going to answer that question." Dr. Fry looked at the nurse practitioner, annoyed at me and wanting backup. "Your sister is fragile. Your sister's brain has not responded well to any of the neurological tests or stimuli that we've given her. You'll have to make your own decision based upon that information."

"I take that as a ninety percent chance that my sister is going to stop breathing the moment the tube is removed."

"I told you that I'm not answering that, because I don't know. It's unpredictable." Dr. Fry looked at his watch. "I have to do my rounds. When you make a decision, please let me know." With that he handed control of the meeting to the nurse practitioner and left, the neurologist following right behind him.

After the conference room door closed, we sat in silence for a minute. The nurse practitioner eventually forced a smile. "Dr. Fry is obviously busy with many patients." She folded her hands in front of herself, trying to salvage what was left. "Now, let's walk through the options one more time."

CHAPTER SIX

We waited an hour for my father to arrive. My mother, Jackson, and I had taken over the corner of the family waiting room. Every television show on every channel annoyed us. So, when one of the other families had left the room, we turned the television off and hid the remote control in order to preserve some peace.

My father's hands were in his pockets. His eyes were red and puffy, but he had stopped crying. He never wanted anyone to see him as anything but in control. Mom got up from the couch and walked over to him, and they embraced. Then Dad looked at my brother and me. "Suppose we better do this."

We followed him into Allison's room and gathered around her bed. The nurse stopped in, and I told her that she should get Dr. Fry. We stood there, watching her as the machines beeped and the external pump rose and fell, tick-tock.

This would've been the time for a priest to arrive and give Allison her last rites and for us to say a prayer, but that didn't happen. We'd never been good Catholics, and, like a suicide, this situation seemed different than a heart attack or dying of old age. An overdose felt like a betrayal of God. Even though we'd grown up with the promise of grace, the church had given the impression that such grace was only offered under certain conditions, whether intended or not.

I'm not saying that's right. I'm not even saying that's what I believed, but, growing up Catholic, there was always an ongoing dialogue about who was worthy and who was not, who could partake and who would be excluded. As I stood next to Allison's bed, the last thing I wanted to hear was a prayer, because I knew, regardless, there wasn't going to be a miracle and nobody was going to provide me comfort.

Dr. Fry came into the room, introduced himself to my father, then came over to me and shook my hand. "I know you were just looking for information earlier today, and I apologize for not handling that very well." He looked at Allison, then back at me. "I've seen too many people like your sister lately." He took a deep breath, and it was almost as if I could see the memories pass through. "I'm sorry," he said.

Dr. Fry then confirmed what the family wanted to do as the nurse circulated a form for my mother and father to sign. With the documentation finalized, he went over to the ventilator and turned off the machine. We stood back, out of the way, watching as the nurse removed the tape holding the tube in place. Then she and the doctor slowly pulled the tube from my sister's throat.

When they were done, Dr. Fry stepped aside. He whispered, "Come closer."

Each of us put our hands on Allison as we watched her stomach slowly rise and fall. I waited for her eyes to open and for her to start coughing, like in the movies, but that didn't happen. The beats on the heart rate monitor grew farther and farther apart, dropping from eighty to sixty to forty a minute. Space expanded between each ping from the monitor.

The nurse turned off the sound, sparing us from hearing the monitor's steady drone when Allison's heart finally stopped.

That was how my sister died.

I stood there, looking down at her, filled with sadness and loss. Even though it wasn't a surprise, the immediate surge of emptiness was unexpected. I had never experienced a feeling so deep. She was now gone, leaving only fading memories.

CHAPTER SEVEN

My mother and father left us to meet with one of the hospital's care coordinators to discuss funeral arrangements. As they disappeared into a small room at the end of the hallway, I felt numb. I asked Jackson what he wanted to do.

"Get out of here." Jackson started to walk down the corridor toward the elevators. "We can figure it out when we get to the truck."

I began to follow him, but I was stopped by the young nurse who had been in the room with us when Allison had died. "Excuse me." In her hand she held a brown paper sack. "I don't know if your parents have left yet, but I wanted to give them this."

I looked at the bag. "What is it?"

"Your sister's clothes," the nurse said. "What she was wearing when she was admitted to the hospital, along with her purse, phone, and a few other things."

"Thank you." I took the bag.

The nurse tilted her head to the side. "I'm very sorry for your loss."

◆ ◆ ◆

As Jackson turned onto Kingshighway Boulevard, he said we were going to a nearby dive bar called the Royale. With no better suggestion, I acquiesced, and as we drove past Forest Park, I sifted through the large brown paper bag the nurse had given us.

I don't know what I had expected to find, but I didn't see anything unusual—a pair of worn tennis shoes, jeans, a shirt. The hospital had put Allison's underwear and bra into a ziplock bag. Then, buried deep, I found a small purse.

I removed the purse and set the bag down at my feet. "Think I should look inside?"

Jackson glanced over as he drove through the intersection at Shaw. "Why?"

"I don't know." I unzipped the purse and took out a wallet with Allison's driver's license, a couple of credit cards, and a few random receipts. The only thing remaining in the purse was a half-empty pack of gum, some spare change, and a key chain with a single key and a baby-blue plastic tag in the shape of a diamond. On one side of the tag was the logo for a motel near the airport on Woodson Road. It was called the Lindbergh Inn, and as a sure indication that the place was sketchy, it advertised affordable weekly and monthly rates. On the other side of the tag was a room number.

"Do you think this was where she was staying?"

Jackson turned into a parking lot next to a nondescript brick building. "Gotta sleep someplace."

I looked up at the bar. It was definitely not Le Canard. Thirty motorcycles were parked out front. A group of bikers were smoking in a huddle, arguing about something. "So this is the Royale?"

"Too lowbrow for you?"

I stuck the motel room key in my pocket and put the purse back in the paper bag. "If it works for you"—I opened the door—"it works for me."

Inside, Jackson pointed at an empty table by the dartboard. "I'm going to the bar to get some shots. Grab a seat for us and I'll be right back."

I did as instructed, sitting and waiting. It was a good place for people watching. I'm no expert, but the bikers didn't look like weekend warriors. These weren't dentists and insurance salesmen who dressed up in leather for the weekend. I'd never met a Hells Angel, but I imagined this was what they looked like. I made a mental note to stay out of their way.

Jackson soon arrived with two shots of tequila and a pair of Budweisers. "Take it." He pointed at one of the shot glasses and picked up the other.

"Seriously?"

"Shut up, man, and be a brother." Jackson held up his shot glass. "To Allison."

I picked up the other shot glass and raised it. "To Allison." We clinked and kicked it back. The cheap tequila burned all the way down, and it didn't stop burning once it hit my stomach. I grimaced as the fire continued. "That's awful."

"That's why you chase it with a beer." He picked up the Budweiser and downed it in four large gulps. He inhaled deeply, and exhaled slowly. "That's how it's done."

I picked up my beer and took a much more cautious sip. If I slammed it, I was sure that whatever was in my stomach would soon make a reappearance.

Jackson studied me. Once he was satisfied with my progress, he ordered another round of shots and leaned back. "OK," he said. "Favorite memory of Allison."

"Favorite memory?" I closed my eyes, thinking. "We're really doing this now?"

"We are." Jackson paused as the waitress delivered our drinks. Once she left, he continued. "I need to get the hospital out of my head, man. I want something to make me smile."

I opened my eyes, then picked up the shot. "I guess we all deal with our grief differently." I drank it down, chasing it with a few gulps of beer, less cautious this time. "OK." I smiled. "Remember Allison's first boyfriend?"

"The skinny cross-country dude?"

"Yes." I started to laugh, picturing Allison's boyfriend. His name was Bjorn, skinny and tall with cheeks pocked with acne. "He was way out of his league with Allison, and he knew it."

"He tried to be all friendly with us, like our long-lost big brother."

"And then for some reason he kept egging us on to wrestle him." Jackson drank a little of his beer. "How old were we?"

"I couldn't have been more than eleven," I said. "You were in junior high."

Jackson started to laugh. "Remember when he's in our kitchen, and Bjorn is yelling at me to bring it on in a Randy 'Macho Man' Savage voice, and I'm kinda circling him—"

"And I come in from behind and give him a massive nutpunch." I started to laugh, and Jackson howled.

"And the dude just hits the floor." Jackson is now laughing so hard, he's crying. "He's rolling around on the ground and he's yelling, 'Why? Why did you do that? Why would somebody do that?'"

"Then Allison comes in and sees Bjorn on the floor and starts yelling at us and comforting him like he was just shot."

"And Mom comes in and starts yelling at us, and finally Dad gets up from watching television because he can't hear his show and he, like, walks into the kitchen like this . . ." Jackson sat up straighter, furrowed his brow, and, with great deliberation, moved his head from side to side. "He, like, surveys the scene, puts it all together, then just turns around and walks away. Not a single word." He shook his head. "It was the only time in my life that I thought Dad was proud of me."

"He was not a Bjorn fan."

"None of us were," he said. "Although nobody was ever good enough for her." He took a drink, and we fell into silence again. As grief began creeping back, Jackson interrupted it before the feeling could take root. "How about this? First night after Allison gets her driver's license."

I smiled. "You mean the night a pole at Taco Bell jumped out and hit her?"

"That's right," Jackson said. "And she never stopped. She kept going forward and backward, so then the whole side of the car gets wrecked by the time she got away."

"Dad was pissed," I said. "I swear that's why he never finished the Mustang."

"It was the sweet-sixteen gift that never materialized," he said. "But it's the thought that counts."

I thought about the rusted shell of the 1964 Mustang that had sat untouched in my parents' garage for decades. "I don't think he wanted to put in the work and then have her wreck it."

"Probably." Jackson shook his head. "Or he wanted it for himself."

We ordered a third round, then a fourth. Between them, I thought about all the stories that weren't really stories at all, little moments where Allison protected and mothered us between our teasing and bickering over television shows and music. The times when she'd change the subject at the dinner table when my mother started to peck. The evenings when she'd shield me from the darker elements of our parents' marriage.

That was the loss.

Our conversation devolved from fully developed anecdotes with a beginning, middle, and end to fragments, sometimes just a word or two: homecoming, curlers, John Travolta, Journey. By our fifth round, I needed a little break. I attempted a little more coherent conversation. "So what is it that you do now?"

"Work construction when I want to," he said. "Got a lady friend out in Troy who I crash with, but mostly I travel around, hooking up with protests and talking with people, organizing."

"What are you protesting?"

"Everything." Jackson signaled for a waitress to bring us another round of beers. I may have needed a break, but Jackson had just gotten started. "Our society is messed up, man. Human beings are the true parasites of the world, no natural habitat. All we do is destroy 'em. We're like an invasive species that just grows and grows, crowding out the things that were living just fine without us for thousands of years. We're killing the earth and killing each other."

I knew Jackson was serious, so I didn't try to crack a joke. His struggles with school and steady employment were never due to a lack of intelligence. He was well read and curious, despite his best efforts to come off as a Hoosier—which, in Saint Louis, had nothing to do with being from Indiana. It was slang for a country redneck or white trash, take your pick, and I think Jackson took perverse pleasure in being the only Hoosier at a Black Lives Matter protest. My guess was that it also piqued the curiosity of young, liberal college women looking for a romantic adventure, but that was just a guess.

After the waitress came and went, Jackson turned the question back on me. "So what kind of law do you do?"

"Business litigation." I kept it vague.

"Business litigation." He took a drink. "Sounds like two rich white guys pissing back and forth about money they don't actually need."

I smiled. "That's pretty close. Mind if I use that for our next marketing brochure?"

"For a fee," Jackson said. "I gotta keep gas in the tank, you know?"

CHAPTER EIGHT

My phone woke me up, even though I had only vague memories of going to sleep in the first place. I tried to piece together how my night with Jackson ended, remembering that I forced myself to drink a couple of large glasses of water as well as take a preemptive ibuprofen.

None of that worked. My body still felt as if I'd run a marathon. Every muscle was sore. My neck was stiff. My head hurt with every breath. I just wanted to lie still in complete silence. The phone, however, continued to ring.

As I rolled over to fetch it from the nightstand, I noticed Jackson sleeping in his old bed on the other side of our basement bedroom. He was on his side, buck naked. His feet hung well over the end of the small single bed.

I checked my phone screen: Tess. "Hello?"

"Where are you?"

I hesitated. She sounded intense, annoyed. "Home," I said. "I spent the night at my parents' house."

"I thought you were picking me up."

"Picking you up? Picking you up from where?"

"The airport," she said. "Last night you said that you'd pick me up from the airport. I texted my flight information to you, and I've been waiting for you here at the airport for thirty minutes."

"Wait . . . I called . . . We texted last night?" I tried to remember more details about what I'd done at the Royale, but there were only fragments, nothing specific.

"You forgot?"

"No . . . not really, sort of. But I'm pretty tired . . . overslept." I sat up, swung my legs around, and tried to stand. "I'll be there in a few minutes. OK? You said you texted me the flight information?" Tess confirmed, and I hung up.

Upstairs, in the kitchen sink, I stuck my head under a stream of cold water. Then I smoothed my hair back and put on a clean shirt as I walked out the back door. From Benton Park in the southside of Saint Louis to the airport was not a quick trip, and by the time I arrived, Tess was not happy.

"If you forgot, just say you forgot, and I would've taken a cab." She got into the passenger side of the rental. "Instead I'm waiting here for over an hour. I would've taken a cab, but I didn't know where to go." She flipped down the sun visor and examined herself in the mirror.

"I apologize." I looked for oncoming traffic, then pulled out. "I was with my brother last night after we left the hospital, and things got a little out of hand." I put my hand on her leg and looked at her. "It's been difficult."

She shook her head, then put her hand on mine. "I suppose." She pressed a few of the cheap plastic buttons on the console, as if proving its poor construction, and I caught her trying to hide a sneer. "So where are we staying? It'd be nice if, wherever it is, it has a laundry service."

Since I had no reservations and hadn't even thought of making reservations, I decided I'd use her request to my advantage. "I'll check on that. I'll run into the hotel and talk to the concierge while you wait in the car, and if the hotel doesn't have it, we'll go someplace else." I leaned over and pecked Tess on the cheek. "I promise."

◆ ◆ ◆

For the next two days, I worked hard to minimize my fiancée's contact with my family. It actually wasn't hard to do, since Tess wasn't really interested in getting to know them. I got us a suite at a boutique hotel near Saint Louis University that offered in-room massages, manicures and pedicures, and a full business center. In the mornings, Tess and I had coffee and pastries at a trendy café along the rejuvenated Washington Avenue, then she spent the rest of the day billing clients. In the afternoon, I usually spent some time with my family and relatives in Benton Park before meeting Tess again for a nice dinner at one of the city's growing number of farm-to-table restaurants.

It was odd, shuttling back and forth between two worlds. One moment I'd be sitting on the twenty-year-old couch in my parents' living room. The next I'd be eating a grass-fed, organic lamb chop sourced from a family cooperative in Lincoln County, Missouri, and later sipping a handcrafted cocktail at Atomic Cowboy. When I was with my family, I couldn't wait to leave, but then when I was with Tess, I felt guilty.

My father didn't seem to care whether he'd ever meet Tess, and I think my mother was so busy hosting relatives that she hardly noticed. Whenever the topic came up, I just told her that Tess would be at the funeral reception and that they'd have plenty of time to talk.

The funeral was held at Saint Andrew Catholic Church in the Lemay neighborhood. It wasn't the church where I was baptized. Like a lot of Catholic churches in Saint Louis, the parish where I grew up was now closed. Nothing dramatic. It simply happened over time. Every few months a member or two would pass away from old age or disease, and no new members would walk through the door to replace them. It continued like that for years, until, one day, the people serving Mass numbered the same as the people who were taking it. Bills piled up. The building fell into disrepair, and there weren't enough gifts in the offering plate to keep the parish going anymore.

A priest met Tess and me at the door of Saint Andrew's. He led us into the airy and bright sanctuary and to a back room where my family had congregated. A hunchbacked senior priest, Father John Gallagher, was there describing the logistics of the funeral.

Father Gallagher stopped and turned. "You must be Matthew." He stood up from his chair and walked over to me. He extended his hand, and we shook. "I've heard a lot about you, and I'm so glad that you came. I do wish, however, that we would be meeting under different circumstances."

"Yes, it's a difficult time." I put my hand on Tess's back. "I want to introduce you to Tess Garrity."

Tess stepped forward and extended her hand. "It is a pleasure to meet you, Father. I'm glad I could be here."

Father Gallagher looked down at her large diamond engagement ring. Then he looked at me, and I noticed a little twinkle in his eye. "But of course," he said. "Please have a seat. We were just discussing what scripture will be read and sharing some stories about your sister." He directed us to a set of empty chairs, then turned and began to walk toward a cushioned seat in the corner. About halfway there, he stopped and looked back at me, apparently reflecting upon Allison's death, then he continued across the room. "Tragic," he said. "Too young."

Standing at the pulpit, I stared out at a mostly empty sanctuary. An addict's funeral wasn't like other funerals. For my sister, who was only in her thirties, you'd expect the sanctuary to be filled with high school friends, former teachers, and coworkers. If she'd been struck down by cancer or died tragically in a car accident, that would be the case. This, instead, was a lonely affair. The people in attendance were few, because that was the life of an addict. People got burned.

I didn't volunteer to give the eulogy for her, because I didn't know what I was supposed to say. The task fell to me by default. My father was certainly not capable of doing it. My mother would probably be able to say one sentence, two at most, before breaking down. And Jackson told me that I was "her favorite."

So I got the job.

"We are gathered here today to honor my sister, Allison," I began, "and mourn a loss that neither she nor us deserved. My big sister didn't fit in with any one group. She knew everybody. She liked everybody, and everybody liked her. That was why she hated the high school lunchroom—she didn't have the heart to pick one table over another." I tried to keep my voice steady. I'd break down if I looked at the people in the pews, so I focused my eyes on the church's back wall. "She didn't want to sit with the theater kids or the band geeks or the jocks or the kids who were in all the advanced placement classes. So Allison would get her lunch and walk around the lunchroom, stopping at each of the tables to exchange a few words or a joke or a story before moving to the next—like she was running for president of the United States or something."

I felt the tears build in my eyes, and a few escaped while a lump formed in my throat, but I pushed on. "Not many people know this, but after she made the rounds, Allison would go up to the library and eat her lunch alone. I don't know why I'm sharing this story with you all, but perhaps there's another Allison in your life, someone at work or school or someplace else, and maybe we should pay closer attention to that person who appears to be friends with everyone, and make an effort to make sure they aren't eating alone. Because I think that if my sister would have connected deeply to at least one or two people in that lunchroom, maybe things would've turned out differently."

I wanted to tell stories about how Allison protected me, how she shielded me from my father. I remember him screaming at her. I'd be in my basement bedroom, doing homework or trying to fall asleep.

Through the ceiling I could hear them arguing and my father stomping around the kitchen above me, slamming drawers.

Allison, along with my mother, took the brunt of it so that I didn't have to. She also taught me how to sense when it was coming, so I'd leave. I'd disappear into the basement and turn on the radio so I wouldn't hear it.

She allowed me to focus on school and escape, and I did. I'd run off to New York and created a new life for myself, but maybe I was supposed to bring her with me. For all those times she'd helped me escape, I never repaid the favor.

"The last time Allison and I spoke I was hoping she had found her place, but I could tell she was still searching. It's cruel that her life was cut short and she never found her peace here on earth, but hopefully she's found some peace in heaven." I looked up at a beautiful stained-glass window. "We love you, Allison."

As I returned to the pews, so that the priest could say his homily and administer communion, I saw Perry enter the back of the sanctuary. It took everything in my power not to run back and confront him, but I resisted. When the funeral was over, I looked to see if he was still there, but Perry was gone.

◆ ◆ ◆

People started arriving at my parents' house about an hour after the funeral. Each came with a dish, and soon virtually all available counter space in my parents' small kitchen was filled with food. In addition to the chips and baked beans, there were the Saint Louis potluck classics: a large pan of baked mostaccioli, gooey butter cake, and toasted ravioli from a little Italian grocery in The Hill.

Jackson had taken it upon himself to load the kettle grill with charcoal, and by the time Tess and I arrived it was already filled with pork steaks slathered with Maull's barbecue sauce. After stopping at the cooler for a few beers, Tess took my arm as we walked over to two empty lawn chairs. Both were next to a small metal firepit intended to mitigate the evening chill.

I handed Tess a can of Michelob Golden Light, and she leaned in. "It's been a long time since I've seen that much food in one place without a single vegetable."

I opened my can of beer. "I like that we don't even try to pretend to be healthy." I took a sip and sat down. "Why go to the trouble of making a big salad if nobody is going to eat it?"

"I'd eat it." Tess liked to be contrary.

I hit back: "That's because you're ashamed of your roots."

For the rest of the afternoon and into the evening, people floated in and out. Each paid their respects to Allison, sharing a story of her kindness. By dark, most of the food had been consumed and only a few people besides Tess, my immediate family, a few cousins, and my aunt Connie and uncle Walt remained.

"Tell me about this fancy job in New York City." Uncle Walt was pretty drunk, and I was confident he'd have little recollection of our conversation.

"I'm a lawyer." I decided not to elaborate, hoping the conversation would soon turn to sports or the weather, but Uncle Walt wanted more.

"Like, do you represent criminals? I'm not sure I like lawyers who represent criminals."

Before I could answer, Jackson chimed in. "Now come on, Uncle Walt, you sure didn't mind that lawyer who represented you on that DWI." Jackson laughed, trying as usual to stir the pot. "Seemed like you were pretty happy with him."

"Robbery." Uncle Walt fired up. Jackson had pushed a button. "Cost me four thousand dollars. Still paying off that credit card bill. Probably be paying it off till I die."

"But he got you off," Aunt Connie said, getting in on the action. Other families played board games, exchanged engaging anecdotes about grandchildren or work, or complained about gridlock in Washington, DC. My family bickered, which always started playfully, and always ended badly. Connie staked out her position: "Seems worth it to me, and you seemed pretty happy at the time."

Uncle Walt's face got red. "The cop had it out for me, and he had no reason to pull me over." The intensity of Uncle Walt's gestures grew, and a little beer spilled from his can. "Of course the lawyer got me off, but I could've represented myself and got the same result." When Jackson looked skeptical, Uncle Walt added, "Judge even said so." Then he pointed at Aunt Connie for corroboration, but she didn't help matters.

"The judge didn't say you should've represented yourself," Aunt Connie said in a singsong voice. "He said it was obvious to anyone that it was a bad stop, but that's different than saying you could've represented yourself. I think your memory is off in your old age."

"My memory ain't off," Uncle Walt said. "My memory is perfect-o, and I know that's what the judge said." Uncle Walt scanned the crowd, looking for anybody to challenge him. When nobody did, he walked over to an empty lawn chair next to Tess. "Whatever." He sat down and turned to her. "So what do you do?"

Tess looked at me, unsure whether she should continue. "I'm an attorney like Matthew."

"Matthew?" Uncle Walt smiled. "Don't know no Matthew, but if you're talking about little Matty, suppose he's a decent guy." Then Uncle Walt turned to me and, in a loud stage whisper, said, "You be careful, son. Beauty and brains is a powerful combination."

"Thanks for the advice," I whispered back, relieved he hadn't directed his anger for his DWI attorney at me or Tess.

My mother walked out the back door and stumbled down the short step, then righted herself at the last possible moment. She hadn't been seen since the funeral. I'd been told that she just needed time to rest, but I knew that was a polite way to say that she was off someplace drinking alone.

"Where is she?" she said, her words slurring as she looked around the yard.

I stood up. "Who, Mom? Who are you looking for?" I walked over, but my mother pushed past me.

"You know who I'm looking for." Her eyes locked on Tess. "You ain't going to take my son. Coming in here uninvited. No, no, missy, you ain't taking my son."

"Mrs. Daley, I'm not trying to take your son." Tess looked past my mother to me, wanting help. "We love each other very much."

My mother moved closer. "You think I'm blind? I saw that ring. You think I don't see? You think I'm dumb, like I don't know." She turned back to me. "You're getting married, and you're not going to invite me? You don't even bother to tell me." She pointed at Tess. "I don't even know this woman, and you bring her into my house. You bring her to your sister's funeral? I can't believe it. I don't even know who you are anymore, Matty."

She repeated herself over and over, different iterations of the same comments, often incoherent. Uncle Walt tried to intervene, coming to Tess's defense, but it didn't work. Mom just got angrier. She pushed him away and took another step toward Tess. "I want you out of my yard and out of my house."

Tess tried to get up, which was what my mother had demanded, but my mom didn't give her enough room. Tess fell back down into her seat, and when she tried to get up again, my mom shoved her back.

Tess wasn't somebody who got shoved around, even if she was thin. She came up quicker this time. My mother was a second too late in her attempt to keep Tess in her chair. Tess had the momentum and strength. When they collided, my mother stumbled and fell backward.

Jackson sprang out of his seat. He wrapped Tess in a bear hug and lifted her off the ground. "I think that's enough." He carried Tess to the edge of the yard and released her. "You apologize to my mother, then I think it's time for you to go back to your ritzy hotel."

"You want *me* to apologize?" Tess put her hands on her hips. "Your mother came after me. I was trying to get away from her."

"You knocked her down." Jackson was just as stubborn as Uncle Walt and the rest of my family. "Accident or not, I seen it and you did it. Apologize."

Tess looked at my mom, who was still on the ground and in the process of pulling herself up to her feet. "I'm not apologizing," Tess said. "It's your mother who—"

"Come on, honey, let's go." I took her hand, but she shook free.

"That's it? You're not going to stand up for me?"

Uncle Walt opened another can of beer, thoroughly entertained. This was what was expected at a Daley family get-together. "Sounds like we got trouble in paradise." He chuckled. "Got to be careful of them lady lawyers." He barked. "Bite you like a dog."

"Shut up, Uncle Walt." I took Tess by the arm and led her away. "We're going."

◆ ◆ ◆

We rode back to the hotel in silence. Not a word was said in the elevator or even once we got inside our room. Tess grabbed a pair of pajamas out of her suitcase and went into the bathroom. After a few minutes I heard the shower start.

I changed into my own pajamas and lay down. Aimlessly flipping through the television channels, I thought about what had happened, wondering why I didn't come to Tess's defense. Everybody had just fallen into their old roles. I was embarrassed for her, my family, and myself. I wanted to leave before any more damage could be done.

Tess eventually came out in one of the white robes provided by the hotel. Her wet hair was wrapped in a towel. All her makeup had been washed away. It was clear that she had been crying.

"Tomorrow, we're going," she said.

"Tomorrow, we're going," I agreed, walking over to her. "Your flight is first thing. I'll catch the afternoon flight, and we'll have dinner together at our favorite little Thai place around the corner."

Tess nodded. "Sounds lovely."

I thought about my return to New York after everything that had happened. "Yes," I said, not entirely convinced. "It does sound lovely." I forced a smile, but below the surface, I was unsettled. The various stages of grief—denial, anger, bargaining, etcetera—are so clean, but what if you feel all of them at once or out of order or not at all? Often, I felt nothing. I'd forget Allison died entirely. I'd be worried about keeping Tess happy, thinking about clients, or returning to New York. Then the grief would surprise me, and I'd feel guilt. Not only had I not been able to save my sister—I couldn't even mourn her properly.

And I didn't know what I needed to do about that.

CHAPTER NINE

The airport's "kiss and ride" lot wasn't very crowded, hadn't been since 2001. That was the year that American Airlines bought the bankrupt Trans World Airlines, otherwise known as TWA. Soon hundreds of employees were laid off, and later American Airlines stopped using the Saint Louis airport as one of its major travel hubs altogether.

Growing up, announcements like this were common. It seemed like a large company downsized, closed, or moved every other month. The local news constantly affirmed a general feeling that there was no future in Saint Louis, and my family's struggles made those feelings even less abstract.

I found a spot near the door while Tess fixed her lipstick.

I popped the trunk and set her luggage on the curb. "I'll be on the next flight, back early afternoon."

"You're not going to come in and see if you can switch your ticket?" She stepped out of the car. "We could fly back together."

"I've got a few things left to take care of," I said. "I'm meeting my brother this morning, and I'm not sure when I'll see him next."

Tess tipped her head to the side, acknowledging my choice, but not approving of it. Tess picked up her bag, and I watched her disappear into the terminal. She never looked back. No final wave, no blown kiss goodbye. Nothing.

◆ ◆ ◆

The Lindbergh Inn was across the highway from the airport. It was marked by a faded sign with the majority of its signature neon lights burned out or buzzing at the end of life. I pulled into the parking lot, dodging potholes and broken bottles, and spotted Jackson in his truck.

We didn't exchange any pleasantries, and I wondered if, like Tess, he still hadn't worked through what had happened the night before. "Got the key?"

"Of course," I said. I pulled out the motel room key, the one I'd found at the bottom of Allison's purse, and tossed it to him.

He caught it with one hand. He hadn't hesitated at all, smooth, always the natural athlete. We walked up the concrete steps to the second floor. Plastic bags filled with fast food containers and other garbage littered the place, waiting for a housekeeping service that may or may not come. Empty beer cans and the occasional ashtray lined the railing overlooking the parking lot.

The motel was quiet now, but I'm sure the night before, in the darkness, the balcony and the rooms of the Lindbergh Inn had been hopping. We walked down to room 209. Jackson stuck the key in the lock and opened the door.

Inside it looked as if a dumpster full of dirty clothes and garbage had been dropped into the room from above. The floor was covered. The air was thick and sour. When I turned on the light, there was movement in the corner. A large rat looked up at us, questioning our presence with no evident fear. After a prolonged stare down, the rat sauntered along the back wall to a hole, disappearing into the adjoining room.

"Hello?" I called as we both went farther inside. "Anybody here?"

No response.

Jackson walked to the back of the room toward a closet. Inside was a black piece of luggage, compact with rollers on the bottom. Jackson pulled the suitcase out and set it on the bed. He unzipped and searched the pockets.

"Empty."

Then he began searching the room for anything worth keeping, a tangible memory of our sister and our life together. We didn't want everything she owned to disappear, like she never existed.

I searched the bathroom, sifting through a countertop littered with cotton balls and empty bottles of free shampoo and conditioner. In the sink a stained shirt floated in dirty water, and beneath the sink sat a duffel bag. Inside were a pair of tennis shoes, a couple of paperback books, some notebooks, and a framed photograph of the Daley kids. I pulled out the framed photograph and looked at it.

This was us.

Snow covered the ground. We stood in front of our house on Pestalozzi with a bare Christmas tree, recently cut down and about to be taken inside for decoration. Jackson was on one side, already towering over Allison. Allison's cheeks were red, and her arm was around me. I was the little brother with a broken grin. It was the year I had lost four teeth over the Thanksgiving holiday.

"Check this out." I handed the picture to Jackson.

He looked at it and smiled. "I remember that day." He looked at the bag in front of me. "What else you got in there?"

"Some notebooks." I flipped through them. "Journals." I wanted to stand there and read every page, but I didn't have much time. Soon I needed to get back to the airport and through security.

I continued in the bathroom as Jackson sifted through the things on the floor near and under the bed. When he was done, Jackson went outside for fresh air, and I joined him when I'd finished. For our efforts, we'd retrieved only the photograph and three spiral notebooks. I don't know why, but I'd expected more.

Jackson wiped away a tear. "You glad we came?"

"I am." I looked back at the motel room. "Now I know. I would've always wondered what we left behind. Not sure how I feel about it, but at least I'm not speculating about where she was at."

Together we walked back to the truck, and Jackson held up the photograph. "Mind if I hang on to this?"

"I don't mind," I said. "If you don't mind me hanging on to these for a little while." I looked down at the notebooks in my hand. "I'd like to read them on the plane."

"That's cool."

There was an awkward silence as we both tried to figure out how to say goodbye. Professions of love were not going to happen, but a handshake seemed equally bad. "Well." I waited a beat to see what Jackson would say or do, but he did nothing. So I held out my arms, and we exchanged a stilted hug, complete with two pats on the back.

"I'll give you a call when I land in New York." I turned and started to walk to my rental car, but Jackson stopped me.

"Hey, Matty." I knew something was on his mind. I'd felt it since I had arrived, and now I was going to find out what it was. "Why didn't you tell me what you do for a living?" He didn't ask it harshly. It was soft, but there was still an edge.

"What are you talking about?"

"In the bar, at the Royale, I asked you what kind of lawyer you were."

It took a second, but I remembered the conversation. "I told you what kind of lawyer I was."

He shook his head. "But you didn't tell the whole truth, right?" He stepped forward. "You didn't say, 'I represent companies like the one that killed our sister.'"

I was confused. "Where's this coming from?" I backed up, keeping space between us. "Allison died of a heroin overdose, Jackson. I don't represent heroin dealers. I'm not a criminal defense attorney."

"You don't? Sure sounds like you do." He pointed his finger at me. "I'm not an idiot, Matty. I may not wear fancy clothes or have a bunch of degrees, but I'm not an idiot. The article says that you're the guy—the first person those drug companies call when they get in trouble."

"Article?" The *New York Times* profile must've been published. The reporter had said it was coming out soon, but I didn't think my brother would read it. "I'm a business litigator. That's what I told you. I represent corporations. That's what business litigators do. Most people don't want to hear the details, and so I don't get into it."

"But you specialize, right? You represent a particular kind of corporation. You represent these drug companies when they kill people, am I right?" Jackson waited for me to deny it, and, when I remained silent, he kept going. "Let me ask you this: Do you know how our sister got hooked on heroin? Do you remember the car accident?"

"Of course I remember the car accident."

"And did she tell you about her doctor or the pain medications, or did you not bother to ask her, figuring that as long as you wrote her a nice check every once in a while, it gave you permission to not be bothered with the details?"

"When she called me, she needed help, and I gave it to her, because, unlike you, I could."

Anger flashed across Jackson's face. He grabbed hold of my shirt and spun me into the side of his truck. "Who do you think drove Allison to treatment?" he asked. "Who do you think bailed her out of jail or answered her calls at two in the morning, begging for some money or to pick her up from some abandoned flophouse on the northside?" He pulled me close, then he slammed me into the side of his truck again. "You know nothing about me, Matty, and you knew nothing about our sister. This wasn't even her first overdose." He jerked me to the side as if he was going to slam me into the truck again, but then he stopped. He let me go, separating. "If you really loved her and you really knew her, then you wouldn't do what you do."

He reached through the open window of his truck and into the passenger seat. He pulled out a folded newspaper and tossed it at me.

"Yes," he said. "Your ignorant big brother reads the *New York Times* every damn day, and then I read the *Wall Street Journal* just so I can find out what the enemy is thinking." He turned and began to walk away. "Keep her journals." He waved his hand. "I already know what they say, 'cause I lived it with her."

CHAPTER TEN

I resisted the temptation to get hammered on the flight back to New York. I drank nothing, instead. That's something that kids of alcoholics do sometimes. They give themselves little tests in self-control, just to prove that they aren't alcoholics like their mom or dad. That's not really how it works. My dry flight home didn't prove anything one way or the other, but, in the moment, passing that test was important.

Economy and business class were full, but I got lucky in first class. The seat next to me was empty. With room to spread, I got out my stuff. I set my carry-on in the empty space, got out my headphones, and settled in with Allison's journals just before the flight took off.

I heard her voice in every word, honest and raw. At times reading them felt like an invasion. I was still too defensive to admit that Jackson was right—ignorance had allowed me to pretend that I was there for my sister when, in reality, I was not.

I didn't know her struggle. Although she used and experimented with all sorts of substances, her addiction didn't take hold until she was prescribed an opioid pain medication called Bentrax. There was a car accident shortly after her thirtieth birthday. Although I was already in New York City, I remember when it happened. Allison wasn't the driver, but she was the one who got hurt when her friend lost control of the car on an icy road. They spun into the other lane and got hit by a truck going in the other direction. Allison broke her collarbone and messed up her back, but I was told that she was going to be all right, and maybe she would've been all right if she hadn't been prescribed Bentrax.

Allison left Central City Hospital after her car accident, her doctor gave her a prescription for fifty pills, and it became the new love of her life. In the journal she'd created while at the Arch Treatment Center, Allison wrote:

> *I took those fifty and then I went back and got fifty more. It went on like that for about a year, then I started crushing the pills and shooting them up. The high got even better. I did that for another year, then the state passed a bunch of new laws and the pills got cut off. With no more prescriptions, I started buying Bentrax on the street. But the price kept going up, and, sometime around there, that's when I was offered a free hit of heroin. The high was just as clean, but heroin was cheaper and easier to get than Bentrax, and so I switched. If alcohol made me feel normal, Bentrax and heroin made me feel great. And who doesn't want to feel great?*

I set the journal down. It was just like Jackson had said. Allison probably didn't need it, but the doctor prescribed Bentrax anyway, then when the medication got harder and harder to get, she turned to the street equivalent, heroin.

As the plane landed in New York, the internal compartments that I'd built up between different aspects of my personal and professional life began to fracture. The walls separating what I did for a living, my beliefs, and the people who made me had begun to crack.

The cab stopped in front of my apartment, a six-story building on Orchard Street in Chinatown. When I came through our apartment door, Tess was on the couch typing something on her laptop while also watching a movie on television. Seeing how many minutes we could bill clients while also watching a movie or bingeing a show was always a fun challenge. Those were the games that we had played.

"Hey." I walked across the room and sat beside her. I leaned over and kissed her cheek.

She set her computer aside and paused the movie. "I'm glad you're home." She snuggled closer to me, and I could smell her favorite perfume. "I'm sorry if I was a little harsh," she said.

I put my hand on her knee. "It was hard going back," I said, "but I'm glad I was there." I thought about telling her about the motel and the journals, but what would I say? "My brother gave me a hard time about the article."

"He's just jealous." She picked up the *Times* from the end table. It was folded in half with my profile on top. "This is awesome." Tess waved the paper in the air and cleared her throat, preparing for a dramatic reading.

"In a country with over one point three million lawyers," she read aloud, "Matthew K. Daley has become the one lawyer that major pharmaceutical companies call when they make headlines for all the wrong reasons. His most recent victory on behalf of BioPrint Pharmaceuticals cut short a major class action related to BioPrint's most profitable cancer drug before it even got started. The lawsuit's dismissal cemented Daley as the young 'Judge Whisperer.' Clients gush that he is able to calm hostile judicial officers with a broad smile and a large dose of Midwestern charm."

Tess laughed. "I can't believe it." She set the paper down. "Tomorrow morning the firm is going to change the name from Baxter, Speller & Tuft to Baxter, Speller, Tuft & *Daley*."

"I wouldn't go that far."

"I would." She was excited now. Money had a tendency to do that. All the bluster and annoyance that she'd exhibited in Saint Louis was gone, and I could tell that she was already dreaming about a summerhouse in the Hamptons. When the provider provides, sins were forgiven.

Uncomfortable, I got up off the couch. "I'm going to take a shower now."

"You know I'm right," she called to me as I went into the bathroom. "You know you're a rock star."

My face turned red. "Whatever."

"I'll be waiting in the bedroom when you emerge all clean," she teased. "Candles will be lit."

◆ ◆ ◆

I woke up an hour earlier than usual the next morning and went for a run. Most New Yorkers stayed up late and got up late. So I couldn't help feeling like I was part of a secret club as I ran along the Hudson River and witnessed the sunrise.

For the first time that I could remember, I didn't want to go to work. There had certainly been moments over the past seven years that I would have rather been on the beach than billing clients, but those moments passed. This feeling was something different. I didn't quite hate my job. I just didn't want to go. I was off, and I knew it. My hope was that the run would clear my head.

An hour later, it was a little better. I had recaptured some energy and convinced myself that everything was going to be fine, although thoughts about Allison and my brother lingered in the background. I fixed myself some toast and made a smoothie out of a bag of frozen fruit and yogurt, then showered.

When Tess was ready, we went to a new coffee shop on the corner called GRIND. It was the latest addition to our ever-gentrifying neighborhood. Tess picked up her skinny latte from the counter, and I made a promise to call her if anything exciting happened at work.

"I just have a feeling." Her eyes sparkled. "No delays. I'll be waiting." She kissed me more passionately than I think she'd ever kissed me in public, then turned and headed north to her firm, Nelson Rockler.

I walked in the opposite direction to Baxter, Speller & Tuft, and ten minutes later I was sitting behind my desk. Even though I had been gone for less than a week, the aquarium felt different. The law firm was all-consuming, and to step out of the boiling pot for even a short time made you realize just how hot it ran.

I was glad that I had gotten to work even earlier than usual, because I didn't want to talk to everybody on my way to my office. Although Francis Kirsch knew what had happened to my sister, I didn't want to explain my dysfunctional family to others. I had decided that if asked, I'd just say that there was a family medical emergency, but everything's fine now. Nobody would ask a follow-up question, partly because they didn't care and partly because every minute they were talking to me, they weren't billing clients.

By midmorning I had begun to find my old groove. Emails were returned, clients' questions were answered, and I made progress on a few urgent legal research projects. The aquarium life was simple. Expectations were clear: make money. Focus on that one goal, and everything else fell into place. Time for regret was limited.

I'd almost pushed my sister and my family out of my mind, but not entirely, when Francis dropped by in the late afternoon. He sat down in the chair next to my desk and leaned back. "Got some good news for you, Matthew." Francis was a short man, thin and balding. He knocked two times on the edge of my desk and smiled. "The executive team met this morning, and a big part of the discussion was about you."

"The firm's doubling my bonus?"

"To be honest," Francis said, "that could happen." His eyes got bigger. "There are some strategic meetings going on, and Tuft is thinking about how to leverage your recent success."

"Like what?"

Francis shook his head. "I'm not telling," he said. "You'll have to hear it from the man himself."

"Tuft?"

"Exactly," Francis said. "He wanted me to invite you to the Yankees game tonight. It's the home opener. The firm has a box. I'll be there, a few other guys on the executive committee, and some potential clients."

"I don't know, Francis, I just got back from Saint Louis yesterday," I said. "I'm really tired."

"I'm not hearing it." Francis stood up. "I'm sorry about your sister, but this is big. You're coming to the game tonight. The firm will arrange a car for you, and I'll email you the details."

"Francis, I really . . ." I held out my hands, pleading my case, but Francis heard none of it.

CHAPTER ELEVEN

The Lincoln Town Car dropped me off at the VIP entrance at Yankee Stadium. On the way over, I had called Tess. She was working late and told me not to wait up for her, but she sounded very excited. Tess also took the opportunity to remind me numerous times that she knew something big was going to happen as a result of the article in the *Times* and I hadn't believed her.

An off-duty cop opened the door and greeted me. He checked my name against a list and scanned my ticket. After I made it through security, a concierge wearing a blue sport coat with the New York Yankees logo on the pocket guided me to a private elevator. It brought me directly to the executive suites. Even though the game was well underway, there were no crowds or lines. Unlike the rest of the stadium, the back entrance and suite level were quiet.

Another concierge was waiting when the elevator doors slid open, and I stepped out. The gray-and-blue carpeted hallway was brightly lit and clean. There were no people milling about or waiting to use the bathroom. There were no food stands or barking vendors or overpriced sodas served in gigantic souvenir cups. This was a premium experience. Food was ordered and brought directly by a waitstaff. Cocktails and beer were served in glassware. No money exchanged hands. It was all included in the cost of the suite.

"You're right this way." The concierge guided me past black-and-white photographs of Yankees legends. She stopped in front of a frosted glass door next to a stainless steel sign with the law firm's name and logo. She opened the door for me. "Here we are."

The suite was on the third base line, with a direct view of the Yankees dugout across the field. About twenty people mingled and grazed on a table filled with appetizers. Francis Kirsch saw me and immediately brought me over to the wide, leather-cushioned seats overlooking the field.

I may not have met them, but I knew them all. It was most of the firm's executive committee, three division heads—one flown in from California—two of the firm's biggest litigators, and the head of the DC office, himself a former congressman.

At the end of the row, closest to the aisle, was Tobias Tuft. He had started at the firm, then known simply as Baxter & Speller, in the mailroom—of course—pushing a cart from one floor to the next. It wasn't glamorous, but it paid for college and law school. Eventually the firm hired him as a lawyer, and he kept clawing his way up until they put his name on the door.

"Mr. Daley." Tuft pointed at the empty seat next to him. "First let me extend my condolences regarding your sister."

I looked over at Francis, but he didn't make eye contact with me. I looked at the others seated next to Tuft, wondering if they all knew.

What did Francis tell them? He promised to keep the details private.

Unsure of what to say, I fell back on the expected response. "Thank you. I loved her very much."

Tuft then complimented my work ethic and the fact that I had billed a record number of hours for the firm over the past two years. "I read your profile in the *Times*," he said. "If you're not careful, I might get a little jealous." He began to laugh, and the former congressman sitting next to him robotically laughed along. Tuft smiled. "There can only be so many big egos in this firm, and I think we already have quite a few." On cue, there were a few more forced guffaws.

Tuft looked down at the field and watched the Yankees' new shortstop swing at a curve ball and foul back into the netting behind home plate. As the pitcher collected himself, Tuft turned back to me. "I'm told Francis already gave you a clue as to why you are here, and so I better just cut to the chase." He leaned forward. "I'd like to form a pharmaceutical litigation division, and I'd like you to run it. You can assemble your team from existing attorneys, or you can go out there and steal some from other law firms. Of course, being a head of one of our divisions would mean that you'd get a higher distribution of the firm's profits, because there is extra responsibility, as well as a seat on the executive committee."

I looked back at Francis. He was still standing in the aisle, his arms folded, listening. To Tuft I said, "That's truly an honor." A few more garbled words came out of my mouth before I fully regained my composure.

"I've put together a working group to hammer out the details," Tuft continued. "It'll take some time, but there's one opportunity that I want you to hit hard right away. Time is of the essence, and I want you to really go after it. Show me that I'm not making a mistake."

"What's that?"

"I was at the club the other day and had a few drinks with our US attorney for New York. He told me that he's getting pressure to do something about the heroin epidemic, and that there are some state attorneys general, class action lawyers, and even some cities that are on the cusp of suing the manufacturers of opioid pain medications."

My stomach dropped. It was like a sick joke. I thought, *The timing couldn't be worse.*

"The timing is perfect," Tuft said. "Given your personal connection to the crisis, you'd be the ideal person to push back against these ridiculous attempts to find a scapegoat."

"Isn't this premature?" I asked. "Nobody has filed any lawsuit. We don't even know what we're defending."

Tuft waved his hand dismissively. "That's the value you bring to the table. You know what they'll claim because you can think like they can. You understand." He looked for confirmation down the row, and, whether they were even listening or not, each one of them nodded in agreement with the head of the firm.

Tobias Tuft glanced up at Francis. "Kirsch has already been in touch with several reporters who are ready to roll with another story, like a follow-up to the one in the *Times*. We want the reporter to go back to Saint Louis with you and talk to your family, really dig deep, and then, of course, you'd get a platform to defend our clients and explain why civil lawsuits will be a waste of time and money." Tuft looked at the other men next to him, and each agreed that the plan was brilliant. "Then you can tell them that the government needs to go after the Mexican drug cartels who are manufacturing enormous amounts of heroin and smuggling it across the border or start cracking down on these dealers or helping to pay for treatment."

"You mean acknowledge the emotion, redirect the focus toward dry legal issues, and shift the responsibility to somebody else." My tone was flat.

"Exactly." Tuft snapped his fingers, then clapped as a Yankee hit a single into right field. "See, you know exactly what to do." As Tuft talked more about the position, I found myself rationalizing that I could somehow do it. I sat silently next to him, performing mental gymnastics. *Why not me? Somebody is going to do it—why shouldn't I get the money?*

"Carol?" Tuft shouted, and an attractive woman suddenly appeared with a large manila envelope. Tuft pointed at it. "Go ahead, take it and look inside."

The top page was a term sheet. It highlighted the major components of becoming a managing partner at the firm and a member of the executive team. There was also a brief job description that outlined what would be expected of me as the head of the firm's pharmaceutical litigation division and a noncompete clause that warned me against stealing clients and competing against the firm for two years after separation.

The term sheet went on to break down the percentage of revenue that I would receive as a result of hours billed by the division's partners and associates. In many ways, I realized at that moment, the firm was less like a traditional company and more like a Ponzi scheme. Just like a housewife selling cosmetics or a gym rat hustling supplements to his friends, I got richer the more people that I recruited and the more money that they brought into the law firm. There was no reward for being small or going slow.

Printed at the bottom of the sheet was a minimum annual base salary: $2 million.

I looked up at Tuft. "That's a fabulous opportunity with a lot of responsibility."

"You remind me of myself at your age," Tuft said. "You're hungry and driven. Doesn't hurt that you're talented." He pointed at the term sheet and the formal, detailed agreement underneath it. "Don't feel any pressure to sign that right now, but I want you to know that I'm moving forward with this division, whether you're with me or not. Strategically it's the right move for the firm, and I need to get there first, before other firms figure out what's going on."

I put the contract and term sheet back inside the envelope. "You mind if I take this? I'd like to read it carefully."

"I don't mind." Tuft was shrewd. He wanted me to know that he wasn't desperate. His attitude was exactly what Francis had said it would be: you're replaceable. He called to Carol to retrieve the envelope from me. "She'll give it back to you when you leave tonight," Tuft said. "In the meantime, I need you to mingle."

"Mingle?"

"Up in the suite, I've invited some people who are very interested in meeting you."

"Who?"

"The North American president and general counsel for Synanthem," Tuft said. "It's a Swedish pharmaceutical company. And then there's a few from HarperPharm and NexBeaux."

"NexBeaux?"

"That's right," Tuft said. "The makers of Bentrax."

I nodded, then slowly got up from my seat. It was all happening too fast. Francis Kirsch tried to talk to me as I walked past him into the suite, but I didn't stop. As the crowd behind me stood up and began to sing "Take Me Out to the Ball Game," a big, flushed man stopped me. "You are Matthew 'Big Dick' Daley." He pointed at my chest and laughed. "Sign me up, my little judge whisperer."

People were watching now, curious how I'd handle this very rich, and very drunk, man. "It's pretty simple, sir." I put my hand on his shoulder. "All it takes is a six-figure retainer check, and I'm all yours."

The man's head jerked back, and his eyes narrowed. When it finally clicked that I was joking, he smiled and howled with laughter. "Good one." He slapped my back. "I just might get you a check before the night is through."

"Great." I looked over his shoulder at the bathroom, feeling sicker by the second. "If you don't mind, I need to take a little potty break."

"Don't mind at all." He held out his hand. "Chandler Hawkes, NexBeaux Pharmaceuticals."

My skin crawled as we shook. I thought about my sister. "I've read a lot about you." I released his hand and began walking past him. I thought I had gracefully gotten away, but then Hawkes swung his arm around me and pulled me back.

His face was uncomfortably close to mine. His breath was heavy, and I could smell the Jack Daniels. "Right over there is my chief financial officer as well as my general counsel," he said. "You tell them you're hired. 'Cause I said so."

"Thank you."

"I'm serious." He released me. "You're the guy I need." He shook his head. "Those ambulance chasers are coming after me. I'm telling you."

"If that's the case, I'm sure we'll be happy to help." I forced a smile, moved quickly into the bathroom, and locked the door behind me. My hands were shaking, and a bead of sweat rolled down my neck. My stomach felt queasy, and I was thankful that I hadn't drunk any alcohol.

I sat down on the toilet, waiting for my heartbeat to slow.

So that's the guy.

Although there were only three major drug companies that manufactured and sold opioid pain medication, NexBeaux was the largest. I couldn't believe the company's CEO was here. He was like a cartoon villain. As a client, he'd be an absolute disaster on the witness stand. I thought about Allison and Jackson. The longer I sat in the bathroom, the more I heard Jackson's voice whispering in my ear and encouraging me to go into the other room and throw a drink in the guy's face—or something worse.

What am I doing? I don't belong here.

I'm working at a law firm that wants to exploit my sister's overdose. Nobody voiced any concern that maybe it would be inappropriate to do such a thing just days after her funeral. They all assumed I'd go along, provided I got a nice paycheck. It was ridiculous.

I walked back into the suite and over to the two executives that Hawkes had pointed out to me. "Hey," I said. "I'm Matthew Daley. Your boss thought we should talk." I smiled, then I bluffed. "He told me you guys had been exchanging some pretty hilarious jokes."

The general counsel and chief financial officer—both drunk, clearly—exchanged looks and began to giggle. I leaned in and whispered, "I could use a good laugh. Can you forward me your best ones?"

The chief financial officer's mouth bent into a sly, conspiratorial smile. "If you can handle it." He took out his cell phone. "What's your email?" I told him my personal address, and a few seconds later I felt my phone vibrate. Message received.

"Thanks," I said. "We'll be talking soon."

I left the party. I didn't say goodbye to Tuft or anyone else. I quit. No more firm. I was done. I went out the door and was halfway to the elevator when Francis called my name.

I stopped and turned as he walked toward me.

"Where are you going?" Francis looked confused.

"Home."

Francis took in my hard stare and realized that I wasn't happy. "Are you mad or something?" Francis put his hands on his hips. "You should be saying thank you."

"Thank you?" I turned away from him and looked at the elevator. As my hands balled into tight fists, I just wanted to get away. "I told you to keep what happened to my sister private, and instead you tell the entire executive team, and then, just to take it a step further, you call reporters and pitch a story about my dead sister and my bizarre passion for representing the people who killed her. Doesn't that strike you as a horrible, messed-up idea?"

"Tuft liked it," Francis said. "Everybody liked it, and I was hoping you'd understand the opportunity that I created. It's great for you, and it's great for the firm."

"And part of the plan is to introduce her to my family and let her interview them, is it? Have you any idea who my family is?"

"The whole go-back-to-Saint-Louis-thing was Tuft's deal. I didn't come up with that."

"But you obviously didn't oppose or bother to run it past me first. My brother is not going to say nice things about drug companies. Do you know what he does for a living? Drives around in a truck and protests about half of this firm's clients."

I began to walk away. "Hold up." Francis put his hand on my shoulder, stopping me. "You're not thinking clearly, Matthew. With this you can go places that you never dreamed. I saw that opportunity for you, and I helped it along. If you accept it, in five or ten years you can write your own ticket. You can start your own law firm. You could become a federal judge, or one of these pharmaceutical companies would hire you in a second to be their general counsel. Do you know how much that pays?" He didn't wait for an answer. "Instead of making a few million here, you'd make triple that plus stock options."

"You had no right to tell everybody about my sister."

"I'm your mentor and I'm mentoring you. I'm helping you succeed."

I took his hand off my shoulder and began walking away. "What you did isn't helping me succeed. I'm not doing it."

Francis followed behind me, continuing to plead his case. "Tobias Tuft may have presented this as a proposal," he whispered, "but I'm telling you, Matthew, this is not a voluntary mission. You either get on board or leave."

"Then I'm leaving."

"That's a huge mistake," Francis said as the elevator doors opened. "I'm not just saying that because I don't want you to go. I'm saying that as your mentor and as someone who, whether you agree or disagree, poured a lot of time and effort into making you the lawyer that you are today."

"I wasn't going to last here much longer anyway." I got into the elevator.

"But at least try," Francis said. "You're not even trying to stay here. You're just throwing it away. Everything that you worked for."

"Maybe things have changed." I pressed the button for the main floor. "I can't do this anymore."

The elevator doors began to slide closed, but Francis stuck his hand between them. A bell sounded, and the doors jerked back. "Listen,"

Francis said. "You've had an awful month. There's no turning back from this. Just stop for a second and think about what you're doing."

"I have thought about it." The doors began to close again. "When I die, I don't want to be known as the lawyer who helped hurt people. There has to be a better way. I don't know what it is, but I know this isn't it." The doors shut, and the elevator began to fall.

CHAPTER TWELVE

It took a few minutes, but my driver soon arrived, and I got into the back of the Lincoln Town Car. "Where to?"

I thought for a second. "Nelson Rockler." I leaned back, suddenly tired and drained. "Take Twelfth up to Forty-Fourth. It's by the Harvard Club." I rolled down the window to take in some fresh air, and I crawled back inside my head for the ride. I thought about calling Tess, but what would I say? *Hey, honey, I just wanted to check in and let you know that I committed career suicide tonight.* No, that wouldn't be good.

For more than seven years, people at the firm told me how special I was, how essential I was to the firm. Affirmation I desperately craved. I certainly never got that from my dad. And I never really got much from Mom, either, apart from the occasional obligatory "Good job."

Baxter, Speller & Tuft was different. It was like a cult, indoctrinating me. They fed my ego. During my three months as a summer associate between my second and third years of law school, partners bought me lunches at expensive restaurants and took me to Broadway shows. After graduation, I became an associate, and they kept telling me I was "chosen" and "among the best and brightest." The constant praise assuaged my insecurities and drove me to work harder and bill even more hours for the firm. As a poor kid from Saint Louis, I didn't want to disappoint them. I didn't want to be revealed as a fraud.

The cycle continued, every day them telling me I was distinguishing myself at the best law firm in the world. They were the elite, the rich and powerful, and I could be, too, they told me. Then I made partner, and now they wanted more.

New York City's night sky clouded over. I heard a clap of thunder in the distance, but it still hadn't started to rain. I checked my watch, wondering if the Yankees game was over or whether there'd be a delay. *Not a good way to start the season,* I thought. Then I closed my eyes for a second to rest, and, when I opened them, twenty minutes had passed. We were there.

I gave the driver a tip and got out of the car. Nelson Rockler was in a skyscraper about five blocks from Times Square. Tess worked for a notoriously ruthless attorney, Shirley Glade. Her nickname was "Glade the Blade." Most associates lasted only two years, but Tess had made it five.

After signing in at security, I knew where to go. I stepped off the elevator and walked past the overnight receptionist. Even though I didn't work at Nelson Rockler, they didn't stop me. I was a white guy in a suit who didn't appear to be lost. When I made it to her office, I paused at the closed door, still trying to figure out what to say.

Good news, I'm going to have a lot more time to do things around the apartment and cook. Bad news, that beautiful brownstone isn't going to happen, and the wedding reception just got smaller.

I opened the door, ready to—hopefully—receive some comfort from the woman I loved. I needed support, somebody I could trust to talk through how I felt and how I should go forward. If it were a movie, there would be violins, maybe a harp. Even though it was nighttime, sunshine from the window would miraculously bathe the office in a soft, golden light. Tess would be confused and startled by my sudden appearance, then the camera would cut to me, and I'd say something witty and self-deprecating. Channeling my inner Hugh Grant, I'd say, "I guess my new job is just loving you." The audience would groan but wouldn't be able to resist bursting into applause as we embraced. It would be perfect. Everything would be OK.

Instead I opened the door and saw Tess and another man kissing. Her shirt was untucked. His hand was up her bare back. They must have seen the movement or sensed a change in the room, because the man immediately pulled away. He was tall and dressed in an expensive three-piece suit. He looked about ten, maybe fifteen years older, probably a partner at the firm.

Every law student had to take a class in criminal law, regardless of whether they ever wanted to prosecute or defend criminals. I don't remember much from the class, but I did remember that "heat of passion" was a defense to murder.

My class had found a certain antiquated humor in the defense. *Le crime passionnel* was rooted in the idea that a person completely overcome with the unexpected betrayal of a lover lost the ability to commit premeditated murder. So a man who comes home to find another man in bed with his wife could pull out a gun and shoot them both. It wasn't a complete defense, but often enough to avoid the death penalty.

Seeing Tess and this man together *did* cause me to lose my mind. I never believed that our relationship was perfect, but I loved her. Even with all her flaws, she was a partner who I chose because she understood where I wanted to go. Trust, now, was broken.

I staggered away from the open door. Everything moved in slow motion. The man receded into the corner, staring at the ground. Tess opened her mouth and started to speak, but I didn't understand a word, the sounds jumbling in my head.

I should have punched that guy in the face, but there was no bloodshed, no violence. Instead I walked out of her office in a state of mind that I had never experienced before—the "heat of passion," just as we'd imagined in law school. Colors were too bright. Sounds too loud. Temperatures rose and fell in waves. So much adrenaline coursed through me that I think I could have lifted a car and thrown it across the street, Superman-style.

I cabbed back to our apartment. Everything seemed to take place at warp speed. I walked through the door and then out again with a suitcase filled with clothes, a duffel bag filled with shoes and ties, and a cardboard box filled with my favorite books, Allison's journals, and some personal items. That was it. Tess could have the dishes. She could have the television, the furniture, and anything else. I was going back to Saint Louis. The airline would charge extra for the box, but I didn't care.

CHAPTER THIRTEEN

On the flight, I didn't listen to music or read a magazine or play with an electronic screen. Instead I just stared out the window and watched the specks of light below become fewer and fewer the farther away we got from the city.

As the other passengers on the red-eye went to sleep, I listened to my breath. I counted my heartbeats, and I waited for my hands to stop shaking. My life at a big firm as a New York attorney was over. The closing date for the brownstone in Park Slope would come and go without me, earnest money lost. I figured that it wouldn't take long for Tess to move in with her new man. She had a plan for her life, and I had no doubt that she would stick to it, with or without me. Now I had to figure out who I really was.

To Francis, I'm sure that I had sounded confident, like a person who'd found his moral compass. Truthfully, however, that compass was doing nothing but spinning. My head was a muddle of thoughts and emotions, highs and lows. I had to start over.

During a five-hour layover in Chicago, I called my brother. It was four in the morning, but he answered. After he told me that I should've waited for a direct flight, I explained everything that had happened, and why I'd rather be in an airport than in New York City. When I was done, there was silence. Then he said, "Sue 'em."

"Excuse me?"

"I said you should sue all the bastards, every single one. If your boss—Tufty or Tufter or Toffee or whatever—thinks there's going to be a bunch of lawsuits against these drug companies pushing pain pills, why don't you just sue them yourself?"

"Because it's not that easy." I watched a frazzled mother hustle her young son down the terminal, then added, "The case is impossible."

In my mind, I cycled through the most common causes of action brought by class action attorneys against pharmaceutical companies. None of the claims fit. There was a weak element in each one, causation the most obvious of them. A plaintiff had to prove direct causation—that the injury would not have occurred absent the manufacturer's negligence.

"There are too many intervening factors, and all the victims are different," I said. "They come from different walks of life, different circumstances. A class action would start to fall apart the moment it was filed. That's why Tuft was so jazzed about the idea. It was low risk, high reward. He knows defending these lawsuits will generate thousands of dollars in billable hours, and in the end they all will be dismissed or fade away with a minimal payout, nuisance value."

"Then don't do a class action," Jackson said. "Just focus on Allison, man. Just hold them accountable for our sister." Jackson was fully awake. His voice grew louder and a little higher.

"Are you asking to be exploited?"

"In order to jack these corporate bastards up, I am. Exploit me."

"But Mom and Dad would have to sign on," I said. "I can't imagine that."

"I can," Jackson said. "They trust you."

"I'm not so sure about that."

"At first they'll be resistant," Jackson said. "But in the end, they'll go along, even Dad."

After we finished talking, I checked the time. There were still several hours before the second leg of my flight. I found a Starbucks near a set of bathrooms and a place for a walk-in massage that hadn't opened yet. I decided to kill time by drinking coffee and surfing the internet until boarding.

As I sat, exhausted and angry, I thought about what it would be like to be a plaintiff's attorney suing a giant pharmaceutical company. I'd have an advantage, of course, because I knew all the defenses. I'd see the punches and counterpunches coming. The challenge intrigued me, the risk and redemption. After my brief interactions with the NexBeaux executives at the Yankees game, I already knew they were idiots—and I had an email containing inappropriate jokes to prove it.

As I pulled up various news websites on my phone, I combed through the archives and read more about opioid pain medications. With each article, I began to identify important events and key pieces of information. An outline for a potential lawsuit began to take shape in my head. I took the initial set of facts and tried to think of different ways of distilling the history and nature of opioid painkillers to my advantage. It was all a cycle. Nothing was new. NexBeaux was just doing what every drug company had done since the chemical compounds were discovered over a hundred years ago.

Opioid was just an umbrella term encompassing a variety of drugs with similar elements, most importantly diacetylmorphine hydrochloride, that activate the same part of the brain. It started with morphine. Initially morphine was considered harmless, then people realized that it wasn't. In the 1890s, the German pharmaceutical company Bayer decided to commercialize a new variation of the chemicals, naming it heroin. Like those who first sold morphine, Bayer marketed heroin as harmless. It was supposedly a nonaddictive form of morphine, but that wasn't true.

A hundred years later, pharmaceutical companies like NexBeaux tried again. A new batch of opioid products came on the market, and, just like morphine and heroin before it, Bentrax was sold as a wonder drug.

Television commercials encouraged people to "ask your doctor about the benefits of Bentrax and how Bentrax can help you better manage your pain" and promised that the drug was "trusted by doctors" and "less addictive than the leading pain medications." And just like the original marketing of morphine and heroin, the claims made by NexBeaux about Bentrax were wrong.

This would be the basis of any lawsuit. *Keep it simple,* I told myself. *Don't overreach.* Stray too far or ask for too much and I'd lose.

I kept thinking about the lawsuit and the different angles I could play during the flight home. Eventually I heard the panels open beneath the plane as we descended toward the runway. The wheels fought the wind as they were lowered into position. The captain turned off the cabin lights and rang the bell to prepare for landing. As my ears popped, we fell, bounced twice on the runway, and slowed to a stop.

Just like that, I was back home in Saint Louis.

Jackson met me at the baggage claim, a huge smile on his face. Now that I was unemployed, my brother was finally proud of me. We loaded up his truck with my things and headed to our parents' house in Benton Park. I looked at the time on the dashboard display, and I was relieved that they'd both likely be gone for the day when I arrived.

"Did you call them like I asked?"

"I did," Jackson said. "They didn't say much when I told them that you had quit and were coming home for a little while." When the music broke for commercials, Jackson turned off the radio. "Want me to come in with you?" He signaled at the exit for I-70 east.

"No," I said. "I'll be fine. I'm just going to shower and lie down for a little bit."

"I've been thinking about what we talked about . . . the lawsuit and all." Jackson accelerated around one car and then another. "I was just shooting my mouth," he said. "If you don't want to do it, that's cool." Jackson rubbed the morning stubble on his chin. "That's just what I do. When I'm in a corner, I just wanna fight my way out. Figured you should too."

"No," I said. "Don't apologize. I've been defending these people for so long, my perspective is all screwed up. The firm pounds it into your head that the 'client is always right' and 'never tell a client no.' It wears you down, and you start to minimize and rationalize because everybody around you is minimizing and rationalizing."

"So you're actually thinking about doing it?" Jackson's face brightened, but it was obvious that he was trying to stay level. He didn't want to scare me off. "You're gonna take 'em on?"

"I'm definitely thinking about it," I said. "It may be due to sleep deprivation, but I'm definitely thinking about it."

"Hot damn." Jackson honked his horn a few times and accelerated past a large delivery truck. "Maybe you ain't so bad after all." Jackson put his hand on my shoulder and gave it a squeeze. "All you gotta do is convince Mom and Dad."

I nodded as we drove past a broken-down Toyota Corolla. There always seemed to be a car broken down on the side of the road about five miles from the Forty interchange. I pictured Harold Cantor, Megan's father, and how he probably felt when his attorneys told him that Judge Platte had granted my motion to dismiss the BioPrint case. I wondered if my parents could handle the scrutiny that would come with a lawsuit like this. Could they handle losing? "Let's just take it one step at a time."

I was trying to keep both our expectations low and grounded in reality. In addition to convincing my parents, if I was really going to do this, I needed help. Although I was licensed to practice law in Missouri, I couldn't file a major lawsuit from my parents' basement. NexBeaux would have an army of lawyers. The thought of facing them alone was frightening. I needed to find an army of my own.

As Jackson exited the highway, I had an idea. Even if it was a small army, at least it would be something.

◆ ◆ ◆

By early afternoon, I was ready. A little sleep, followed by a shower and a shave, had given me some life. I went out the back door and ventured into our detached garage. Junk was piled everywhere. What room was left was taken up by the Mustang, inoperable due to its lack of an engine or wheels. Other than the occasional push from my mother to sell it, the Mustang had been largely forgotten.

I squeezed past the car, sidestepping boxes of Christmas ornaments and random tools. In the back, hanging from the rafters, was my old Trek mountain bike. I had mowed lawns and done odd jobs for an entire summer to afford it. In junior high and high school, that bike had given me freedom.

With some effort, I managed to lift the bicycle off the hooks without knocking everything down. I put it on my shoulder and hauled it outside. In the light, I could better assess its condition. As expected, the tires were flat. Cobwebs draped across the frame and crowded the spokes. Overall, however, not bad. The gears and chain seemed OK. My worst fear was that they would have been covered in rust, but the garage had kept the bike dry. With a little solvent, the gears and chain would shine again.

I found my father's toolbox and a half-full can of WD-40 on the garage's workbench. I checked my watch—a quarter past one. Plenty of time. According to the law school's online schedule, Professor Sherman Friedman's class met at three.

Sherman and I had met our first day of law school. Incoming students were divided into four-person study groups during orientation. Sherman was one of the three others who were in my group. He came from a prominent Jewish family in Saint Louis, generations of lawyers. From day one, Sherman made it clear to everyone that he was only getting his law license because his father had told him that he'd get cut out of his will if he didn't carry on the family tradition.

I figured if I could get the bike going, I'd be able to catch him before class.

Forty minutes later, I was on the road. It'd been more than ten years since I'd been on a bike, and the feeling was wonderful. At a stop sign, I looked down at my hands and smiled at the bit of grease on my knuckles. Two weeks ago I couldn't have imagined being back in Saint Louis and living in my parents' basement, much less pedaling my old Trek through the neighborhood.

I cut down to Broadway and fifteen minutes later took Chouteau Avenue to the Riverfront Trail. I biked along the river, past the Arch, and up to the Eads Bridge. As cars passed at sixty miles an hour, I couldn't help wondering what would happen if I got clipped. Only a few feet separated me from the railing—I could easily topple over the side and fall into the Mississippi—but I pushed those thoughts out of my mind as I crossed. Although the wind rocked me back and forth, cars gave me plenty of space. It helped that I wasn't trying to cross at rush hour.

◆ ◆ ◆

The Cahokia College of Law was not Harvard. If Harvard was a Lamborghini, then Cahokia was a 1970s Eastern European moped. Don't get me wrong; I'm not a snob. Not every lawyer from a top-tier law school became a brilliant attorney, but Cahokia occupied a precarious position in the manufacturing and minting of baby lawyers in America.

According to *U.S. News & World Report*, Cahokia ranked dead last among law schools. Its accreditation was under review, and the federal Department of Education was investigating it for violations of student lending practices because too many kids were taking out loans and defaulting soon after graduation—if they ever graduated at all.

Founded in the late 1970s, Cahokia was meant to provide an opportunity to individuals who wanted to become a lawyer as a second career. A night school, it catered to men and women in their late thirties and early forties. Its early life wasn't bad. Few, if any, Cahokia graduates became judges or occupied prestigious positions in the Bar Association, but the school did provide hundreds of competent, affordable lawyers who'd eventually hang out their shingles in old neighborhood storefronts. These solo practitioners, these one-attorney shops, would represent people going through divorce, drafting a will, or seeking affordable representation for a low-level criminal offense. Their clients didn't care whether their lawyer could successfully petition the United States Supreme Court or whether they were members of the local country club—they just wanted some help navigating the courts.

I locked my bike next to the entrance of the building in East Saint Louis, not far from the hospital. This was considered the nice part of town, although it still looked pretty rough to me. East Saint Louis was distinct from Saint Louis. Located just across the river in Illinois, East Saint Louis had always played second fiddle to its bigger cousin. When Saint Louis prospered, East Saint Louis prospered a little less. When Saint Louis struggled, East Saint Louis collapsed. While some might already know that from Jonathan Kozol's profile of the city's crumbling schools in his seminal book, *Savage Inequalities*, for most, the problems facing East Saint Louis were best illuminated by the theft of the Griswold family's hubcaps in Chevy Chase's classic comedy *National Lampoon's Vacation*.

Inside the law school's entryway, a security officer was stationed at a desk. I signed in and was directed to the clinic offices and classroom in the basement. When I eventually found the Civil Litigation Clinic, Sherman was standing in front of a small group of his students—very small. Three in all. I had expected more, but it made sense. When trying to find information about Sherman, I found a recent newspaper article that stated that enrollment at Cahokia had dropped 300 percent in the past five years, partly due to the economy and partly due to accreditation issues.

I stood in the back and listened to Sherman rail against the excesses of capitalism, like an overweight Bernie Sanders. "Don't buy into the myth that our country is bankrupt. Don't buy into the myth that we can't afford to provide housing and health care and education to the poor. Are we not wealthier than France and Canada and Norway? Are we not ten times more powerful? Then why can't we do it? These are the ideas you must keep in the forefront of your mind when asking a jury for damages. To most people, ten thousand dollars sounds like a lottery jackpot, but it's nothing to these companies. They spend more than that on paper clips."

The students, a ragtag bunch, laughed and nodded. Each of them had at least one visible tattoo. The skinny woman in the front row had purple spiked hair and what appeared to be a nail through her nose. Even Sherman wasn't wearing a suit, not even khakis or a dress shirt. Just jeans, sandals, and a faded pink T-shirt from his niece's bat mitzvah.

I gotta get Sherman and Jackson together. The world will never be the same.

When Sherman noticed me, he did a double take. I'd rarely seen him this speechless. "My God," he said, recovering, "speaking of the capitalist bourgeoisie." The class turned to see who Sherman was talking about. "Ladies and gentlemen, we have here a real bona fide corporate blood-sucking lawyer." Sherman bowed his head slightly. "I want to introduce you to my friend and former law school classmate, Matthew Daley."

Sherman clapped, and his students clapped along with him. He pointed to a seat near his desk. "Please come forward and sit. The force is a powerful thing, young Jedi. Perhaps I can teach you how to use your powers for good instead of evil."

"Thanks," I said as I sat down. "I need all the help I can get."

◆ ◆ ◆

Later, the students filed out, leaving Sherman and me to ourselves. "I can see why you love to teach," I said.

Sherman walked over to the desk where I was sitting. "It never gets old." He gathered up his notes. "Too bad they're probably going to shut this place down. I'm not sure what'll happen." He paused, and his shoulders slumped. "I doubt I'll be able to find another teaching gig." Sherman walked toward the door, and I followed. "Let's lock up, and I can show you my fancy office with a view of a parking lot and a self-storage facility. Sort of give you the grand tour."

He guided me up to the third floor. His office was filled with treatises and biographies of various lawyers, particularly Clarence Darrow. Even in law school, Sherman loved Clarence Darrow, the lawyer who famously took on William Jennings Bryan in defense of a teacher who taught the theory of evolution in violation of Tennessee law.

I sat down in a chair across from Sherman's cluttered desk. "Are you serious about the school closing down?"

"Did you see my class? When I started working here, I'd have twenty kids. Now it's three." Sherman picked up a pen and started fiddling. "It's all wrapped up in the crackdown on those for-profit technical schools. You know the ones—they take out a bunch of cheap television ads during the afternoon reality shows and charge kids who don't know any better about twenty thousand dollars to learn how to frost a cake or install computer software, but the degree doesn't actually improve their job prospects." Sherman looked around him. "We got lumped into that, and I have to admit that sometimes I don't think this school *is* much different. There are too many lawyers, and the world doesn't necessarily need this school. We aren't for-profit scum, but our graduates certainly struggle, no denying that."

Sherman looked out the window. The law school's lawn was filled with bare trees anxiously waiting for those first few days of real Missouri heat to fully come alive. It wouldn't be long. Sherman then turned and looked at me. "But you saw them and heard them in there. Those kids are going to end up taking cases nobody else will. They're going to represent people at an affordable price or probably for free." He set his pen back down on his desk. "I don't know if that justifies the student loans that every single one of them has or not. I've got a lot of mixed emotions about it . . . Maybe I'm just rationalizing my own existence."

"So you're going to close if the school loses its accreditation?"

"No. There are lots of unaccredited law schools in the United States. California has dozens of them. So the lack of accreditation will probably just mean even fewer students and some layoffs. The killer is if the Department of Education no longer guarantees our student loans. No student loans, no law school. It takes money to operate this place, and nobody's paying cash up front. Nobody."

He paused, lost in his own thoughts. I didn't break the silence, because we'd been friends long enough for me to know that he'd come around—and he did. His eyes narrowed, as if he just realized how odd it was for me to suddenly appear in his classroom after not speaking for years. "So, like, what's going on with you?"

I told him about my sister and Tobias Tuft's plan. "Disgusting," he said when I was done. "I would've quit too." He shook his head. "But what your fiancée did, man—that's just cold."

"I know."

"Did you get the ring back?"

"No," I said. "It, like, just happened . . . haven't seen her since, and I don't plan to."

Sherman agreed. "What's next?"

"Well, I want to sue the drug company that introduced my sister to heroin." I handed the folder to him. "Their name is NexBeaux, and they sell the pain medication Bentrax."

Sherman laughed. "You know that's like one of the biggest pharmaceutical companies in the world."

"I know," I said. "That's why I'm here. I was hoping that you and your students could help."

"Go to court?" He pushed his chair back, as if actually practicing law was a disease. "That's not my thing."

"You don't have to go to court or even put on a tie if you don't want to," I said. "But I need space to work, and I need your brain. You're one of the smartest people I know."

"Flattery." Sherman hesitated, then he leaned back. "Do you have the lawsuit written?"

"No," I said. "Not yet. I've done some of the preliminary research," I lied. "But I expect it'll be done soon."

Sherman took a deep breath, then exhaled slowly. "I'll tell you what I'll do," he said. "Let me take a look when you're done. Email it to me, and I'll read it, but only as a friend. Then we can go from there."

"That's all I ask."

◆ ◆ ◆

On the way home, I approached the forty-five-acre cemetery coming up from the river. When I'd decided to visit Sherman, I hadn't planned on this, but I felt drawn. Saint Matthews Cemetery wasn't far from Benton Park, but it was in a slightly wealthier part of town. The houses lining Holly Hills Boulevard were bigger. They went beyond shelter. Everybody had more space.

I biked through the cemetery gate and wound through the grounds toward Allison's gravestone. I knew where to go. My family had been buried here since my great-great-grandfather immigrated to Saint Louis 110 years ago. Amid the other tombstones, Allison's was a simple black marker.

I walked the bike across the green lawn, set it aside, and sat next to the grave. It was a cool spot, shielded from the sun by a large shadow cast by a nearby oak. I was alone. The cemetery was quiet. It was too early in the season for anyone to be out mowing the lawn or trimming weeds.

I reached out and ran my fingers across Allison's name, engraved on a granite stone along with the years of her life. I stared at that gravestone a long time, lost, and started to cry. Not just one tear or two—the tears came uncontrollably.

The walls of those compartments within me were no longer just fractured. They had fallen, broken down. It was something that I hadn't allowed myself to do until then, but alone, here, it felt like it was time.

I sat there, looking down at Allison's grave, filled with sadness and loss as well as anger. I'd never felt rage so deep as in that moment. Her death was wrong and unfair, and NexBeaux was going to pay the price.

On the way home, I stopped at the Venice Café to use their free Wi-Fi and get started drafting the complaint. The café was still quiet, and it'd be a few hours before the music and party really started. I sat on the patio under a large propane heater, mostly by myself, surrounded only by concrete and mosaic sculptures, a pond with two happy turtles, and a diverse collection of rusted license plates, as well as an odd lawn ornament or two. If a revolution was going to start, the Venice Café was a good place to begin.

I removed the laptop from my backpack and started to type. I wanted to get it out as quickly as possible. There'd be time for adding dates and details later. I felt a drive that I hadn't before. I wanted to tell my sister's story. I wanted to expose NexBeaux for what it really was and the dangerous game that it played with thousands of people's lives.

There was little doubt in my mind that they knew the risks, because the active ingredients in Bentrax weren't new. A beautiful television advertisement and the reassuring words of a product spokesperson didn't change the fact that the chemicals that were Bentrax's foundation, like morphine and heroin, were highly addictive. And when the prescription ran out, people would seek alternatives. They'd turn to street drugs, and that's what happened to Allison.

◆ ◆ ◆

I brought my bike back into the garage, then I walked up the back steps and turned the knob. I had been at the café for a few hours, and it was later than I had planned. "Hello?" I said as I stepped through the door. "Anybody home?"

"Little Matty, is that you?" my mother asked. She and my father were in the living room watching television.

"Yes, Mom, it's me." I put my backpack with my computer down and walked toward her. She got up from the couch, came over, and gave me a hug.

"Jackson told us you were coming, but I was wondering what happened when you weren't here when I got home." She gave me another quick hug, then we walked back to her place on the couch. "I thought maybe you decided to stay in that fancy hotel again."

I sat down next to her. "No," I said. "I think those days are over for now."

"But you were doing so well." My mother shook her head. "I find it very hard to believe that they would fire you."

"They didn't fire me, Mom," I said. "I quit."

While my mom looked confused, my dad just nodded his head. "Big decision." He muted the television and leaned back in his big, overstuffed recliner. "Didn't know you were unhappy."

"I didn't know I was unhappy either," I said. "But after I came back from the funeral, things started to change."

"Things changed that fast in a few days?" My father was skeptical. He glanced at the television, checking to make sure it was still a commercial break, then back to me. "What's your little fiancée think about all this?"

"I don't think she's my fiancée anymore." I scratched my head, thinking about a positive spin to put on the last forty-eight hours of my life. Thinking of none, I just decided to tell the truth. "She was cheating on me," I said. "And my law firm wanted me to defend people that I didn't want to defend."

"Like who?" This got my dad's attention. He set the remote control in his lap and gave me his full attention, focused.

"It's a drug company called NexBeaux," I said. "Allison was prescribed their stuff after her car accident. It's addicting, and I think that's what got her started."

My father's eyes narrowed. "Addicted?" He waved away the idea. "If she had wanted to stop, then she just needed to stop hanging out with all those losers. It's not that complicated." He picked up the remote again, anticipating the end of the commercial break. His finger rested on the button, ready to unmute the television the moment the show returned. "Guy at work that I know, he was a drunk for years, then one day his wife said that she would leave him if he didn't stop drinking, and he begged her. He says, 'I'll stop.' And he did." He completed his little story with a quick wave, like it was easy and smooth. "Never had another drink after that. Started going to church. Decided to change his life, and it was over. No freakin' drama."

"I don't think it's that easy," I said. "Some people can do that. Some people can't. Getting off heroin is hard."

My father stopped listening to me. His show was back, and our conversation had grown tiresome. Even though I had wanted to talk to both of my parents about the lawsuit, it was obviously not a good time. It would only lead to trouble if I got between my father and his shows.

Instead I decided to divide and conquer. "Mom," I said. "Can we talk in the kitchen?"

She looked at me and nodded ever so slightly but didn't say the words. The things that my father had said about Allison . . . I knew that he had said the same things to my mother many times for decades. As a boy, I had heard him screaming. I'd be in my basement bedroom, maybe doing my homework or lying in bed, trying to fall asleep. Through the ceiling I could hear them arguing and my father stomping around the kitchen above me, slamming drawers.

My dad was always furious about the money that my mom spent on alcohol, ignoring the fact that he drank just as much as she did, then the complaints about money led to further complaints about the house not being clean and dinners not being cooked and laundry not being folded. It was all because my mom, unlike him, had no willpower. Then, more often than not, it became physical.

My mother and I got up from the couch and went into the kitchen. She walked over to the sink and began to fill it with hot water and soap. As she began to wash the dirty dinner plates, I took the dish towel off the hook. "I can dry."

"You don't have to, I can handle it." She shut off the water.

"No, I'd love to help." I joined her at the sink. As we scraped and scrubbed, we fell into a rhythm. About halfway through, I told my mother about Sherman and his class and a potential lawsuit on behalf of Allison.

"I don't know." She handed me a wet dish. "Bad things happen to good people." Then she picked up another dish to scrub. "It's not always somebody else's fault."

"But sometimes it is, right?"

"Really? Nobody made her do it." She handed me another dish. "It's not like people were tying her down and making her do those things." She stepped away from the sink and took another towel out of the drawer to dry her hands. "I just can't talk about this right now. It's too soon."

Like with my father, the conversation had run its course. My mom wasn't going to engage any further. I watched her as she walked over to the narrow closet by the telephone. Inside the closet, there was the vacuum cleaner. A mop and broom hung on the door. On the bottom shelf there were all sorts of cleaning products, most of which were rarely used. And then on the next shelf there was alcohol. My mom got the bottle of vodka, then she went into the refrigerator and got a bottle of juice. That was all she needed.

"You don't need to do that, Mom," I said.

"Sometimes your father is right," she said. "People change. People quit. Your father doesn't drink like he used to. He doesn't do the things he used to." She began walking toward the hallway leading to the bedrooms. "Some people don't have the will." Then she disappeared for the night with her bottle.

I put together a plate of leftover food from the refrigerator and went into the backyard with my laptop. It was dark now. The sun had set, and the neighborhood was quiet. I set up on the picnic table and continued drafting my lawsuit against NexBeaux. I wondered what would've happened if NexBeaux required doctors to explain that Bentrax was just another form of heroin. How many fewer prescriptions would've been written if doctors had said to their patients, "I'm sorry to hear about your back pain. How about a little heroin to ease your discomfort?" If that would've happened, NexBeaux would've made a lot less money, there probably wouldn't be an opioid crisis, and Allison would probably be alive.

I just needed to convince my parents that while willpower helps, sometimes it wasn't enough.

CHAPTER FOURTEEN

It took another week to finish my draft of the NexBeaux lawsuit. I emailed it to Sherman, as promised, and we arranged to meet at McGurk's, an Irish bar in Soulard. The bar had been there a long time, but the neighborhood had been given a second life in recent years. Its proximity to downtown Saint Louis made the area ideal for wealthy professionals with no kids and a love of historic homes. The high per capita ratio of pubs to residents also didn't hurt.

Jackson wanted to come along, and I didn't see any reason to say no, especially since he was willing to drive. The bar was crowded when we arrived. To my left, a young woman with big plastic glasses played a pennywhistle on a small stage. Two bearded hipsters accompanied her; one played a guitar, the other a button accordion.

Sherman texted me to meet him around back. Jackson and I took a right through a bachelorette party and found that the patio was just as crowded as the bar. We waded through the mix of college kids and yuppies until I spotted Sherman in the corner.

"Beautiful night." He held up his beer, toasting my presence. "I think spring has finally sprung."

I introduced Sherman to my brother.

"Are you the socialist?" Jackson asked.

"Democratic socialist," Sherman clarified.

"Close enough." Jackson smiled. "It's good to find another enlightened soul in the Show-Me State." He sat down next to Sherman, and the two of them immediately started talking about raising the minimum wage to some astronomical level that would bankrupt every small business in America. Instead of participating in a debate about economics, I kept my mouth shut and looked for a waitress to bring me a beer.

As the night continued, the three of us scoped out the women. A married man, Sherman urged us to flirt. "I have an opportunity to live vicariously through you guys," he said. "You two are at the perfect age for legendary hookups."

"I don't know," I said. "Remember that engagement we talked about?"

"Doesn't matter," Sherman said. "Rebound city. You've got all the superhot women our age. The ones who rejected us in high school and are now divorced. You can go older and date some rich executive who put her professional life first, and you can go all the way down to recent college grads and not be super creepy."

"But it's still creepy," I said.

"But not *super* creepy." Jackson exchanged looks with Sherman, lending support to his new best friend. "I think I'll go give it a try."

"Yes." Sherman slapped Jackson on the back. "Do it."

"I'm doing it." Jackson got up and wandered toward a group of women standing near the patio bar. We watched him for a little while, then I turned to Sherman.

"I could never do that," I said. "I have never picked up a girl in a bar."

"What about Laura? I thought you two met in a bar, like a law school mixer or something."

Laura Bauer. We had started dating during our first year in law school. She had joined our study group after hers had fallen apart. "We met in the law library," I said. "Where all love blossoms."

"Yeah, right," Sherman said. "I never met any women in the library."

"Maybe you weren't hanging out in the right section."

"Maybe," Sherman said. "Or maybe you're just a better-looking nerd than me."

"Why thank you," I said. "I'll take that as a compliment."

"Have you stayed in touch?"

"With Laura?" I shook my head. "We didn't exactly end on good terms."

"Everybody figured you two would get married."

"I can see that," I said. "But then I got the job at Baxter, Speller & Tuft in New York, and my mentor advised me to ditch her. He said she'd distract me, and, like a fool, I followed his advice."

"Well," Sherman said. "She's still around. You should look her up."

"That ship's probably sailed." I remembered Laura's expression when we broke up. It was the day after graduation when I told her it was over. I was too much of a coward to drop any hints beforehand, and she never saw it coming. I broke her heart. "How about we change topics?"

"The lawsuit?"

"What'd you think of the draft I sent over?"

Sherman, now Professor Sherman, brought his hands together and lifted his nose in the air, preparing himself to pontificate. "It was brilliant, as expected." He chose his words carefully. "Well written, concise, and you identified all the legal claims that I think are applicable, but . . . if you look at it objectively, Matt, you have to admit that this case has a lot of problems."

I sipped on my Guinness. "I prefer to use the term *opportunities* rather than *problems*. *Problems* has very negative connotations."

"That's because not every problem is an opportunity," Sherman said. "Some problems are exactly that—problems. It's one thing to talk about taking on the evil corporations over a beer on a patio or in a nice cozy classroom, like I do, but this is a high-profile case, and, as you know, these companies don't play nice."

"So are you saying I shouldn't do it?"

Sherman avoided answering the question. "Do your parents and brother really know what they're getting into?"

"He's on board." I watched Jackson dancing with a woman to a Gaelic version of Adele's "Hello." "My parents aren't quite there yet."

"I don't blame them." Sherman looked at me, now sympathetic. "I know you're hurting, but, even setting aside the legal challenges—I mean, opportunities—personally and professionally it's crazy."

I sunk a little lower in my chair, but Sherman wasn't done. "This isn't some random client who found you in the phone book or who golfs with the managing partner at your firm. This case is about *your* sister." He took a drink. "Think about that for a second. What are you going to do when NexBeaux wants to depose your mom, or if they force her to testify at trial? What about your brother?" Sherman looked at Jackson, who was now dancing an Irish jig, clicking his heels in the air. "Don't get me wrong, because he seems like a lot of fun to be around, but what's he going to say on the stand? And what about you? What if they call you to testify? Have you thought about that?"

I sat there and took it all in. Sherman was right about everything. I needed to hear it, but it wasn't changing my mind.

"Addiction is personal," Sherman said. "That type of discovery in this case is relevant. The judge is going to allow it, and their lawyers are not going to respect your family's privacy at all. In fact, the more they pry, the more likely it'll be that you'll cave or your parents will quit. NexBeaux has an incentive to go nasty, early and often."

"And so do I." I leaned back, finding the resolve that I had at Allison's grave. "I'm not going to cave. I'm at rock bottom. What can they do to me?"

"Matt, they will do whatever it takes to destroy you, and you know it." Sherman finished his beer. "You can totally get a job. It hasn't been that long, and you haven't exactly tried. You were profiled in the *Times*, for Pete's sake. But this case will mess all that up. You'll look a little unhinged."

"Now you sound like my dad."

"No," Sherman said. "I sound like somebody who knows you."

"Are you bailing on me?" I asked.

"No," Sherman said. "But I *am* trying to protect you, because you're my friend. You asked for my help for a reason, and I figured the best thing I can provide is a little perspective."

"Thank you," I said. "Because if I'm really going to do this, and for all the reasons you just rattled off, I need you there with me. I lied about you never coming to court, like I said in your office. I need you to be all in with me in order to pull this off. I need my Clarence Darrow."

"You had to go there." He looked up at the sky. "That's really low, you know that? Invoking the name of Clarence Darrow on me. I mean, that's really, truly manipulative." He ran his finger around the edge of his pint glass, thinking. "OK, if you really want to do this, I'm in, and I'll make my students work for you too. If you don't want to do this, I support that too. Maybe it's just the Guinness talking, but I got your back. I'll even put on a suit and tie and dance around for the amusement of a judge."

"Excellent." I raised my hand to get the attention of the waitress. "One more round."

CHAPTER FIFTEEN

The night before we filed our lawsuit, we gathered in the Cahokia basement classroom for a pizza party. It had taken a few more weeks to finalize the theories of liability, but the complaint looked good. In the morning, we'd file it at the historic courthouse in downtown Saint Louis. Known as the 22nd—because Missouri was divided into circuits and the city of Saint Louis was the 22nd of 46 circuit courts—it was the busiest courthouse in the state. More lawsuits were filed and more jury trials occurred in the 22nd than anywhere else, and ours would now be one of them.

Certain legal requirements were necessary to file a lawsuit, and particular language needed to be used in the lawsuit itself. I decided to satisfy those technicalities at the end, rather than the beginning. Using eighteenth-century language in the complaint's introduction would be difficult for nonlawyers to understand, and I wanted at least its first paragraphs to read like a press release—reporters and the general public needed to understand who we were, what we wanted, and why our claims were valid. Plus, it was never too early to begin educating potential jurors.

I stood up on a chair in the middle of the classroom. Jackson, Sherman, and the three students from Sherman's class stood around me. "Ladies and gentlemen," I pronounced, "tomorrow is going to be a historic day." They all burst into applause. "I don't know who's going to represent NexBeaux, but I guarantee that the lawyers are going to work for a massive law firm and get paid a ridiculous amount of money to make us go away. They will call our lawsuit frivolous and our claims ridiculous, but we will press forward. Maybe the judge will agree with them, and our lawsuit will be dismissed. But while other people sit on the sidelines and complain and wonder why nobody is doing anything, we'll go to bed at night knowing that we did what President Theodore Roosevelt encouraged everyone to do, which is to get into the arena and get dirty."

There was more applause. "I want to thank Professor Sherman Friedman for giving me the opportunity to work with you all on such an important case. As I've recently gotten to know you, I've been impressed with your legal research and your comments. I feel pride in a way that I never felt pride while working for a law firm that shall not be named in New York City." I raised an invisible glass. "To Professor Friedman."

Jackson and the students shouted and raised their bottles of water and soda. "To Professor Friedman."

"We have a few more things to do before going home," I continued. "Sherman, I need you to follow up with the reporter from the *St. Louis Post-Dispatch*. Make sure she has an advance copy of our lawsuit, but remind her that she can't make it public until after our press conference."

To Cynthia Sanchez, one of Sherman's students and a mother of two, I said, "Ms. Sanchez, I need you to follow up with KWMU and KMOX. See if they are sending a reporter or whether they just want to call us for an interview."

Then I turned to Jeff Grant, a star college football player whose knee blew out his senior year, and Screw, the girl with the purple hair. "You two are in charge of reading the Rules of Civil Procedure and the local rules to make sure that we have all the documents that we need. Find out if we need to file any other forms along with our lawsuit."

I clapped my hands like a coach who just finished giving his team a halftime pep talk. "Here we go," I said. "There's lots of pizza here to keep us going, and when we're done let's clean up the room, because this is where we're going to have our press conference tomorrow morning at ten a.m. OK?"

Everybody gave another cheer, and I got down off the chair. As the students got busy making their phone calls, I walked over to Sherman and Jackson. "Looks like we're really doing this."

Jackson pulled me in for a bear hug. When I was released, he went over to talk with Cynthia and Screw. Sherman patted me on the back. "I can't believe you sucked me into this, but I love you for it."

"It's getting real," I said. "It's crazy."

Then Sherman whispered, "Can we talk in the hallway? Someplace a little more private."

I nodded, and we left the party. Once we were alone, Sherman looked around, then he began with an expression of concern. "I was reviewing the documents that we're filing tomorrow," he said. "And we're missing an important piece."

I knew exactly what he was talking about. "I know," I said. "I'll have it tomorrow."

"That's not what you were supposed to say." Sherman gave me a look of disappointment. "We've busted our asses over the past month to line this up. I got it cleared through the law school's bureaucracy. You got free student labor until the end of the school year and even through the summer, work space, and now you're telling me that your parents haven't agreed. I thought you locked that down right away."

"They've sort of agreed," I said. "We've had a lot of conversations over the past few weeks, and I think they're coming around."

"But they haven't signed the certificate of representation," Sherman said. "Which tells me that they haven't actually come around, because if they'd come around, then we'd have the certificate of representation and the retainer agreement."

"Don't get mad at me," I said. "I'll get it."

"I thought you had it, Matt," Sherman said. "What am I going to do tomorrow when people start showing up for a press conference about a lawsuit that doesn't exist?"

"It will exist," I said. "And it does exist."

"No, it doesn't," Sherman said. "If it existed, we would have a retainer agreement and a certificate of representation, but we don't." He stepped away. He began to rub the back of his neck, kneading out the stress knots. "Matt, I know this law school is sort of a joke, which means that I'm sort of a joke, but this is my job, and I think I'm pretty good at it. You convinced me, as a friend, to help you. Now you need to get that retainer agreement and certificate of representation, and let's make this real."

"I agree," I said. "I'll get it."

When I got home that night, my parents were in the living room watching television. My dad was in his La-Z-Boy recliner, and my mother was on the couch. I sat down on a chair off to the side. In my hand were two pieces of paper. The first was a retainer agreement. The second was a certificate of representation that I would file with the court.

I waited patiently for the television show to be over. When the final credits rolled and the commercials began, I got up and walked over to the coffee table in front of the couch. I took the remote control and turned off the television.

"What's the deal?" Dad said. "We're watching that."

"I know." I returned the remote to the table. "It's just that I have something to talk to you about."

"If it's about your sister and the lawsuit again . . ." My father's face knotted in disgust, and he looked at my mom. "And your mother doesn't want to hear it either." He pointed at the remote. "Give me that."

"No, Dad." I looked at my mother, then back at him. "I quit my job in New York because I couldn't defend these companies anymore. The people that run NexBeaux are awful. I met them." I pulled out my phone. "This is an email that I got from Duncan Stewart. He's senior vice president of the company that makes Bentrax, the painkiller that Allison took after the car accident." I cleared my throat. "Question: What does a person on Bentrax do for exercise?" I looked at my mother. "Answer: Open her eyes." I looked at my father. "What did the Oxy addict get on his IQ test?" I paused. "Drool." Then I read the last one. "What do a hockey player and a woman hooked on Bentrax have in common?" I waited. "Answer: They both change their clothes after three periods."

I shook my head. "These are pharmaceutical executives. Can you believe that? They make enormous amounts of money, then they joke about people, like Allison, who get addicted to their product." I ran my hand through my hair. "I want to file a lawsuit against them. If I don't, I'm going to have a hard time moving forward. I have to do this for her, and I have to do this for me. I can't just let it go."

My mom and dad exchanged looks, and my father glanced at his watch. I figured I had about a minute before he gave up on the television, got up, and left.

"I love you two very much," I said, pressing forward, "and I know that things have been complicated. I know it seemed like I've been running away from you all these years, ashamed, but now I've gotten a different perspective."

I started to go on but stopped myself and tried to focus. "I'm sorry if I ever made you two feel bad. I know that I've made mistakes, and you've made mistakes, but there's nothing we can do about it. I know you don't understand the lawsuit. I know it's painful to talk about Allison, but I need to tell Allison's story. I don't want to be silent. I want to hold somebody accountable, or at least try to." A lump formed in my throat. "Allison wasn't perfect, but she didn't deserve to die."

I took out a pen and set it on the table next to the remote control. Then I took the retainer agreement along with the certificate of representation and put both documents down next to the pen. Then I stepped back.

"I can only do this if you agree. I want to file this lawsuit tomorrow. People have worked very hard to do this. Jackson is on board, but I really need you to agree. You have to agree to let me do this for Allison. Without you, I can't do it."

Neither of my parents said anything, which may or may not have been a good sign. "Thank you for hearing me out, and I hope that you can trust me. I can't guarantee that we're going to win. In fact, we probably are going to lose, but I won't embarrass you, and I won't embarrass Allison. I'm not going to embarrass anyone. Especially you, Pops. Nobody down at work is going to laugh at you. The Daley family has to take a stand, and when we do, we could help a lot of people."

That was all I had to say. I turned and went down to the basement. That night I tried to get some sleep, unsuccessfully. In the morning, I walked up the stairs to find the place empty. My mother and father had already left for work, and I had a sinking feeling in the pit of my stomach that I'd need to call Sherman and tell him that the press conference was off.

In the living room, the table was empty. I wondered whether my father had taken the retainer agreement and certificate of representation, torn them up, and thrown them away. That was certainly not out of the question.

On the kitchen table, however, at the seat where Allison had sat hundreds of times, I found the documents. Both were signed. Relief rolled through me as I realized that my parents had agreed to let me file the lawsuit. On the table was a yellow sticky note too. On it, my mom had written in her sprawling script, "We Love You."

I called Jackson. "They did it. We're really doing this."

He let out a hoot. "I told you that they trusted you. What's next?"

I thought about it for a moment. "It's time to go to war."

CHAPTER SIXTEEN

When I arrived at the law school, I was surprised to see Cahokia's parking lot fuller than ever and the law school's president, Arthur McIntosh, standing next to Sherman. They were waiting for me near the entrance to a large atrium.

McIntosh, a tall, thin man with a bushy mustache and a receding hairline, walked up to me and shook my hand. "Professor Friedman has just been telling me about how you have most graciously volunteered your time this semester to help us with our civil litigation clinic. I so appreciate the support from lawyers in the community like you."

I exchanged a look with Sherman, unsure of what lies and exaggerations he had told his boss. Then I smiled. "You're welcome. I think I'm actually getting more out of the experience than the students."

"Well"—McIntosh leaned back, impressed—"what a wonderful sentiment. If you could add something like that to your remarks during the press conference, I would be eternally grateful." He leaned in and lowered his voice as if passing along a secret. "These are challenging times for our law school, and you are doing us a great favor."

"I was just telling President McIntosh that this is a very unique lawsuit," Sherman said. "This is one of the first, if not the very first, lawsuits of its kind filed in Missouri. What we were hoping was for you to give President McIntosh an opportunity to acknowledge the creativity and intellect of the students who have worked on this lawsuit at some point during the press conference. I told him that you wouldn't mind."

"Of course," I said. "Why don't you go first, President McIntosh, then you can introduce Professor Friedman, then Sherman can introduce me, and then some of the students will have a turn."

A big grin flashed across McIntosh's face. Rarely had the Cahokia College of Law generated any good news, and he was eager to take the lead. "Sounds like a good plan to me." Unfortunately, I was likely leading him and his students off a cliff, but that wouldn't happen for a few months.

Then my phone vibrated. I read the text and looked up at McIntosh and Sherman. "Looks like the lawsuit has officially been filed and accepted by the clerk of courts. We should get the press conference started."

The conference room was packed. Up front was a podium emblazoned with the college's logo, and behind the podium hung a rich-blue fabric backdrop. I had no idea where the podium or the background had come from, but, if you didn't know any better, it almost looked like we knew what we were doing.

Reporters from the local newspapers and television stations were gathered. We'd given each a blue folder embossed with the law school's logo, and inside the folder were a press release; a brief biography of Sherman Friedman, the law students, and myself; and a copy of the lawsuit filed with the court that morning. Toward the back of the room were television cameras from the local stations and photographers from the Associated Press and the *St. Louis Post-Dispatch*. Curious students, administrators, and professors filled the rest of the space. Seeing all those people gathered in one room as a result of my work—which I'd kept telling myself was meaningful and important—almost made me cry.

I stood along the wall with the students, including Cynthia and Jeff, while President McIntosh welcomed everyone. He gave a brief history of the law school. Then he praised its students and faculty, and finally concluded. "I think you will see a different side of the Cahokia College of Law this morning, and I know that the public will be impressed by their passion, creativity, and intellect." His moment in the spotlight complete, McIntosh introduced Sherman.

After briefly explaining the purpose of the civil litigation clinic and praising the students who chose to take that class, Sherman introduced me with a quote from Clarence Darrow. I felt my knees go a little weak as I walked to the front of the room. I had never been nervous speaking in public before, but this was different.

I adjusted the microphone, cleared my throat, and began, getting right to the point. "This lawsuit is for and on behalf of my sister," I said. "She died of an overdose, after getting addicted to heroin after her doctor prescribed her Bentrax. Allison may be the focus and the subject of this lawsuit, but she is not alone. Over sixty-five thousand people died last year from a drug overdose, nearly a thousand of them from Missouri, and the rate hasn't slowed this year. That's more than the total number of Americans who died during the entire Vietnam War. In fact, about seven people will die in America today from an opioid overdose while we're in here talking about this lawsuit. On average, seven people an hour."

I took a step to the side of the podium and began to speak more personally. "I'm blessed my family has allowed me and the law students here to represent them and to seek justice and accountability for my sister. She wasn't perfect, just like I am not perfect, and just like nobody in this room is perfect. But every once in a while you get an opportunity to do what's right, and I believe that pursuing this lawsuit is what is right."

I looked at the reporters in the front row. "If you open your folder, you'll find a description of the lawsuit. We allege that NexBeaux violated Missouri's consumer protection laws through its false and misleading marketing and sale of Bentrax. We also allege that NexBeaux breached its common-law duty to provide a safe and effective medication. And finally, we allege that NexBeaux has created a public nuisance in the State of Missouri, much like an environmental disaster, and my sister, Allison, died as a result."

CHAPTER SEVENTEEN

I spent the rest of the afternoon with Sherman and Jackson, fielding questions from reporters, then Jackson drove me back to the house. I, physically, felt lighter. I was liberated, a true break from Baxter, Speller & Tuft.

"You want to come inside for dinner?" I asked.

Jackson shook his head. "Nadine's boy has a soccer game tonight."

"That's cool," I said, realizing he had never told me his girlfriend's name. He had always referred to her as his "girl" or his "honey over in Troy." I'd been left with the impression that it wasn't that serious, and, for that reason as well as my complete self-absorption over the past month, I had never asked him more about her. "I'd like to meet her."

"Meet who?"

"Nadine," I said, "and her kids. Maybe we could go out for pizza or something."

"She works a lot," Jackson said. "She's a nurse at the hospital out there, but we might be able to find a time."

"Good." I opened the door and climbed out of the truck. "Thanks for all your help today, and with everything since I've come back," I said through the open window.

He nodded his head. "I hope . . . ," he said after a moment. "I hope with this lawsuit and stuff . . . I mean, I hope I didn't like . . . pressure you to mess up your life or anything."

"You didn't," I said. "So don't worry about that." I knocked on the top of the truck's cab for good luck. "It'll all work out. I needed a course correction, and I got it."

Jackson raised his eyebrow. "OK, brother." He shifted the truck into drive and slowly lurched away. "I'll talk to Nadine about some pizza."

When I went into the house, it was quiet inside. Mom and Dad weren't watching television. I thought maybe they were eating their microwave dinners around the kitchen table, but there was nobody in the kitchen either. Then I heard some sounds out back.

Through the window I saw that the door to the garage was open, and, curious, I went outside. There was more scraping and pounding. The usually dark garage was all lit up. My father had strung three high-powered work lights above the Mustang, and he was bent over the back fender with a piece of sandpaper in one hand and a rubber mallet in the other. I couldn't remember the last time that I'd seen my father work on the thing.

I made some noise so as to not surprise him. "Hey, Dad," I said. "Nice setup."

He looked up at me. A bead of sweat rolled down his cheek. "Can you hand me that can of putty and the trowel?"

"Sure." I spotted them on the floor and brought them to my father. "It's looking pretty cool."

"Yeah, well . . . it's sort of a myth that you can pound the dents out, but I can try." He pointed at the rusted metal around the taillights. "Gotta get rid of the rust completely, though, before slapping any putty on there. Otherwise the putty falls off and the rust comes back."

"Where's Mom?"

"Resting." Dad carefully applied a bit of putty to a little hole near the fender that had been sanded clean. It wasn't much, but it was progress. "She had a long day."

I knew what "resting" meant—she was in their bedroom with a bottle of vodka—so I didn't pry. "We filed the lawsuit today."

"As planned." He sounded satisfied. "I heard them talking about it on the radio." He set the can down and got back to sanding the rust while the putty he had just applied hardened. "Hope you know what you're getting into with all this."

"I hope so too." I rolled up my sleeves and picked up a piece of sandpaper off the floor. "I know it's difficult, hearing people talk about Allison, because it's difficult for me, but people have been supportive today. Nothing but compliments and congratulations." I began sanding an area above the rear wheel.

"You know that guy at work? The one who was drunk for years and then flipped a switch?" My father turned to me. "I kept waiting for Allison to do that, you know? I sorta did it. I don't drink the way I used to. I figured that she could too."

"Some people can," I said. "Some people can't."

"Then why couldn't your sister be one of the people who could?" He started sanding again, harder and more vigorous than before. "That's what I'm saying."

"I'm not sure anybody can answer that question. Whether some-body is an abuser of drugs or an addict, it's hard to tell from the outside."

"Well"—he pulled himself up and let out a heavy sigh—"I'm sure that drug company will tell us why it's Allison's fault and not theirs."

I thought about it, and my dad was exactly right. "I'm sure they will," I said, and we both laughed, because it was better than admitting we were scared.

"Hey, Dad," I said. "Why did you finally agree? Why'd you sign the papers?"

"Because I know I wasn't the best father in the world. I ain't getting no awards, that's for sure, but I sorta realized that there's no such thing as fate. Like this Mustang." My father put his hand on the trunk. "The Mustang ain't gonna fix itself. Maybe it'll never run again, maybe it will, but I'm never gonna know if I don't get out here and try." My father wiped the sweat off his forehead with a red bandanna that he'd retrieved from his pocket. "Just figured this lawsuit of yours was sorta like your Mustang." My father nodded slightly. "That's all."

It was as close to a real conversation as we'd ever had. For a brief moment, we were almost normal. "I appreciate it, Dad. I really do." I started walking toward the door, then stopped. "After I change clothes, do you need any more help out here?"

He surveyed the beat-up car. "Son, I need all the help I can get."

◆ ◆ ◆

That night was different. Since walking away from the firm, I had woken up every three or four hours, only to fall back into a shallow rest until morning. But not that night. My dreams were vivid and real.

In one, I was back in New York at the aquarium. It was dark outside, and the office was lit. Inside, everything was the same, except all the office doors were stainless steel rather than wood, as if each were a bank vault. I walked quickly down the hallway. Attorneys and paralegals noticed me and nodded. Some would say, "How have you been?" or "What have you been up to?" It was as if I had just been on vacation, but I knew that I wasn't supposed to be there. I looked over my shoulder, waiting for a security guard to arrive or a police officer to arrest me.

I walked into a large storage room filled with cardboard boxes. My heart pounded and my hands trembled as I looked for something, one box after another. A woman came in, looked at me, and left. Not knowing whether she recognized me or knew that I was someplace I didn't belong, I searched even faster.

Then I found it. I didn't know what the document said or who it was from. I hustled out of the storage room and ran toward the elevator.

I pressed the button to go down, waited, and pressed the button again. Time moved slowly now. I needed to leave. I needed to get out, but the elevator wouldn't come.

Someone shouted my name. I turned and saw Francis Kirsch and Tobias Tuft coming toward me. They ran down the hallway, but the hallway had grown longer and it wasn't clear whether they'd get to me in time. I heard the doors slide open, and I took a step inside without looking first.

I fell into an open elevator shaft.

I let go of the document and it floated into the air, catching one light breeze after another. I reached out and grabbed for it, but I was falling too fast. The document floated above me as I continued down the shaft, farther and farther away.

Panic grew. My heart beat faster as I sensed the end. I got hold of one of the thick steel cords that lifted the elevators up and down, but I was falling too fast. The cords just slipped through my hands, cutting and blistering them as my grip failed.

I landed at the bottom of the shaft with a thump. The crack of my spine echoed up and then back on me. I lay there paralyzed, then pills poured out of a hole in the wall, like grain brought in from harvest. I commanded my body to move, but it didn't. Pills covered my legs, then my stomach. I lifted my head to keep from drowning, but the pile kept rising.

Then there was a hand. "Please." I reached for it, but our fingers barely touched. It was a woman. She called for me. Maybe it was Tess. Maybe it was Laura. Maybe it was Allison or even my mother. Whoever it was, she couldn't save me.

The pills kept coming. My heart beat even faster. I closed my mouth so the pills couldn't get in. Now breathing only through my nose, I thrashed my head. Hyperventilating, I had to open my mouth. I had to take a deep breath as the pressure built. I had no choice but to take it all in as the pills finally buried me alive.

When I woke up, my sheets were soaked in sweat. It had sunk through to the mattress, and I was clammy and cold.

The dream was real. I'm in a fight for my life.

Despite the rough night, my mood brightened a little as I read the morning newspaper online and clicked through the various local television news clips. As I had expected, the press coverage of our lawsuit was excellent. Most of the articles simply recycled material from our press release. The television stories prominently featured the law students, as well as commentary from local nurses and police officers who worked on the front line of the opioid epidemic every day.

The best part of the news coverage was that it was completely one-sided. After spending 99.9 percent of the time talking about our allegations against NexBeaux, each story ended with a bland statement issued by NexBeaux: "We have not seen or received a copy of the lawsuit, and we will have no comment until it has been reviewed."

I called Sherman. "How do you feel?"

"Excited and a little jittery," he said. "But it's hard to tell what's real and what's just the three doughnuts and double espresso I had this morning."

"Seeing it in the papers makes it real."

"Definitely," he said. "But now comes the hard part."

CHAPTER EIGHTEEN

I got the call while Jackson was teaching me how to properly fish. Up until that point, it had been a great day. Jackson had picked me up early in the morning and driven to Nadine's place in Troy, where we filled a cooler with beer and boarded his boat.

The weather was good. Since it was early May, the weather hadn't gotten too hot and the famous Saint Louis humidity hadn't yet arrived. I watched as Jackson pulled one largemouth bass after another out of Lake Lincoln with little difficulty. After an hour, I hadn't caught one. "You got a bobber?"

"Hell yes, I got bobbers." Jackson flipped open his tackle box. "Right there."

I began to reach for one, but Jackson flipped the top back down. My fingers almost got snapped off. "But those are for kids."

"Right," I said. "How foolish I am."

"Are you a man or not?" Before I could answer, my phone rang, and Jackson rolled his eyes. "You brought a cell phone fishing? The whole point is to be out in nature, brother."

I answered the call anyway. "Hello?"

"Got two bits of new information for you," Sherman said.

I felt a little tug on my fishing line, which surprised me. Jackson noticed it, too, and he gestured for me to slowly start reeling it in.

"What's the news? Good, I hope." There was another little tug, and I felt a tingle of excitement.

"We've got a judge, and we've got opposing counsel."

"Great." I watched my fishing line for more movement, but there wasn't anything, so I figured it was just a false alarm.

"Actually, it's not so great," Sherman said. "We got the original rocket man, Judge B. J. Waxman. His clerk already called us to set up a time for an early case management review teleconference. The guy is notorious for moving cases at lightning-fast speed, even complicated ones like this, hence the nickname."

I pulled in a little more of my line, a taunt. I wanted to lure the fish back, trying to create some movement like Jackson had instructed. "Let me guess," I said with a tiny jerk of my line. "He's always looking for ways and reasons to dismiss a case."

"Exactly," Sherman said. "How'd you know?"

I thought of Judge Platte and the BioPrint case. "It's pretty common, but some judges are more aggressive than others. Often goes along with Black Robe Disease."

"BRD." Sherman laughed. "An affliction of arrogance for which there is no cure."

"So that's our judge. That's not good, but it might be overcome. How about our attorney? And please tell me that it's not Baxter, Speller & Tuft."

"Then this may come as good news," Sherman said as I felt a tug on my line. The fish was back. "It's not your old law firm, but it is one from New York." I heard him tapping on his computer keyboard. "Their website is pretty cool."

"What's the name?" I studied the water. The surface was calm, and I began to relax.

"Nelson Rockler." The name was said at the same time the fish hit the line hard. My pole bent. The reel screamed. I don't know how big the fish was, but it felt like I had caught a small child. Jackson yelled at me to reel it in. Sherman, oblivious to what was happening, continued with his report. "The attorney's name is Shirley Glade. You ever heard of her?"

The fish was fighting me now. I pulled on the line, but every time I made some progress, the fish pulled back. It was a fight to the death. With the phone, the pole, and my beer, I desperately needed a third hand.

"Looks like Glade and a guy named Quinton B. Newhouse III— that's a pretentious name—and then there's an associate of hers that's going to be on the call." I continued to fight as Sherman kept talking. "Another woman. Let me click on her profile." A pause. "Hey, she's pretty attractive." The fight between the fish and me went back and forth, blow for blow. "Her name is Tess . . . Tess Garrity." Jackson now tried to get to my seat with a net, and the boat almost tipped over as he went from the back to the front. "Tess . . . Hey, wasn't your fiancée's name Tess?"

At that moment, I got up out of my seat just a few inches, more like a crouch. I didn't get up all the way, because I knew enough to know that a person does not stand in a boat. It was, however, just enough for me to step on the edge of an unused life preserver.

My ankle rolled, shooting pain up my leg. I tried to regain my balance, but the boat rocked. The phone began to slip. I reached for it, letting go of the pole. The fish, now sensing an opportunity for freedom, took advantage. It swam hard, and the loose fishing rod slid along the bottom of the boat. The fish almost pulled it over, but the reel caught on the edge. More line was released as the fish got farther away. The rod balanced precariously, tipping back and forth.

Jackson shouted, "Get it! Get it!"

With the phone safely in hand, I took another crouched step to save the pole before it went overboard, forgetting my twisted ankle. It rolled again, and my knee buckled. As pain shot up my leg, I dropped the phone and spun around before falling face-first into the water.

CHAPTER NINETEEN

Judge B. J. Waxman scheduled the first teleconference for 10:00 a.m. just one week after we'd filed the lawsuit. A judge typically waited until the opposing party filed its answer to the complaint before setting any discovery deadlines or scheduling motion hearings. The rocket man, however, was not one to wait. He viewed civil cases like a cancer—if he didn't eradicate them as soon as possible, the cancer would spread and would ultimately be fatal.

The house was quiet. My parents were at work, and I was alone. I could have called in to the teleconference in my underwear, but I wanted to be sharp, so I showered and shaved and put on my best suit and tie, even though nobody except me would see it. I also set up a little workstation at the kitchen table.

I made sure I had a copy of the lawsuit readily available, as well as any pertinent documents. With the clinic students, we had drafted a proposed timeline for the litigation. I wasn't sure whether Judge Waxman would ask our opinion or just set the dates himself, but if he wanted me to propose a deadline for all depositions to be completed, I was prepared.

At 9:55 a.m., I decided to call. Being early was better than being late. I dialed the conference number and suffered through a few minutes of loud instrumental music. Promptly at ten, the music stopped, and I heard the sound of shuffling paper.

"Hello, this is Judge Waxman." He cleared his throat. "Before we go on the record, I just want to make sure everyone is here."

I was the first to speak up. "This is Matthew Daley representing the plaintiff. I believe that my cocounsel Sherman Friedman is on the line, as well as some students from our civil litigation clinic. I, however, will be the only one formally participating in this hearing."

"This is Shirley Glade from Nelson Rockler, and Quinton Newhouse, and I also have here with me my associate, Tess Garrity."

Just hearing her name made me sick. Even though I had known she was probably going to participate in the teleconference, my immediate visceral reaction surprised me. I thought I'd be more in control, but the fact that she was there, listening, threw me off-balance.

That's probably what they wanted.

"Good." Judge Waxman called the case and walked us through some opening formalities before moving on. "I have reviewed the complaint, and I have some ideas as to how we should proceed. I do, however, want to get a sense from the defense about their intentions."

Glade took the lead. "Thank you, Your Honor. It's my feeling that setting a full schedule at this point may be premature. The plaintiffs set forth some"—Glade paused and forced a condescending laugh—"how shall I say? *Novel* legal theories. So our intention is to file a motion to dismiss as a matter of law. Because the plaintiff has not set forth any legal claim upon which relief may be granted, I really do not want to go through the expense as well as burdening the court, who is already overburdened, with discovery disputes and other motions, if this lawsuit cannot stand on its own four corners."

"Mr. Daley," Judge Waxman said, "your response to this proposal?"

"While I disagree with the characterization of our legal claims, I don't see any problem with going forward with the motion to dismiss. Then we can assess where we are once that motion has been decided." I didn't have to agree so readily, but I knew Judge Waxman would side with Shirley Glade regardless of what I said, and I didn't want the court to see me as slowing things down or being an obstructionist right from the start.

"Excellent." Judge Waxman sounded excited. "We have an agreement. How long do you need to file your motion to dismiss?"

"I think we can have it prepared in thirty days, Your Honor, and schedule the hearing thirty days after that."

The judge made a deflated sound. "Given the size of your law firm, Ms. Glade, I think you can have your motion papers filed in fourteen days. I'll give the plaintiff one week to respond to your written motion, then I'll schedule the hearing nine days later. Thirty days is plenty of time to have this properly briefed and argued."

I'd never heard a more aggressive briefing schedule, but nobody felt comfortable objecting. The rocket man had won again.

That was fast.

CHAPTER TWENTY

The civil litigation clinic met the next day to talk about the case, set a schedule, and assign tasks. "What most people don't realize," I said, "is that the law is dynamic. It changes over time, slowly building and adjusting to different scenarios and difficult facts. The purpose of the defense attorney is to slow that change down. NexBeaux and Shirley Glade will spend a lot of time talking about unintended consequences as well as telling Judge Waxman, either expressly or implicitly, that he's going to get overturned on appeal if he rules in our favor. Our job is to keep the case alive by squeezing it into existing legal theories, and, ultimately, get it to trial."

"Trial? Aren't they going to settle?" Screw asked. Since the filing of the lawsuit, her hair had gone from purple to pink. "I mean, I thought all cases settled."

The idea of a big cash settlement caught Jeff's attention. "Yeah, what do we want from them? Like a million dollars or something?"

"To be honest"—I just decided to level with them—"I filed this case for my sister. The point was never to make a million dollars. The point was to hold NexBeaux accountable, to raise awareness."

"But every case is about money." Jeff looked at Sherman. "That's what Professor Friedman told us on day one. It's all about the Benjamins."

"True." Sherman had been standing off to the side, and he now stepped forward to bail me out. "Although this is a bit different. It's what I'd classify as social-impact litigation rather than solely for compensation. We do, however, need to get a better handle on our damages, both direct and punitive. So why don't you take that assignment, Mr. Grant? Research medical malpractice claims as well as the larger lawsuits against pharmaceutical companies and write it up before the next class. We need to know the value of the case."

Cynthia raised her hand. "I'd like to help with that."

"Great." Sherman turned back to me. "What other research do you need?"

"We need to start identifying witnesses and interviewing them," I said. The only person left for the assignment was Screw, and I wondered how people were going to react to a student attorney with ever-changing hair color and multiple piercings. I didn't, however, have much of a choice. "Screw, you'll have to take this one. Take an initial cut, then we'll help you out."

She opened her notebook and took out her pen. "Where do I start?"

"Start with the journals." The thought of sharing Allison's journals with her or anyone made me feel uneasy, but if this was going to be a real case, I needed to treat it like one, objectively evaluating and separating out the emotion. I had to rebuild those internal walls, at least partially, to do the job. "There will be plenty of names and places in Allison's journals. Start by making lists."

With Sherman's help, we spent the rest of the class going over a timeline and brainstorming future tasks. When the hour had passed, the students filed out of the classroom, leaving Sherman and me alone.

"So I realize that this seems a little bit like stalking," Sherman said, opening his bag. "But this came in the mail a few days ago, and I thought it might be something you'd want to check out." He reached in and removed a half-sheet advertisement printed on heavy cardstock. "You might need the continuing education credit."

I took it from him and soon understood why he had taken a sudden interest in whether I was fulfilling my licensure requirements. There before me was a large photograph of Laura Bauer, my law school girlfriend and our old study group partner. She was the featured speaker on "High-Conflict Family Matters" as part of a fall lecture series sponsored by the Bar Association of Metropolitan St. Louis.

"Just a few days away," Sherman said. "Perfect timing and conveniently located downtown, so close you can ride your cute little bike."

"I'm sure that will impress her."

Sherman laughed. "Women love dudes on bikes."

With class over and tasks assigned, I knew that I had to take advantage of the brief calm before the storm. It was time that I could use to research and prepare without distraction, but it was difficult. The quiet allowed the grief and sadness to creep back. In the last two months, I'd lost a sister, a fiancée, and a job.

I went from nearly realizing a dream of owning my own luxury brownstone to sleeping in my parents' basement. My bank account had some money, but I was shocked at how little I'd saved during my years as an associate. Every day the balance shrank, and I felt like I needed to do something but didn't know where to begin.

I decided to retreat to the downtown Central Library to take my mind off the future. Being among books had always comforted me. I used to bike there alone as a kid, something that would never be allowed today, to escape my family and dream of getting out. It seemed like something I needed now just like I needed back then.

The building itself was a work of art. Designed by Cass Gilbert, the same architect who designed the United States Supreme Court building in Washington, DC, the Central Library represented a different era in the relationship between the government and its people. Its arched windows and three huge doors were aspirational, built at a time filled with hope. Anything was possible.

When I arrived, I wandered through the whole library, exploring and rediscovering spaces that I'd forgotten. I spent hours bothering the librarians to help me navigate the electronic research tools, and they gladly helped me find books on addiction, treatment, brain development, and the war on drugs. After working my way through that material, I read government reports and investigative journalism on the growing opioid epidemic.

I'm not sure whether the librarians truly liked me or were just glad someone in the library was doing real research. If given a choice between helping find obscure medical journal articles for me or servicing the downtown homeless population that spent their days among the stacks and sleeping in the library's many nooks, I'd like to think they'd prefer the former.

At closing time I walked back up to the main desk, returning a book of bound medical journal articles that included a study that found common aspirin was just as effective, if not more effective, than Bentrax and other opioid pain medications.

The librarian took everything off my hands. "Anything else?"

"There is, actually," I said. "Do you have any books about restoring classic cars, like really basic? I need to learn how to get started."

"What kind of car?"

"Mustang."

"I'm sure there's something." She walked over to her computer. "Let's take a look."

I smiled as she typed the search terms into her computer. I thought about the day we filed the lawsuit against NexBeaux, the day my father began working on the car again. Although he was probably never going to have a deeply personal conversation with me about the mistakes he'd made or the regrets he had, I felt like he made a little invitation that day. He opened the door, just slightly, to make amends. The garage was a safe space. All I had to do was show up.

◆ ◆ ◆

At the end of the week, Jackson pulled up to the front of the house. With the engine running and the truck spewing smoke, he honked his horn. When I emerged from the house wearing a full suit, he hooted at me out his open window. "What's with the fancy outfit?"

"This old thing?" I brushed off some imaginary lint. "If I'm going to be meeting with a potential witness, I don't want to wear shorts and a T-shirt. I need to look credible." What I didn't tell Jackson was that, after our meeting with the director of the Arch Treatment Center, I was going to Laura Bauer's presentation.

After I got inside, Jackson pulled away from the curb. "So where is this place?"

"About forty-five minutes east," I said. "Beautiful southern Illinois."

Jackson drove up to I-270, then across the New Chain of Rocks Bridge into Illinois. We kept going past Edwardsville and continued straight until my phone told us to take a sharp left onto a dirt road.

After bumping along for a bit, Jackson looked over at me. "I hope the GPS on your phone isn't leading us off a cliff."

The blue dot on my screen traced the planned route north into nothing. Jackson's truck continued to kick up gravel and dust as we wound through cornfields and past farmhouses and horse barns. After taking two more side roads, I wondered whether, if my phone battery died, we'd ever be able to find our way back to Saint Louis.

Soon we found a small nondescript sign at the beginning of a long driveway. If you weren't looking for it or weren't paying attention, you'd never know it was there. We turned up the drive, and I soon saw the Arch Treatment Center, a cluster of buildings overlooking a pond fed by a narrow creek.

The director met us at the door. I introduced myself and Jackson. "Pleasure to meet you in person," Director Merriam Glasby said. "Let's talk in my office." She turned and led us back to the administrative area. As she sat down, I closed the door and sat across from her. Jackson did the same.

"Thank you for meeting with us." I wondered how many other family members came back to the Arch after losing a loved one, and how many of the people accepted into the program relapsed. It had to be high. I probably should have asked before paying to send Allison there, but I'd been desperate and hadn't given it a second thought. I was just so thankful that they were going to take the burden away from me.

"As I told your assistant when I called to schedule this meeting, I'm a lawyer," I said, "and I'm working with a legal clinic at one of the local law schools." I didn't say which one, recognizing that Cahokia College of Law was not exactly an impressive name to drop. I also figured that it was equally unimpressive to tell her that I was living in my parents' basement. "We recently sued NexBeaux. They are the ones who manufactured Bentrax, the ones I believe are responsible for Allison's death."

"I read about your lawsuit in the newspaper." I'm sure Glasby had her opinions regarding the merits of my case, but she didn't immediately challenge me. Instead she circled back from the side. "I've been the director here for over twenty years, Mr. Daley, and I've seen a lot of heartbreak and disappointment." Her eyes fell a little. How many times had I seen that look? There was the doctor and the priest, even the expression on Harold Cantor's face at the BioPrint hearing. People who've seen the loss of others dying too young.

"For all of them," Glasby said, "the most common emotion is always anger. You may not be yelling, but I know you're angry, and I'm not sure I can tell you who to blame or how to rid yourself of that anger."

"It isn't you that I'm interested in suing," I said, a little too defensively, "if that's what you're worried about."

Glasby waved away the thought. "I'm not worried. I'm just not sure that you'll be able to meet your objective. Legally, well, that's not my area of expertise, but with regard to the other objectives." She reached into a desk drawer and removed a thick file. "Your sister signed a release of information. It was fairly limited, but I think there is an argument that the release is broader than that." She suddenly looked quite old. She was tired and perhaps resigned to let someone else fight for a little while. "If I'm wrong and there's a problem, I'll let the attorneys deal with it."

She pushed the file across the desk to me. "Allison was not with us very long, compared with others, but she was here long enough. You two were both important to her." Glasby looked at Jackson, then back to me. "I think she would want you to do whatever it is that you think is right."

I picked up the file and stood. "Thank you." As the director opened the door for us, I asked, "Did she really want to change? I mean, she told me that she wanted to change, but did she *really* want it?"

Glasby tilted her head to the side and closed her eyes, serene. "That is perhaps the greatest unanswered question that I grapple with here every day. Twenty years ago, the answer would've been that your sister did not surrender, that she did not submit to a higher power and follow all the steps." The director shook her head. "But I no longer believe that, and neither do you."

"The chemicals, Bentrax—I think it changed her brain, physically, and she couldn't stop."

"Perhaps," Glasby said. "But others have taken Bentrax and any number of other painkillers and they did not become heroin addicts. So what's the difference?"

I didn't have a good answer to the question, and I was certain that NexBeaux and Shirley Glade would soon be asking the same thing.

◆ ◆ ◆

Neither Jackson nor I said much as we bounced back down the gravel road. I'm not sure what I had expected Glasby to say, but I felt disappointed. Maybe Jackson felt the same way. I wasn't expecting to be treated like a hero, but I assumed Glasby would be more openly supportive of our lawsuit. Because she worked the front lines, I thought she'd be just as angry with NexBeaux as I was.

Maybe she was just numb.

"I'm not sure Glasby is going to be a good witness for us," I said. "She was a mix. On the one hand, she said that she no longer believes that willpower is enough, but then she didn't assign any blame to NexBeaux either."

"Do you think she's like a genetics person?" Jackson slowed down and pulled into the right lane as a semitruck barreled past on the left. "You know what I'm saying? Mom's a drunk. Dad's a drunk. So Allison must be a drunk."

"I don't know." I thought about it. "We probably should interview her another time before any deposition or testimony. Based on what I just saw, I don't think she's going to be our star witness."

Since we were going downtown, Jackson drove further south in Illinois and then west. The iconic Saint Louis Arch in the distance slowly grew larger as we approached. Sunlight reflected off its metallic skin, and I began to wonder. "Hey, Jackson," I proceeded cautiously, "do you think Allison ever used heroin before her car accident? I mean, that's the whole premise of our case. Is NexBeaux going to find a doctor's note or something else? I don't think she did, but I don't know."

"I don't know either." Jackson glanced over at me, then he turned his attention to the cars in front of him. "She partied," he said, "and she bounced around from job to job. So she drank and probably smoked a lot of weed . . ." Jackson shrugged. "Does it matter?"

"It does," I said. "I'm not pretending that Allison was like this straight A student until Bentrax sent her off the rails, but it's an opening that Glade the Blade will try to exploit. We need to start figuring out how to defend it. We need to find Allison's friends, people who will testify about what she was like before."

"I'll start poking around." Jackson signaled a turn, and we exited the highway into downtown Saint Louis. After we drove past the new Busch stadium, I pointed at the ornate building on the corner of Sixth and Washington Avenue. It used to be the May Company Department Store and the Crawford Department Store before that. Now it was where the local bar association managed its membership and hosted continuing legal education courses.

"This is it."

Jackson pulled to a stop. "You got a meeting or what?"

"Class," I said. "I need to take a certain number of classes every year to keep my license to practice law."

"Shoot," he said. "Thought you'd be smart enough to be done with school by now." He smiled. "Let me know what else I need to do for the case, OK? I always thought it'd be cool to be an investigator."

"Just finding out who Allison's friends were before that car accident would be great. She never had a lot of them, but there has to be somebody." I opened the door and stepped out. "And say hello to Nadine and the kids for me."

"Will do," Jackson said as the driver of the car behind him honked the horn. "Gotta go."

I walked inside and found my way to the small auditorium on the first floor. About twenty people were already seated, and I found a place in the back. Up front, a woman was attaching a microphone to Laura's suit jacket. When everything was set, the woman came to the podium.

"OK, everybody," she said. "Let's get started. My name is Marin Holt, and I am the assistant director of the Bar Association of Metropolitan St. Louis. I want to welcome everyone to this afternoon's program. We have here Ms. Laura Bauer. She is a partner at the law firm of O'Malley & Schmidt, in Clayton, and she specializes in family law. Today, Ms. Bauer will focus on high-conflict personalities, particularly people who are representing themselves, in contentious and personal family law proceedings. Please welcome Ms. Laura Bauer."

With that, Laura came up to the podium and began her PowerPoint presentation. Instantly her voice brought back a flood of memories. For the next forty minutes, I just watched and listened to the same Laura I'd fallen in love with, only now she was more mature and confident. While I'd succumbed to my worst traits since law school—competitiveness, greed, and a thirst for validation from all the wrong people—she had come into her own.

After the question-and-answer period, I made my way to the front and, nervous about how she'd react, waited my turn while a few others spoke to Laura first.

Laura gave a man her business card, then turned to me. "Matty." She smiled, but she wasn't overly enthused. "Sherman warned me that you might be coming."

"He did?"

"Yes. He told me you'd had a rough month and that I shouldn't punch you in the face."

"I appreciate that." I rubbed my jaw. "And I also appreciate that you heeded his advice."

"So far," Laura said. "There's still plenty of time."

"I'll be careful. I know this is out of the blue, but I'm glad I came today. You were great."

"Thank you. I read about your lawsuit, and I'm sorry to hear about your sister."

"It's been difficult. A lot of change." I noticed Laura look at her watch, so I took the hint: less is more. "I know you have to go, but I hope sometime we can get together and talk. I understand if you don't want to, and I don't blame you, but I'd love to hear about what's been going on."

Laura shifted uncomfortably from one foot to the other. "Look, Matty, I've got to get back to the office," she said. "I want to beat rush hour traffic, and I have a client coming in for a late afternoon meeting."

"I totally understand." I accepted her noncommitment, and I considered the fact that she did not expressly reject the idea as a success. "It's good to see you."

CHAPTER TWENTY-ONE

Over the next three weeks, I was essentially a law firm of one. The students in the clinic were enthusiastic, but there were just three of them and only so much that they could do. Judge Waxman had put us under enormous time pressure.

As predicted, the memo produced by Shirley Glade, my ex-fiancée, and the army of Nelson Rockler associates was well written, thorough, and convincing. It was fifty pages long and contained an appendix of treatise articles, appellate decisions, and unpublished orders all intended to cast our legal claims in the worst light. I read everything, trying to find a little something in each case to distinguish it from our lawsuit, which wasn't easy.

The day before the hearing, I decided that I needed to get away from the desk for a while, do something different. I put on my work clothes after breakfast and went out to the garage. My old boom box was set up on the workbench, and I turned on the classic rock radio station and got to work on the Mustang. While I sanded and scrubbed, I practiced my oral argument out loud and answered hypothetical questions, from the most expected to the most random. I put myself in the mind of Judge Waxman.

How would I convince him that my lawsuit was not a waste of time?

"Some cases are not cancers. Some cases deserve consideration."

While I talked to myself, I continued to sand away all the rust, pound out the dents, and fill the holes with putty. My father and I had been making good progress, and my goal was to finish by the end of the day. I wanted to surprise him when he got home from work, and I also wanted something to celebrate when I went out with Laura later that night for our nondate.

I hadn't seen her since her presentation for the bar association. It'd taken multiple phone calls and, I suspect, some more intervention from Sherman. After weeks, she finally agreed, and I was determined not to blow it.

◆ ◆ ◆

We met at a small Central West End Italian restaurant wedged between an antiques store and a dry cleaner. The restaurant had only ten tables, so I spotted Laura by the window almost immediately. The evening light made the edges of her hair glow and softened every feature of her face.

I pointed at her wineglass as I sat. "What are you having?"

She picked up the glass, swirled the red wine, and took a sip. "I looked at the wine list, and I found the most expensive wine. Then I found the least expensive one, and when the waiter asked for my order, I picked the wine that was priced in the middle of those two."

"Pretty sophisticated," I said. "Is it any good?"

Laura swirled the wine again. "Good to me."

The conversation flowed easily through dinner and into dessert. I learned about Laura's work and about her law firm. She also told me about all the places she had traveled to since law school. After we broke up, she decided to run a marathon on every continent. She already completed one in North America, of course, in Mexico City seven years ago. Three years ago she ran one in London, then one in Cairo last year, and now she was training for one in Sydney, Australia.

"Have you dated anybody?"

"That's very personal." Laura took a bite of her tiramisu. "But yes, despite your best efforts to permanently break my heart and sour me on men forever, I dated a couple guys for over a year, but they were too boring. One was an accountant. The other guy designed software for credit card companies." She scrunched up her nose. "I couldn't do it. I was exhausted trying to pretend like I was interested in what they did during the day."

She took another bite of her dessert and sipped her cappuccino. "So now that you know a little about my post–law school love life, how do you feel about that?"

"I'm not sure I feel anything, but I'm glad you told me." I smiled. "It means that you trust me just a little bit, and that trust makes me happy, because it means that maybe in the future you'd trust me even more."

"Maybe." Laura smiled, toying with me a little.

The waiter came with our check, and Laura looked at her watch. "It looks like you better call it a night. You've got a big day tomorrow."

"I'm afraid I'll get my ass kicked."

"But at least you tried," she said.

My heart swelled, but I tried to keep it in check. I reached out and took her hand. "Thank you."

CHAPTER TWENTY-TWO

I instructed all the law students to come to court wearing the official lawyer costume: a dark-blue suit and a starched white or light-blue shirt. Neither the fabric of the suit nor the shirt was to have any discernible pattern. From a distance of three feet or more, the color should appear solid. A man's tie should not have any lines that cross, wild patterns, or images of cartoon characters. The tie should have two colors—that's it. According to Francis, who was responsible for brainwashing me, any deviation from the official lawyer costume would render the attorney a two-bit hack and undignified.

Women were to wear a skirt that fell just below the knee. Anything lower would make her look like a member of a religious cult. Anything higher would make her look flighty. Again, according to Francis, women in pantsuits were simply a joke and all pantsuits should be burned. While I did not necessarily agree, if a young attorney wanted to survive, it was best he or she wasn't remembered for their wardrobe. Boring was better.

Among the class, we had organized a betting pool. Every participant put in five dollars. We each got one guess at how many total lawyers and senior executives would come to this motion hearing from NexBeaux. My guess was ten, but some were as high as eighteen. Later, I learned that Cynthia had won the pool. She guessed correctly: sixteen. Although it was never clear who was an attorney and who was just an executive.

Sherman and I decided we'd be the ones to sit at the counsel table, along with one student. The class drew names, and Cynthia won. She got a front row seat to see her professor get grilled. The rest of the class sat in the seats behind the counsel table.

While we waited for Judge Waxman, I scribbled notes on my notepad and ignored defense counsel. I didn't want to look at them. Then Sherman leaned over and whispered in my ear, "Is that your old fiancée sitting over there?"

I purposely dropped my pen on the floor. When I bent over to pick it up, I looked at opposing counsel. There was Shirley Glade and another partner at Nelson Rockler, Quinton B. Newhouse III. He was the man who was making out with Tess while I had been at the Yankees game. The image of those two together was one that I'll never forget.

I must've shuddered, because I felt Sherman's hand on my shoulder. "You OK?"

"I'm fine," I said as I sat back up in my chair, just as three associates, including Tess, sat down behind Glade the Blade and Newhouse.

I adjusted my tie and leaned over to Sherman. "That is my lovely, *former* bride-to-be over there, and the middle-aged guy at the table is the asshole she was having an affair with."

Sherman raised his eyebrows. "Really?"

"Really."

The bailiff graveled the court to order. "All rise, the Honorable B. J. Waxman presiding." Judge Waxman entered the courtroom and took his seat at the bench. He was probably in his early sixties, but he looked younger, with his full head of hair, strong jaw, and sparkling blue eyes. He had energy. There was a bounce to his step, smiling all the way. It was clear that he loved his job, which, unfortunately, he viewed as making lawsuits disappear.

Judge Waxman held out his hand and directed us to take our seats. "Please sit down. Thank you." He paused while everyone took their seats. "We are on the record in the case of Daley versus NexBeaux

Pharmaceuticals. We're here this morning for oral arguments on the defendant's motion to dismiss. Let the record show that I have read all the memoranda and reviewed the defendant's very thorough appendix of legal authority, and I am now prepared to go forward with oral arguments."

The judge acknowledged each of the attorneys present, making eye contact with each of us. Then he focused on me.

"I don't think that judges should be state legislators. Courts are not where public policy should be made. In reviewing the plaintiff's complaint, that is what comes to mind. I worry that the plaintiff might be pushing an agenda in a forum that is reserved for the law, not politics. So I want to take a break and allow the parties to reevaluate their positions, particularly the plaintiff's. Both parties should know that if I dismiss this case after this hearing, I will assess costs to the losing side, including attorneys' fees. Of course, if a party voluntarily withdraws, this motion becomes moot. Think about that before we expend any more energy or time this morning."

The bailiff struck the gavel three times. "The court is now in recess." Judge Waxman stood and strode off the bench, leaving Sherman and me in shock. Neither of us had expected that.

"Let's go find a conference room." I stood up and walked out. Sherman and the clinic students trailed behind. I found a conference room down the hall, and as soon as I closed the door behind us, people started making comments and shouting questions at one another.

"Everybody be quiet," I said. The room settled down. "First I want to say that what I saw in there was a disgrace. I don't think that we are entitled to win, but the code of professional conduct calls upon us, requires us, to be vigorous advocates for our clients and to make good-faith arguments for the modification of existing law. Yet this judge might assess costs to a nonprofit law school clinic or me personally. That's crazy."

"Judge Waxman is sending a message," Sherman said. "He doesn't want expansions or modifications of existing law, and he certainly doesn't want a party who is not motivated by money. We scare him, because this lawsuit isn't about money. It's about more than that."

"If we lose and end up having to pay all those lawyers," Screw asked, "who's responsible for that?"

"Maybe us." I didn't know how to answer. "When you have two corporations battling it out, presumably the client pays the fees, but here there's no way that my mom and dad are going to be able to pay the legal bill for that fifty-page monstrosity filed by Nelson Rockler."

"So we're going to voluntarily dismiss our lawsuit?" Cynthia said. "But we worked so hard on it."

"But we also knew that we were walking a fine line, right on the edge," Jeff said. "That doesn't mean that our case is frivolous, but the judge seems to think so."

"Thank you all for your thoughts." Sherman must have thought the same thing as me—that the conversation wasn't helping, and we were running out of time. "I think Mr. Daley and I need some time to talk alone."

Once we were alone, Sherman turned to me. "What do you want to do?"

"I have no idea, but I'll tell you what, between Tobias Tuft and Judge Waxman, I'm getting pretty tired of people bossing me around."

"If we lose, how much do you think it will cost us?"

I ran some numbers in my head. There were sixteen people present at the hearing for NexBeaux. I presumed the majority were executives and people from the general counsel's office, but at least five of the sixteen were attorneys, which would be five flights from New York City, round-trip during the week, plus hotel rooms, transportation, and food. Then each of the attorneys charged an average of $300 to $600 an hour.

This will be a two-hour hearing, let's say that works out to be about $5,000 for attorneys' fees.

"I'm thinking more around nine thousand dollars, just for today's hearing, and that's not counting all the time for the associates who drafted the motion to dismiss, the memorandum in support of the motion to dismiss, and that crazy appendix."

Sherman shook his head. "So it's not unrealistic to think that Judge Waxman could order us to pay well over twenty thousand dollars in fees with everything included, if this case gets dismissed."

"That's what it sounds like."

"We have to pull the plug," Sherman said. "I don't know who would be on the hook for it, but whether it's the law school or us or your parents, it's not good."

"And what makes me even more mad is that if we voluntarily dismiss our own lawsuit, there's no appeal. We can't appeal ourselves."

"Judge Waxman is an evil genius," Sherman concluded. "It's the perfect scenario. He gets rid of the case and he doesn't have to write anything. There's also no possibility that he'll be overturned on appeal, because we withdrew the lawsuit ourselves."

"That's true," I said, "but isn't it interesting that he might be afraid of getting overturned on appeal? He'll grant the motion to dismiss, no doubt, but maybe something in our memo is making him think twice. Because he doesn't want to be the judge who dismissed, in error, one of the most important lawsuits in our state."

"It's too huge of a risk, Matt. We have to pull out." Sherman went for the door. "When we decided to do this, I thought we had nothing to lose, but now I'm starting to think we do."

◆ ◆ ◆

On our way back to the courtroom, fully intending to withdraw our lawsuit, I saw Tess and Quinton Newhouse. He was a man I'd never formally met but hated. They were near the door to the courtroom, too close to one another. People walking by may not notice, but I did.

Newhouse was flirting with her. Tess was touching his arm, in the same affectionate way that she used to touch my arm.

What are they doing out here? They had to have known that I was in that conference room, right?

Newhouse kissed Tess on the neck just as I walked past them.

My emotions got the best of me, and, during the walk from the courtroom door to the table, I changed my mind. I wasn't voluntarily dismissing anything. NexBeaux was a bad company. It marketed a dangerous drug with lies and deception. It bribed doctors to prescribe a painkiller that most people didn't need. And as a result, the city's morgue was running out of room because every night the paramedics brought in another person who died of an overdose.

The bailiff hit the gavel three times. "All rise, court is now back in session."

Judge Waxman instructed us all to sit down and got comfortable on the bench once again. He was smug. He thought he was clever, but he was the worst kind of judge. He may not scream at people, but he was still a bully. The fundamental role of a judge was to provide people their day in court, a moment to be heard and to be listened to, even if, ultimately, they lost.

I wasn't going to play that game.

"My understanding is that both parties have had an opportunity now to take into consideration my intention to assess attorneys' fees if the defendant prevails in their motion to dismiss," the judge said. "Of course I will keep an open mind until I've heard all the arguments, but I wanted to be fair and transparent." He looked at me. "Counsel, how would you like to proceed?"

I stood and looked to Tess and Newhouse. "Your Honor"—I turned back to him—"I have a question, because your comments are a little unclear. If the plaintiff prevails in this motion, meaning that the defendant's motion to dismiss is denied, then will the court also award the plaintiff its attorneys' fees?"

Snickers came from the defense table. Judge Waxman smiled as well. "Sure," Judge Waxman said, playing along, "if the motion to dismiss is denied, I would award you attorneys' fees related to your opposition to NexBeaux's motion."

"Just to be clear, Your Honor, we're obviously representing the plaintiff pro bono. So I would assume that you would require the defendant to pay my market rate, which was most recently the hourly billable rate for a partner at Baxter, Speller & Tuft in New York City, and also comparable rates based on experience for Professor Sherman Friedman and the certified student attorneys who have put in countless hours drafting and revising and researching our response in opposition to the defendant's motion to dismiss."

More quiet snickers from the defendant's table. Sherman leaned over and whispered, "What are you doing?"

I didn't answer.

I waited as Judge Waxman considered my question, and once again with a smirk on his face, he agreed. "Sure, I would assess attorneys' fees related to your work as you have set forth on the record. Knowing this information, how would you like to proceed, counsel?"

I kept my feet firmly planted and my back straight. "If you don't mind, Your Honor, my answer is somewhat dependent upon what the defendants would like to do. I'd like to know whether or not they are withdrawing their motion to dismiss."

I'm pretty sure that, at this point in time, everybody in the courtroom was sure that I was severely mentally ill and should likely be disbarred. Nevertheless, I was not howling at the moon, and I had not stripped down to my underwear and donned a tinfoil hat. Therefore, the hearing continued.

Judge Waxman's patience waned. What had once been cute and moderately humorous now started to annoy him. "OK," he said. "Ms. Glade, do you or your client have any intention on withdrawing your motion to dismiss the plaintiff's lawsuit here today?"

"No, Your Honor. We would like to proceed."

The judge turned back to me. "Mr. Daley, you now know the defendant's position. What would you like to do?"

"I would like to proceed as well." I wish I would have been able to take a picture of Judge Waxman's face, because it looked like someone had shoved a lemon in his mouth.

Judge Waxman took a second to recover, but when the hearing got started, it went exactly as expected. The judge treated Glade the Blade as if she had descended from the mountaintop with all the legal answers chiseled onto stone tablets. He was solicitous and unrestrained in his compliments of her arguments. Her logic was brilliant.

Then it was my turn.

I fully expected aggressive questioning, but Judge Waxman barely allowed me to finish an answer or complete a sentence. He sat there, smug. He exhibited open disdain for my very presence in his courtroom. When I was done, I almost expected him to rule from the bench immediately, but Judge Waxman was careful and calculating.

He took a deep breath and announced his intentions, padding the record. "I want to thank counsel for their arguments here this morning. I will take this matter under advisement, and I will issue my order shortly."

The bailiff banged the gavel, and Judge Waxman exited the courtroom through the side door. Nelson Rockler and NexBeaux were obviously pleased. They actually clapped before looking my way and sharing a good laugh.

Sherman stood up and gave me a hug. "You are the bravest guy I know, and I cannot believe what I just witnessed. It was tragic." He put his hands on his hips. "I'm so glad that you didn't voluntarily dismiss our lawsuit and cave to that guy. Waxman is a major prick, and I think it is now my purpose in life to torment him in every way I can think of."

Sherman was soon joined by the clinic students, who were equally as effusive. Strange how everybody on my side of the room was proud of the fight regardless of outcome, whereas everybody on the other side thought that fighting for something you believed in was a joke.

CHAPTER TWENTY-THREE

Biking to and from the court hearing would have been too impractical, riding the bus too depressing. Thankfully Sherman offered to give me a ride.

He slowed as we approached my parents' house. "Is that who I think it is?"

I looked at what had caught his attention. My jaw dropped. "I'm afraid so." Tess was standing outside my house. The last and only time we had been there together was after my sister's funeral.

Sherman pulled to a stop. "Are you OK doing this? I can stay."

"No." I opened the door. "I can handle it. Go home to your family." I stepped outside and slowly walked over to Tess as Sherman drove away. "Hey." I put on a brave face. "I'm surprised to see you here." Neither of us offered a warm embrace.

"Me too." She looked around. "It still smells funny."

"It will always smell funny," I said. "It's Benton Park." From my pocket, I pulled out my key to the front door. "Look, I don't mean to be rude, but this has been an exhausting day. Is there something that you want from me?" I tried hard to keep it civil. I wanted to be the better person.

"I don't really want anything from you," she said. "But I did want to apologize about how it ended, provide a little closure."

"I consider it already closed, but if you need something more formal, that's fine. You can go ahead and do what you need to do, because we're both here." I didn't push it. I waited for what seemed like too long for Tess to make amends or provide an explanation. As painful as it was probably going to be, I was curious. Just like Laura Bauer never really saw it coming when I broke up with her and moved to New York City after law school, I never thought Tess would cheat. We weren't perfect, but we had a connection. We had shared goals and ideas about who we wanted to be. I thought that would be enough.

"It just sort of happened," she said.

"And sometimes people just let it happen too." I looked beyond her to the front door. If that was all she was going to say, then it wasn't worth it. I thought about ending the conversation and simply going inside, but, instead, I asked her a question that had nagged me from the moment I saw her and Newhouse together. "How long was it going on before I found out?"

"Not too long," Tess said. "We got together at a conference last year, a one-time deal. Then it picked up again."

"Before or after Allison went to treatment?"

"Around the same time." She started to cry. "I know you might not believe me, but I planned on marrying you. I loved you." She opened her purse and got out a small black box. "Here's the ring. I want you to have it back. I don't know if they will buy it back from you or what, but I don't deserve it."

I took the box from her and opened the lid. The diamond sparkled in the light, and I found the whole thing absurd. "You know, I actually did some legal research," I said, "and under the law you were entitled to keep this."

"No breach of contract?"

I shook my head. "Surprisingly, no. It turns out that judges no longer want to require a woman to get married against her will simply because she accepted a diamond ring. I think it was all too Jane Austen for judges to handle."

Her lips curled into a familiar sly smile.

I put the ring in my briefcase. "Are you happy with him, happy with Mr. Quinton B. Newhouse III?"

Tess didn't answer, which I knew meant that she wasn't.

"Are you going to leave him or leave the firm?" I asked.

"I'm thinking about both."

There was silence. I watched as tears began to fill her eyes, then Tess turned and started to leave. When she had gotten to her rental car, I stopped her. "Can I ask you a final question? You don't have to answer if you don't want to."

Tess looked back at me and then leaned against her car. "OK, I'll answer it, even if I don't want to. It'll be my penance."

"Today, in the hallway outside the courtroom, were you and Quinton doing that just to mess with me?"

Her face tightened as it reddened, and she looked down at the ground in shame. "That's what I hate about Nelson Rockler. That's what I hate about the firm. They're just mean. When the other Nelson Rockler attorneys started joking about it, that was all it was, a joke, but then Shirley Glade—Glade the Blade—was like, 'You got to do that, it'll be great.' Even though everybody knew you'd lose today, it didn't matter. Winning wasn't enough—the Blade wanted to push it. I'm not sure Quinton wanted to do it, either, but once Shirley tells you to do something, it's not a choice." She shook her head and walked back toward me. Tess wrapped her arms around me and cried, burying her head in my chest. "I'm sorry," she said, over and over.

I didn't want to ask any more questions. I was done tormenting myself and her. Instead I took her hand in mine. "I know that you are a much better person than that." I leaned over and kissed her on the cheek. "Thank you for returning the ring." I smiled then, kindly. "I'm probably going to need to sell it in order to pay all those attorneys' fees."

She conjured a resigned laugh amid her tears. "You're a good guy, Mr. Daley." Then she got into her rental car and drove away. The judge's ruling to dismiss the case was now inevitable, and I figured that was the last time I was ever going to see or hear from Tess again.

CHAPTER TWENTY-FOUR

A few days after the hearing, Judge Waxman issued an order. He didn't directly rule on the defendant's motion to dismiss. Instead Judge Waxman simply scheduled another hearing date for two weeks later and instructed NexBeaux and Nelson Rockler to prepare an itemized accounting of their fees and costs associated with the motion to dismiss.

I called Sherman, and we tried to figure out our next move. "Why would he do this?" he said. "It's weird. Normally a judge rules, then there might be a hearing about costs. I mean, obviously he's going to grant the motion and make you pay NexBeaux its costs. It's just backward."

"If he hadn't decided," I said, "he would have required me to prepare an itemized accounting of our fees and costs as well, but it's over. Not only is the case going to be dismissed, I'm going to be on the hook for twenty or thirty grand, maybe more."

"It's like Judge Waxman hates you so much that he wants to personally see your face when he grants the motion to dismiss."

"I understood that we had long odds from the very beginning, and I also understood that Waxman liked to dump cases, but this is just so petty."

"I think it was because you wouldn't voluntarily dismiss it, then you made him promise to award you fees if NexBeaux's motion was denied," Sherman said. "The look on his face was epic. He did not like that."

"In hindsight, that was a little too cute."

"But I loved it. I mean, it was totally awesome." Sherman laughed, which was easy for him to do because he still had a job. "Should we see if any of the students want to come?"

"Why not? Maybe they'll get smart and drop out right now before it's too late. Being a lawyer is the worst."

"Or how about this?" Sherman proposed. "We skip it, just blow off the hearing altogether, not show up . . . like a protest thing."

"But then Judge Waxman would probably find us in contempt and try locking us up. Being unemployed and bankrupt is one thing, but being locked up is another. No way."

"Fine," Sherman said. "But afterward we should go to the movies or something. That's what unemployed people are supposed to do, right? Go to the movies in the middle of the day?"

"A movie sounds perfect," I said. "Preferably something violent."

"Yes," Sherman said. "Something very, very violent."

◆ ◆ ◆

The night before the hearing, my whole family had dinner together. I couldn't remember the last time that Mom, Dad, Jackson, and me had all sat around the dinner table. In the middle, there were big bowls of spaghetti and meat sauce. Off to the side was garlic bread, the frozen kind featuring butter an unnaturally bright shade of yellow. Except for the empty chair where Allison used to sit, it was almost normal.

About halfway through, I decided to talk about the hearing. Jackson already knew, but my parents didn't really have any idea about what was coming. "Mom, Dad," I said. "You may have overheard me talking on the telephone, but I wanted to give you an update on the case."

Mom smiled. "You've been working hard."

"I have," I said, "but I'm not sure that's been enough. We had a hearing in front of the judge a few weeks ago. The drug company wants to stop our case—kick us out of court—and I think the judge is going to do what they're asking."

My dad shook his head. "But it just got started." He reached out and grabbed a piece of garlic bread, took a bite, and put it on his plate. "I thought you told us it was going to take a long time, maybe six months or a year or maybe more."

"That's only if this motion is denied," I said. "If the motion is denied, then we eventually go to trial, but I'm not sure we're going to get that far."

My father reached out and took my mother's hand, which was the first time that I'd seen him openly express any concern for my mother in a long time. It made what I knew was going to happen all that much harder.

"I'll fight it," I said. "I'll appeal the decision, but I wanted you all to know that the odds aren't good."

"Little Matty has been kickin' it, Pops," Jackson said. "But when you got a judge in the pocket of these rich companies, you know how it's all going to turn out."

My father looked at my mom and back at me. "When will you know?"

"Tomorrow morning," I said. "I'm pretty sure the judge is going to rule at the hearing tomorrow."

My dad simply nodded, and Mom said nothing.

After dinner, I met Laura in Forest Park to walk the paths. We had exchanged a few emails and talked on the phone, but this was our first time seeing each other in person since our nondate.

"This is sort of becoming a tradition," I said as we started down the trail past Steinberg Skating Rink.

"What is?"

"You and me getting together the night before I have an incredibly painful hearing with Judge Waxman."

She stopped in front of a little pond. "At least it seems like tomorrow will be your last time in front of him for a while." We watched three geese float by.

"Maybe it's for the best." I watched as one of the smaller birds hustled over to the larger ones, fearful that it'd be left behind. "My parents didn't take it well tonight. For people who were so reluctant to file the lawsuit, they seemed disappointed when I told them that it was going to be over . . . I don't know. Maybe I should be thankful that Judge Waxman is going to put me out of my misery."

"Don't say that." Laura turned, and we began walking away from the pond. "Just look at the experience that you gave to those law students. They'll remember it for the rest of their lives. And think about that press conference and all the people that learned about the dangers of these pills. It's a big deal, even though it didn't end the way you wanted."

We talked a little more about Sherman and the precarious future of Cahokia College of Law as we continued down the path. "I think the most frustrating thing for me," I said, "is that I just have no idea what I'm going to do next, besides move out of my parents' basement. I don't know, maybe I should just give up my law license. I mean, what's the point?"

"Well," she said, "I don't think I ever envisioned myself as a lawyer who spent every day drafting wills and dealing with people in messy divorces. It isn't exactly the reason I went to law school. I wanted to do criminal law, remember?"

"I remember." We turned a corner and began to walk between the planetarium and the highway. "You had a great time when you clerked for the city attorney's office. Why did you stop?"

"They didn't hire me," she said. "I applied a couple times, had good references, and always made it to the final round of interviews. But never got the job. Then I graduated, the loans came due, and you take what you can get."

"I think we both need an intervention," I said. "Why don't we open up our own firm, together. I think that my incredibly public and humiliating defeat in this case could be seen as a positive in the eyes of potential clients." I laughed, but I was only partially kidding.

CHAPTER TWENTY-FIVE

Sherman picked me up at nine o'clock the next morning. We both chose black suits with black ties. We were trying to make a profound statement. It was a commentary about the death of justice in America, but most people would probably think we were celebrity impersonators. Just add a black fedora, and we'd look exactly like Jake and Elwood Blues, the Blues Brothers.

At the courthouse, we rode the elevator up to Judge Waxman's courtroom. I hoped that NexBeaux would bring fewer people to this hearing for no other reason than it would likely reduce the attorneys' fees I'd soon be paying. Unfortunately, I saw roughly the same number of highly paid attorneys and executives, including Quinton Newhouse, lingering in the hallway. The good news: my ex-fiancée wasn't there. Tess apparently didn't make the trip this time.

We lifted our heads as we walked past them, and Sherman opened the heavy wooden doors. When I stepped inside, the courtroom erupted with applause. Laura Bauer was there, along with the clinic students, Jackson, and my parents. Jackson was wearing jeans, a dress shirt, and a tie. Mom was in her Sunday best. My dad was in a full suit. I was speechless.

Sherman put his hand on my shoulder. "They're here for you, Matty."

"Thank you," I said. "Now I know why all those drug company people were hanging out in the hallway." I checked my watch. "The judge should be out in ten minutes or so."

They all clapped again, and I even saw the bailiff, who was standing in the corner, smile. *And why not?* I thought. Who in Saint Louis—besides perhaps the judge himself—hadn't the opioid crisis affected? Who didn't think somebody should take a stand, even if they lose?

Sherman and I sat down, and a few minutes later the Nelson Rockler attorneys and NexBeaux executives entered. We fully expected Judge Waxman to come out promptly at ten o'clock, as he always did. But the judge didn't show. Not then, nor 10:15, nor 10:30, nor 10:45. At eleven, I looked at the defense table. "Do you want me to go see what's going on?"

Shirley Glade thought about my offer. "Why don't we both go?" She got up from the table, and we went into the hallway together.

As we walked toward Judge Waxman's chambers, Glade looked over at me. "So are you going to pay my fees with cash or credit?" She laughed, sending a cackle echoing off the courthouse's stone walls. "Sorry, given your employment status at the moment, I'll just assume credit."

"That's very perceptive, Ms. Glade. Everybody always told me you were super smart." When we got to Judge Waxman's outer door, I pressed the buzzer and heard it ring in the distance, but nobody responded. I tried it a second time with the same result. "Now what do you want to do?"

"I'm actually a little worried," Shirley said. "This just doesn't seem like him. He's quite conscientious."

"Conscientious?" I pretended like I was considering it. "I guess that's one way to describe him." Then my cell phone rang.

"Hey, I just sent you a link," Sherman said once I picked up.

I checked my email and found Sherman's message. It linked to a story about Judge Waxman, with a headline that read:

Judge's Failure to Disclose Romantic Relationship
Results in Leave of Absence

◆ ◆ ◆

The bailiff knocked the gavel three times. "All rise for the Honorable Erica P. Bruin." We all stood as Judge Bruin entered the courtroom. As she sat down, she gestured for us to sit as well.

"I want to thank all of you for your patience this morning. Obviously you were expecting Judge Waxman, and I was expecting to be on vacation down at Lake of the Ozarks. But sometimes life has other plans." She took a breath. "The chief judge informed me that Judge Waxman has taken an indefinite leave of absence while the Missouri Commission on Retirement, Removal and Discipline reviews a very serious complaint filed against him."

Judge Bruin looked at Shirley Glade, then at me. "Judge Waxman has been my colleague for many years, and I think that he will ultimately do the right thing once the board has had an opportunity to review the allegations." She looked down at her notes. "Your case has been reassigned, and I will be handling it going forward. Luckily, it's still in the early stages and Judge Waxman has not made any substantive rulings, so the transition should be a smooth one."

I was thrilled that Sherman and I had not skipped the hearing, because I couldn't remember a better time in my entire life. With the absence of Judge Waxman, the whole energy of the room had changed. NexBeaux and the attorneys from Nelson Rockler looked deflated. I glanced back at my students in the gallery and at Jackson and my parents. They all looked very confused, so I gave them a discreet thumbs-up. Laura Bauer, however, already knew what was going on. She had a big smile on her face.

"I recognize," Judge Bruin continued, "that there is a pending motion to dismiss. This morning I read the materials submitted by both parties and reviewed the transcript of the motion hearing. I also spoke with Judge Waxman's law clerk and Judge Waxman about the motion as well, so I am familiar with the issues."

She looked at the defense table and offered a warm smile. "Are there objections to me going forward as planned and ruling on the motion to dismiss today? It seemed pretty straightforward. If there are objections, I'd be willing to schedule another hearing where everyone can personally argue their positions in front of me."

Glade stood, no longer full of confidence, but, because she and her associates hadn't had enough time to properly research the new judge, she was willing to continue. Glade smiled. "I have no objection to you deciding the motion, Your Honor, with no further argument or supplemental briefing."

I popped out of my seat before even being asked. "I also have no objection, Your Honor."

Before we filed our lawsuit, the law students had compiled a list of judges. They had ranked them from first to last, and Judge Bruin was first. According to her profile, the bumper sticker on her cherry-red Chevy Silverado read: "Triple Threat: Big Hair, Big Boobs, Big Brains." She grew up in the bootheel of Missouri, and, as a result, she had a deep skepticism of the government, the United Nations, and large corporations. She was also a recovering alcoholic and self-proclaimed "Drug Warrior for Christ." Now twenty years sober, Judge Bruin was the founder of the city's first Drug Treatment Court and spent her time traveling the country providing technical assistance to other judges who wanted to help drug addicts stay out of prison. If anybody knew the effect of opioid painkillers, like NexBeaux's Bentrax, it was Judge Bruin.

"Good." Judge Bruin nodded. "Then let the record reflect that there has been no objection to me going forward this morning and ruling on the defendant's motion to dismiss." She paused, then dropped a bomb on Glade the Blade and Nelson Rockler. "Based upon the memoranda and legal arguments previously submitted, the motion is denied. As

Mr. Daley pointed out in his argument opposing the motion, when a judge dismisses a lawsuit as a matter of law, it means that there are absolutely no circumstances or discoverable facts that would allow the plaintiff to prevail. That is a very high burden, and the defendant has not met that standard."

I looked at Sherman and smiled, then at the stunned faces at the defense table.

New judge, new day.

"My understanding, from reading the transcript," the judge went on, "is that Judge Waxman was going to award attorneys' fees to whoever prevailed on this motion. Strange, because I can't remember ever awarding fees and costs under such circumstances. I do, however, feel obliged to honor the agreement. In fact, there was a specific colloquy between Judge Waxman and you, Ms. Glade, related to this matter. Therefore, I ask that the plaintiff's counsel prepare an accounting of their costs and fees. Please file it with the court within seven days, and the defense will need to pay these fees within thirty days."

Glade stood. "Your Honor, I believe that the standard for awarding attorneys' fees is quite high and, while I respect your decision, I do not believe our motion to dismiss was frivolous or without merit."

"That may be true, but at the previous hearing, you freely and voluntarily agreed to apply a different standard. The conversation on the record, thanks to the thorough work of Mr. Daley, was quite clear. Therefore, it was more akin to an agreement or contract, and I assume you do not breach your contracts, Ms. Glade, correct?"

"Of course I honor my contracts, Judge Bruin," Glade stammered. "It's just that—"

"Good," Judge Bruin said. "Then you'll need to pay up. In the meantime, I'll issue a new scheduling order, then I'll be out of the office. The Lake of the Ozarks beckons me. Thank you."

CHAPTER TWENTY-SIX

Three months passed in no time. All summer long, Nelson Rockler behaved exactly as I had expected. They inundated us with paper. It seemed like every day a messenger came to the law school and delivered another box filled with emails, reports, financial statements, memos, and marketing materials. None of it was sorted by topic or chronology. Most of it was irrelevant.

After the first fifteen boxes arrived, we developed a general system. Screw had found a dozen old file cabinets in one of the law school's storage closets. Nobody asked how she had gained access to the closet, but she assured us that nobody was going to notice that the file cabinets had been "moved." Each file cabinet related to a broad category of documents. As soon as a new box arrived, we would sort the contents into the proper cabinet, then into specific subcategories. Each cabinet also had a separate folder for "hot documents," files I considered either direct evidence of wrongdoing by NexBeaux or simply embarrassing.

The process worked for a while, but eventually we ran out of file cabinets and had to leave sticky-note-laden stacks on the floor. Our workroom grew smaller by the day. I wished we had the resources I'd taken for granted at Baxter, Speller & Tuft—a scanner and document-management software at the very least—but we didn't, and Glade the Blade knew it.

Nelson Rockler also swamped the court with motion after motion. We could hardly keep up, but Sherman and I managed to respond to each one. We didn't win every time, but we made our deadlines and Judge Bruin managed to minimize the damage.

We survived, barely.

Eventually it was time to begin depositions. Depositions were critical. Cases were won or lost at them, because attorneys had an opportunity to question any witness under oath. No judge was present to keep the depositions fair. Objections were noted, but even if a question was improper, embarrassing, or meant to harass, a witness was expected to answer.

Nelson Rockler had already scheduled the depositions of my family as well as Allison's doctors, therapist, and treatment providers. Then one evening I heard a knock on the door.

"Are you Matthew Daley?" He was a little guy in khaki shorts and a baseball cap.

"I am."

He pressed a packet to my chest. Instinctively I grabbed it before it fell as he turned and walked away. I opened the thick envelope and read the cover page. Nelson Rockler didn't just want to depose my family. They wanted to depose me.

◆ ◆ ◆

That night I went to a movie with Laura at the Tivoli on the Delmar Loop. It was originally a vaudeville theater that had fallen on bad times until it was restored and brought back to life. The eclectic mix of movies distinguished it from the suburban megaplex, and the strong cocktails served along with Junior Mints and popcorn at the concession booth didn't hurt.

"What did you think?" I asked Laura as we walked out of the lobby.

"It was pretty good," she said. "I like Stanley Tucci. He's a great actor. Even if the plot drags, he can make it interesting."

"Do you remember him in *Big Night*?" I asked. "It was about brothers trying to serve authentic Italian food in the 1950s."

Laura's memory sparked. "Oh yeah," she said. "I remember that. Great music, and the food was gorgeous."

"I never understood why that wasn't more popular," I said. "Probably my favorite movie with Stanley Tucci."

"I loved him in *Julie & Julia*," Laura said. "He played Julia Child's husband, and he somehow managed to hold his own with Meryl Streep in that one."

"That was good." I pointed at a new taqueria across the street. "Do you want to get a bite?"

Laura looked at her watch. "Sure," she said, "but then I need to go home. I've got a deposition tomorrow."

"Oh no," I said, "don't say that word." I filled Laura in on the latest strategy from Glade the Blade. "The worst part is the money. For every deposition, I have to order a transcript. It isn't required, but there's no way I can prepare for trial or develop my direct and cross-examination without one."

"What about the attorneys' fees that Judge Bruin awarded you when she denied the motion to dismiss?"

"That money will keep us afloat for a little while, but just one of these deposition transcripts costs a thousand dollars a day. Glade the Blade usually spends a day and a half per witness. She told Sherman that my brother's deposition will last four or five days. It's crazy."

"And now she wants to depose you?"

"I think she wants to make me a witness in the case," I said. "I'm sure they'll take the deposition, then the Nelson Rockler attorneys will file a motion to preclude me from being the lawyer in this case because I'm now purportedly an essential witness—"

"And you can't be both a witness and the attorney in this case because you're not the actual party."

"Exactly. My parents, as representatives of my sister's estate, are the plaintiffs, not me," I said. "If I was suing on behalf of myself, I'd be fine."

Laura shook her head. "That's low." She took my arm and held my hand when the light turned and the signal changed to make it safe to walk across the busy street. I don't even know if Laura realized what she was doing or meant anything by it, but my heart skipped a beat. It was the first time we'd held hands in eight years.

When we got to the restaurant, I reluctantly let go of Laura's hand and opened the door for her.

"Thank you," she said. "You really have to let Judge Bruin know they're doing this. It's wrong. She's not going to be happy."

It was good advice.

The next day, we informed Judge Bruin that the defendants were abusing their right to depose potential witnesses in the case and that they recently served me with a notice of deposition. Laura was right. Judge Bruin wasn't happy. She ordered Nelson Rockler to temporarily stop all scheduled depositions. Then she ordered all parties to appear before her for a settlement conference the following week. Her order required someone with "settlement authority" for each party to attend. For us, that meant my mother and father.

For NexBeaux, it meant the company's CEO, Chandler Hawkes. The drunk slimeball I last saw at Yankee Stadium would have to come to Saint Louis.

CHAPTER TWENTY-SEVEN

After some awkward introductions, Judge Bruin's law clerk set coffee and pastries on a table near the window. I don't know if Judge Bruin arranged for coffee and pastries for all her settlement conferences, but I was thankful. Sherman and I had been debating our strategy late into the night, and I desperately needed the caffeine.

I got up and poured myself a cup, along with another two for my mom and dad. I brought the drinks over to the table, then I filled a plate with doughnuts. Judge Bruin arrived five minutes later in a pair of black dress pants, shiny black cowboy boots, a white blouse, and large silver-and-turquoise earrings.

"I like those earrings," my mom said. She began to talk about why she thought they were beautiful, before stopping. It was as if my mother suddenly realized that perhaps she shouldn't compliment a judge.

Judge Bruin, however, took it in stride. "Why thank you, ma'am." The judge smiled, then she settled in at the head of the table. "Picked these earrings up in Branson a few years back. They are some of my favorites."

My mom nodded, and Judge Bruin got down to business. "I'm concerned." Judge Bruin gave Shirley Glade a hard stare. "We are quickly approaching the point of no return here, folks. Everybody is dug into their positions. Everybody hates everybody, and so much time, money, and effort has been sunk into the case that the parties wouldn't know a good settlement if it came up and bit them in the badonkadonk." She looked at me, then turned her attention back to Shirley Glade. "Have you made any settlement offers?"

Glade shifted uncomfortably in her seat. She looked at her client, Chandler Hawkes, then back at the judge. "No, Your Honor. We were waiting for an offer from the plaintiff."

"Mr. Daley." Judge Bruin looked and acted genuinely surprised. "Is that true? You haven't made a formal offer of settlement to NexBeaux?"

My face flushed. I felt embarrassed, which was exactly what Judge Bruin wanted. She wanted to force me to think about the end. I'd talked a lot about holding people accountable, but I'd done a poor job of defining exactly what that meant. Was it money? Was it a letter of apology? Was it the resignation of the CEO? I didn't know.

"I have not yet, Your Honor."

My parents may not have known much about lawsuits and litigation, but they knew that I hadn't done something that I should've done. They looked at me as if I was back in elementary school and the principal had called them into the office for some misdeed that I'd committed on the playground.

I tried to explain. "Your Honor," I said, "this case has never been entirely about money, and I figured that NexBeaux would not be willing to admit any wrongdoing in this case for fear that it would result in additional lawsuits or a class action. So I've always assumed we would go to trial."

"OK"—Judge Bruin nodded—"that's honest, but misguided. Lawsuits are blunt instruments. My guess is that if NexBeaux made a significant settlement offer, you would consider it."

I looked at my parents, then back at Judge Bruin. "Of course," I said. "We would consider it."

"Good," she said. "That's smart, because these upcoming depositions won't be fun. They will be highly personal, and you'd have to answer some very probing questions by the defense. And ultimately, after going through all that, you could go to trial and still you may walk away with nothing. There's no guarantees with a trial."

Judge Bruin turned to NexBeaux's CEO, Chandler Hawkes. "And you, sir, I don't mean to interfere with your attorney-client relationship with Ms. Glade and other attorneys at Nelson Rockler, but have they given you any estimates as to how much all these depositions and the trial is going to cost? Have you seen the bills that have already been submitted by this law firm? And I'm assuming best case scenario for you is that you win. How much is that win going to cost? And what's your exposure if you lose? Ask your attorney these questions in private, and I hope she gives you an honest answer, because I think it's going to cost you a lot."

Judge Bruin stood up. "I'd like to meet with each of the parties separately to discuss settlement, assuming there are no objections." When the room remained silent, Judge Bruin nodded. "Mr. Daley, why don't you and your cocounsel, along with your parents, come with me."

◆ ◆ ◆

Two cushioned chairs sat in front of Judge Bruin's desk. Her law clerk rolled in two more so that everybody would have a place to sit.

"Listen," Judge Bruin said. "I get that this is personal. If my daughter died, I would be absolutely crushed—heartbroken—but the courts are not a good place to heal. A civil lawsuit, win or lose, will never fill that hole that's been left in your lives."

Mom and Dad eyed each other, unsure of how they should respond.

"I'm not going to put you on the spot to answer me right now," the judge went on. "In a few minutes, I'll be in here giving NexBeaux the hard sell. But I want you to be creative, Mr. Daley. What if NexBeaux publicly apologized to you and your family? What if they donated ten million dollars to provide free or reduced-cost treatment to people suffering from addiction in honor of Allison? What if they did all that and also paid your family one hundred thousand dollars or five hundred thousand dollars or five million dollars? Pick a number. What would it take? When is enough, enough?"

"I'm skeptical that NexBeaux would ever offer something like that," I said. "I'm skeptical that they would even offer us one dollar."

Judge Bruin slapped her hand down on her desk. "Let me worry about NexBeaux." She had an intense look in her eyes. "Because I think your lawsuit is righteous. It took a lot of cojones to file this thing, and *you* know that I've fought back against a lot of their attempts to cut your legs out from under you. But, Mr. Daley, while I might not allow them to call you as a witness at trial, I don't see much basis in preventing you from being deposed." She looked at Sherman. "You gotta talk some sense into him, because, although your motives are righteous, I can't protect you anymore. The law is not in your favor, and I have to follow the law."

◆ ◆ ◆

Negotiations went back and forth for the entire day. In the end, NexBeaux made a final offer. "I'm going to write a number down on this sheet of paper." Judge Bruin picked up a pen and scribbled a figure. "This is it. NexBeaux will pay you this. No admission of guilt. The settlement is confidential, and you cannot talk about the settlement, NexBeaux, or Bentrax to the media or publicly, and the company will also donate twenty-five thousand dollars to the Arch Treatment Center in memory of Allison."

She pushed the piece of paper across the desk to me. Sherman and I read the number before passing it to my parents. My mom and dad looked, then pushed the paper away.

None of us spoke.

"I'm going to step out so that you can discuss this in private," Judge Bruin said. "But hear me out. You do this, and it's over today. Imagine that. No more stress. No more wondering about what's going to happen. You can move forward with your lives." Judge Bruin pointed at the offer on the piece of paper. "This isn't what you proposed, but it's a good offer, especially in light of the challenges of this lawsuit. Causation and damages are just a few hurdles that you will have to overcome at trial."

With that, Judge Bruin got up and left us alone in her chambers. When the door was closed, my dad looked at me. "A hundred and fifty thousand dollars," he said. "That's quite a bit of money. Tax man will take a good chunk, but that's still quite a bit of money."

"So you want to accept the offer?"

My dad didn't say. Instead he looked at my mom. "How about you?"

My mother picked up the piece of paper with the dollar amount scribbled on one side. She studied it, as if trying to read something that wasn't there. "No admission of guilt." She put the paper back down on the table. "I don't care about money. I didn't grow up with it. Don't have it now, and I never will. It ain't about money." She pushed the piece of paper as far away from her as possible. "It's about what's right, and I ain't afraid of no questions or nothing. I say what I say. I'm a southie. I ain't afraid of who I am."

I couldn't help but smile. "OK," I said. "And you know that the odds are against us, right? Judge Bruin wasn't making that up. We'll probably lose, especially if she stops protecting us."

"I get that," Mom said. "But I trust that you'll do your best, represent us real good in court."

"Do you agree?" I asked my dad.

My father nodded. "As much as I'd like to buy a new engine for the Mustang, I'm in. Let's see where it leads, for Allison."

"For Allison," my mom echoed.

CHAPTER TWENTY-EIGHT

If the first three months of the case passed quickly, the final months before trial were a blur. Seasons changed, summer faded into fall, but the work was constant. We spent every day attending depositions, reviewing documents, or responding to evidentiary motions. If I had any spare time, which was rare, I spent it with Laura, rebuilding trust and taking it slow.

Now only one week remained before jury selection. I came up from my room in the basement, tired and a little depressed. The depositions of my family hadn't gone well. Shirley Glade had the right to ask us about the most intimate details of our lives—money, drug and alcohol use, romantic partners, employment history—and she did. It was just a preview of what was to come.

The weight of the case pressed down on me. My mind couldn't stop cycling through the lists of things to do. I felt overwhelmed, and opening my credit card statement didn't help. Although I could still make the minimum monthly payment, the revolving balance had almost maxed out.

At first, the lawsuit against NexBeaux hadn't really cost anything beyond the initial filing fee. Now it pushed me deeper and deeper into debt. After the case didn't settle at mediation, expenses multiplied. I had to pay for copies, filing fees, stenographers, process servers, and transcripts. The depositions of NexBeaux executives took place at the company's New Jersey headquarters. That meant I had to pay for multiple airplane flights and hotel rooms. When I left Baxter, Speller & Tuft, my credit card balance was a little high because of the charges for Allison's treatment and the engagement ring, but it wasn't an insurmountable amount given my income. That changed. The balance now hovered around the cost of a nice new car. I had no income, and the debt was compounding at a 23 percent interest rate.

On my way out the back door, I ripped up the credit card bill and tossed it into the garbage. As I walked back to the garage, I looked forward to getting on my bike and clearing my head. The daily rides to and from the law school had become the highlight of my day. Even in the rain or sleet, I always felt better when I was done.

When I arrived at Cahokia, however, I discovered that this day would be very different. News trucks were parked out front. I rode past them, trying to eavesdrop. A robbery, maybe? I locked up my bike and walked to the front door. I pulled the handle, but the door didn't open. I turned to some nearby students. "Why are the doors locked?"

The tall one answered. "School's closed."

"For today?"

"No, man," he said. "Like forever."

I took out my phone and found multiple emails and texts from Sherman. The first email was a forwarded message from President McIntosh that was sent early in the morning. It acknowledged that the school "has been operating at a deficit for quite some time," admitted that a local financial institution denied a request for credit, and ended with an announcement that the Cahokia College of Law can no longer "maintain operations." All faculty and staff were laid off, and President McIntosh "hopes" that current students can complete their education at neighboring law schools. No promises, however, were made. It was clear that the students were on their own.

Sherman also forwarded me an email circulated by the dean of students, and another panicked email among faculty members who were now suddenly out of a job. The texts were shorter and relayed bits of information as they were being discovered. It began with a message stating that the locks were changed in the middle of the night without advance warning, and ended with: Me and the clinic are at Randy's Roadhouse down on Front Street.

When the riverboat casino opened in East Saint Louis, promises were made about how it would spur future economic development along the Mississippi River. The casino indeed reinvigorated the city's tax base (over half the city's budget comes from it), but very little economic development had occurred along the riverfront over the past twenty-five years. Randy's Roadhouse was the exception.

Originally constructed in the late 1940s as an auto repair shop, Randy's Roadhouse was now the best place for a cheap drink before getting on or off the riverboat, and it served as the go-to after-work place for employees of the nearby hospital.

When I stepped inside, it was packed. Students, faculty, and administrators from Cahokia filled most of the seats. Honky-tonk blasted from the jukebox, and it was evident that most had been there since nine in the morning. The dance floor was packed, like it was a Friday night. One guy was dancing around in his underwear. On his chest, he had written in black magic marker "Help! Donate money for loans here," with an arrow pointed down. Based on the bills shoved into his elastic waistband, it looked like he had already earned over twenty dollars.

A nerdy couple was making out near the restrooms, as if it were their last days on earth, and nearby two guys sat on the floor. Their heads were down. Their hands covered their faces as if they were trying to contain an imminent explosion.

Sherman and the crew were over by the mechanical bull, which was not working, much to the chagrin of many of the drunk law students who had gathered. Due to the very real likelihood that at least one of them would fall off and suffer a traumatic brain injury, that may have been a blessing in disguise.

I sat next to Sherman, flagged the waitress, and ordered a round of drinks for everybody while saying a silent prayer that my credit card wouldn't be declined. "I'm so sorry about all this," I said.

They all nodded, but they clearly didn't want to talk about it. My guess was that the topic had already run its course, and the group had now shifted into simply trying to collectively lose themselves for a little while.

I leaned over to Sherman. "Can we talk?"

He looked up from his beer. "Are you offering me a job?"

"Sure," I said, placing my arm around him. "But it doesn't pay anything."

He nodded, and the edges of his mouth turned upward into a crazy smile. "I'll take it."

We walked outside. Randy's Roadhouse had a dozen picnic tables set up at the edge of the parking lot. At night they were mostly filled with smokers, but since it wasn't even noon, more than half the tables were empty.

I picked one that had a nice view of the river. "I'm sorry about your job."

"I knew it was coming," Sherman said. "I should've been out there looking, but it was just too easy to ignore it. I'd been hearing rumors that the school was going to close for years, and every fall a new class of law students arrived, along with a paycheck every other week. I guess I always figured that the board would find a way to keep it going." He leaned over, picked up a stick, and began snapping it into little pieces as a barge filled with shipping containers floated past us along the Mississippi. "Now I don't know what I'm going to do."

"Can we get into the building?"

Sherman shook his head. "Nothing's changed," he said. "They came in the middle of the night and changed the locks. I guess they want to auction off all of the school's assets, and the board of trustees is worried that the school would get trashed if we were allowed inside."

"But what about your stuff?"

"I don't know." Sherman picked up another twig and broke it into smaller pieces, just like the other. "They've got to let us back inside sometime. Maybe later this week. Maybe next week."

"We start trial next week." My stomach churned, and a slight panic crept into my voice. "All our exhibits are locked up. My trial notebook is in there. We can't get to any of the things we need to prepare. There's no way we can start trial on Monday."

"You have to call Judge Bruin," Sherman said. "Like now."

◆ ◆ ◆

The judge called an emergency hearing for late that afternoon. Sherman and I sat around the kitchen table at my parents' house and waited for Judge Bruin to join the conference call.

After a few minutes, her law clerk came on the line. "Hello, this is Maddie. The judge is in a hearing right now, but she should be wrapping that up very shortly. Is everybody here?"

I informed her that Sherman and I were present, and Shirley Glade and Quinton Newhouse did the same. While we waited for the judge, I was tempted to ask Glade about Tess. She hadn't come to any of the depositions or hearings. Her name hadn't been on any of the signature blocks on any of the law firm's numerous pleadings and memoranda. I wondered whether Tess had quit.

"OK," Maddie said. "Thank you for your patience. Just hang on."

We waited another five minutes, then Judge Bruin finally joined the conference call. "OK." Judge Bruin's speech was clipped, irritated. "I'm here. Y'all are here. What's the crisis?"

Sherman pointed at me.

"I'm afraid that I'm the person with the emergency, Your Honor," I said. "I'm, unfortunately, asking for a continuance of our trial."

"A continuance?" Her mood did not improve. "Mr. Daley, I've blocked off three weeks for this trial. This has been planned for many months. We're now just a week away, and you want a continuance?"

"Yes, Your Honor," I said. "As you know, we've been working with Professor Friedman's students at Cahokia College of Law. That's also where we've been storing our documents and our trial prep materials. For all intents and purposes, the law school is my office."

"OK," she said. "I'm still waiting to hear why you need a continuance."

"Cahokia shut down today. It's locked, and we don't have any access. It would be incredibly difficult to go to trial without having any of the documents we need to prove our case or any of our memoranda, legal research, or files."

The call went silent as the information sank in. Then Shirley Glade cleared her throat. "If you don't mind, Your Honor, may I make a suggestion?"

"Please do," the judge said. "I'd appreciate any ideas that anybody might have."

"Thank you, Judge Bruin." Glade the Blade's voice was so sickeningly sweet that I knew she had something up her sleeve. It was like she knew that the law school was going to close and she had prepared for our teleconference. Given the timing, it wouldn't surprise me if she was somehow involved, even if I didn't know how or could never prove it.

"Why don't we simply duplicate our discovery documents?" Glade said. "It may take a day or two, but we'll overnight them to Mr. Daley and go forward just as the court has planned. While I'm sympathetic, postponing the trial to a later date will just increase costs and allow this case to drag on even further. While it has been difficult for the court to block off three weeks for this trial, it has also been difficult for me and my clients. I'm booked solid for at least the next six months. It wouldn't surprise me, if this continuance is granted, that trial would be delayed until next year."

"You think you can duplicate the documents and get them to Mr. Daley by the end of the week?" Judge Bruin's mood had brightened considerably. "If so, I think that's a good solution. It isn't perfect, but it's a good solution."

"But my trial materials," I said. "It isn't realistic to be ready. I'd have to recreate all—"

"I disagree," Judge Bruin cut in. "We'll start picking the jury on Monday as planned. Thank you, Ms. Glade, for your willingness to help."

"Not a problem, Your Honor," Glade said. "Mr. Daley should expect the duplicates of our discovery in a few days. Someone will be contacting him tomorrow about where it should be sent since the law school is . . . well, the law school is no longer anything."

After the teleconference, Sherman went home to his wife and family. They had a lot to talk about, and I could tell that he was anxious to leave. I called Laura, and she agreed to meet me at a coffee shop on the corner of Skinker and Forest Park Parkway after work.

Most of the tables were filled by Washington University students when I arrived, but, after ordering a large cup of coffee, I found an empty spot in the corner by a gas fireplace. On the wall was a picture of the mountains, and suspended from the ceiling was a kayak.

Laura gave me a cute little wave when she came through the door, and that small gesture almost caused me to forget all my troubles. I watched her order a coffee before coming over to the table, and I couldn't take my eyes off her.

"I can't believe it." Laura set her drink down on the table, then gave me a hug. "I thought Judge Bruin was on your side."

"I don't know," I said. "It was like she was a different person today. Maybe somebody got to her, or maybe she's just tired of this case and regrets not dismissing like Judge Waxman was planning on doing. It's been a lot of work, and I'm sure she's probably falling behind, not clearing her caseload fast enough. A continuance would mean that everything was going to get backed up even further."

"Did you know the state court administrator measures all that stuff?" Laura asked as she sat down. "It's ridiculous. It's all about efficiency and timelines. There's never any measurement for whether a judge treats people well or whether serious cases are given the time and attention they deserve."

"Well," I said, "this tough case just got even tougher. I mean, significantly tougher. I have no notes. All the documents had been sorted, and important documents had been pulled. It took us months, and now we're supposed to do it in three or four days." I pushed away from the table and leaned back, staring at the ceiling. "I want to give up. Maybe I should call Glade the Blade and tell her that we'll settle for half the offer that NexBeaux made at the settlement conference. At least then I'd be able to pay off my credit card."

Laura reached out and took my hand. "You can't give up now, Matty. Think about your sister. You've come this far already. You need to see it through."

"I feel bad for the kids," I said. "I know everybody makes fun of Cahokia, but they're hard workers and they're smart, not like book smart, but savvy. They know how real life works. They have common sense, and they understand what is fair and what isn't."

"Do you think they'll help with the trial?"

"I have no idea. They wouldn't be earning any credit. Plus, they've got a ton of student loan debt, and if I were them I'd never even want to talk to a lawyer, much less be one."

"OK, no more pity party." Laura raised her head and stiffened her upper lip. "You need to take a little break. We shouldn't talk about the case. We shouldn't think about the case. For tonight it's done, and tomorrow morning is going to be a new day. You shouldn't make any decisions or do anything until tomorrow."

"Interesting," I said. "So what am I supposed to do tonight?"

Laura leaned over the table and kissed me on the lips. "Come over to my apartment." Her voice was soft. "We can have a few glasses of wine, play some music, and forget all about it."

CHAPTER TWENTY-NINE

In the morning, after a full night's sleep next to Laura, it didn't seem quite as bad. I rolled over and kissed her. She was naked under the thin sheet, and I couldn't stop myself from watching her. I never thought I would be this close to her again.

I got out of bed, found my clothes, and went into the kitchen. I found a half dozen eggs, a green pepper, and some cheese in the refrigerator. With a small onion I plucked from a hanging basket near the sink, I began working on breakfast.

Coffee gurgled in the pot as I sweated the onion and chopped the pepper. The sounds and aromas must have coaxed Laura out of bed, because she wandered into the kitchen not too much later.

"Look at you." She smiled as she got a mug out of the cabinet. "You're playing house so nicely."

"I'm trying." I picked up the cutting board and scraped the diced green pepper into the frying pan with the onion.

Coffee in hand, Laura pulled a chair into the kitchen so that she could sit while she watched me work. "Did you decide what you're going to do?"

"I have a rough idea." I picked up an egg, cracked it, and slipped it into the pan. "Shirley Glade will be dumping dozens of boxes with thousands of pieces of paper on me in two days, so my first step is to find some cheap office space, month-to-month. I just need a place to work. Once it's found, I'll contact everybody, and, hopefully, Sherman and his students will come help out. I don't expect it, but I'll ask."

"One day at a time," Laura said.

I picked up another egg and held it up, examining it. "One day at a time." Then I cracked it open and fried it in the pan.

◆ ◆ ◆

It took me only a few days to find office space. Before I signed a lease agreement, however, I needed money—and I had just one asset. I dug the small box with the diamond engagement ring out from under my bed mattress, then negotiated a price with a savvy downtown jeweler. There was little doubt that he knew I was desperate, either for the money or to rid myself of any remnant of a relationship gone bad. I eventually settled with him giving me about 40 percent less than what I had paid for it. I could've gotten more, if he took it on consignment, but I needed the immediate cash.

The office space was located by happenstance. I was biking around the neighborhood, trying to get some exercise and settle my nerves, when I saw the sign in the window of a little storefront on Broadway. The building was once a dry goods store, catering to immigrants who worked on the barges going up and down the Mississippi.

It had everything that I was looking for. It was minutes from my parents' house. It was big, and it was cheap. The space had been vacant for so long that the landlord even filled it with some used desks and chairs as a signing bonus.

With that obstacle overcome, I called a meeting. Jury selection began on Monday morning. NexBeaux and Nelson Rockler had almost unlimited resources, and I needed help. I sat by the window, reading a book, and waited for someone to come.

The meeting was scheduled for seven, and by a quarter after, still nobody had arrived. I checked my phone, and there were no messages or emails. I got up and walked back to a little kitchenette next to a dirty bathroom. I threw a bag of popcorn into the microwave, and, halfway through popping, I poked my head out the door. I thought I heard someone come in, but there was still no one.

The popping slowed down, then the microwave buzzed. I removed the hot bag and walked back into the large empty office space in the front of the building. As I sat down, everybody jumped out from behind the furniture and doorways.

"Surprise!" they shouted in unison.

The bag of popcorn flew out of my hand, raining white kernels everywhere, and I swear my heart stopped.

"Not funny," I said as everyone else cheered and laughed. "Not funny at all."

Sherman came forward with champagne and plastic cups. Laura brought a sandwich tray and fruit, and my brother brought a twenty-four pack of beer. The students brought themselves, which was actually the biggest gift of all.

"I talked to Shirley Glade today, and she told me that the boxes of documents will arrive here sometime tomorrow," I said. "We don't have time to sort them. All we can do is go through the boxes as quickly as possible and try and find things that look familiar. Sherman is working with President McIntosh, and he says that we might be allowed back inside the school sometime next week, but we can't assume anything."

Cynthia was the first to volunteer. "So what do you need us to do in the meantime? I can start doing witness prep."

"Sounds good." I looked at Jeff. "Can you work on draft jury instructions?"

"I think I got a copy of the lawsuit on my laptop." Jeff opened his book bag and pulled out his computer. "I'll take a look at our causes of action and then find the MAI at the library tomorrow." The MAI were the Missouri Approved Jury Instructions that were required to be used in any civil case, and I was impressed Jeff knew enough to know that we needed them.

"Just go to the law library at Wash U," I said. "You won't get stopped." Then to Screw I said, "Can you put a binder together of all the pleadings and motions as well as a spreadsheet of all of Judge Bruin's evidentiary decisions?"

Screw jumped to her feet and saluted me. "Yes, sir, right away, sir."

"Perfect, and, Cynthia, since you're working on witness prep, I'm going to need a rough outline of questions. I know we did all this stuff before and I'm hoping we'll get it back from the law school, but, if we don't, I need something to work off during the trial."

"I can do that." Cynthia came across as more confident than I was, which was fine. When I was done handing out the initial assignments and the students dispersed, Jackson came up to me and told me that there had been a development.

"About what?" I asked.

Jackson looked over his shoulder, making sure nobody was listening. "I'd rather not say right here."

"OK." I followed Jackson back to the small kitchenette and shut the door. "What's going on?"

"I got approached yesterday with a very interesting offer."

"What do you mean?" I leaned against the wall, my arms folded across my chest. "I'm tired, Jackson, just tell me what's going on."

"It was Perry." Jackson talked in a whisper. "He says that NexBeaux offered him five thousand dollars, if he testified truthfully and honestly."

"What does that mean?"

"It means," Jackson said, "that NexBeaux is trying to pay off a witness. If he does it, Perry is going to testify that Allison never really took Bentrax. He's going to say that she got a prescription, but only took a few and sold the rest on the street. He's going to say that she was using heroin long before her car accident, and once she'd gotten a taste of the real stuff, she had no interest in a stupid painkiller."

"That's not what her journals say."

"Perry's going to say that she lied in the journals. He's going to say that Allison was always in denial about being a junkie, and that she liked the story about getting hooked on painkillers first because it made her seem more innocent and naive. It absolved her of any responsibility."

"That testimony is going to blow up our case."

"I know," Jackson said, "and so does Perry, and that's why if we outbid NexBeaux and pay him six thousand dollars, then his testimony might be 'refreshed' with other information that helps us out."

I began to pace. "So you're saying that NexBeaux is trying to bribe a witness."

Jackson shook his head. "They ain't *trying*, bro—they *are* bribing a witness, and they may be bribing other witnesses that we just don't know about."

"But, out of the goodness of Perry's heart, he is giving us the opportunity to shape his testimony in our favor."

"Exactly," Jackson said.

"Well, I'm not paying him anything," I said.

"Then we're going to lose." Annoyed, Jackson blew a deep breath out of the corner of his mouth. "If we don't pay Perry what he wants, then there's no point in having your little minions out there run around for the next three weeks."

"I'm not doing it."

"Why not?" Jackson shouted. "You want to win? Then you need to fight 'em in the gutter. That's where they are. If they cheat, then you do too." He took a step toward the door but stopped and pointed at me. "If I had the money, I'd pay Perry myself. But I don't."

"And you think I do?" I asked. "I've already spent thousands on this case, and that's not even counting the cost of this place. My credit card is maxed out. I have no car, and I live in Mom and Dad's basement. What, if anything, did I just say that would suggest I had money lying around?"

CHAPTER THIRTY

The documents didn't come on Thursday, nor did the documents come on Friday. Shirley Glade feigned confusion as to why they had not been delivered. She swore that the duplicates had been shipped on Tuesday, and she promised to get to the bottom of what had happened.

On Saturday morning, just two days before the start of trial, a large white delivery truck pulled up in front of the office. I was there, even though it was just seven thirty in the morning. I had so much to do, there hadn't been any point in going home. I'd purchased a cot, and I now slept at the office.

The initial discovery had originally come in waves, and so I didn't realize how many boxes were going to arrive when they came all at one time. I knew that there would be a lot, but I didn't anticipate sixty Bankers Boxes filled with paper. Stacked one on top of the other, the boxes rose to the ceiling. The large office space filled. The boxes were everywhere, unlabeled and random.

I didn't know whether to even bother calling in Sherman and the students. *What was the point?* I called Laura instead. Whatever I had said or whatever desperate tone was in my voice must've caused her alarm, because it didn't take long for her to arrive.

She found me sitting on the floor in the middle of the room, frozen. "Matty," she said as she surveyed the room, "this is crazy."

"I know." I ran my hand through my hair. "Assuming we just start pawing through these boxes, our chances of getting lucky and finding something are next to nothing." I got up and removed a box's lid. I pulled out a stack of paper and flipped through. "There's no system, just like the first time, maybe worse." I stuffed the paper back into the box and put the lid back on. "And we start jury selection on Monday. Then we've got a day, maybe two or three, before the final jury is selected and we have to start actually trying this case. I mean . . . there's no way."

Laura came over and put her arms around me. "I'm sorry."

I rested my head on hers, still holding Laura tight. "Do you want to hear the best part?" I asked. "Shirley Glade sent a cover letter. It said that these boxes not only contain a duplicate of the documents previously provided, but that there are also 'supplemental responses' to our discovery requests."

Laura took a step back. Her eyes narrowed as she deciphered Shirley Glade's legalese. "So there's also new stuff in here?"

"Exactly," I said. "Somewhere in these boxes are documents that weren't previously disclosed. They are totally new, and I have no idea what they are about or what they say."

"You have to call the judge," she said. "This is completely unfair."

"I can't. That's why this is so brilliant," I said. "Shirley Glade delayed the delivery until Saturday, knowing that Judge Bruin or her clerk wouldn't answer the phone or return a call on the weekend. It was just a big setup."

CHAPTER THIRTY-ONE

Every trial needed a theme, and this theme was David versus Goliath, little versus big. It worked, because it was true. The number of attorneys from Nelson Rockler marshaled against us continued to grow. For the motion to dismiss, there had been about five, two partners and three associates. Now it seemed like there were twenty.

I made a strategic decision to sit alone at the counsel table with my mother and father for the entire trial. Even though I had plenty of support, I wanted us to appear outmatched on every level. If this was David versus Goliath, then I needed to be David *alone* in the lion's den. I hoped that it would work. After all, people were naturally drawn to the underdog. They hated the bully, and I had no doubt that Nelson Rockler was going to come across as the bully.

At nine o'clock, the case was called and Judge Erica Bruin took the bench. After she made some opening remarks, forty-five potential jurors filed into the courtroom. They were sworn in, then one by one they were seated in the jury box for questioning.

"I want you to answer these questions fully and truthfully," Judge Bruin instructed. "If you wonder whether or not something is relevant information, err on the side of overdisclosure. Let the attorneys decide what is important and what is not."

Before handing the questioning off to Shirley Glade and me, Judge Bruin began by asking each juror basic biographical questions and then about their feelings on general legal concepts. Finally, she waded into the most controversial issue.

"How many of you consider yourself to be an addict or you are currently working a program of recovery? Raise your hand." No hands. "OK, then how about this: How many of you have a close friend or relative you consider to be an addict, who has gone to treatment, or who is currently working a program of recovery?"

This time most of the jurors raised their hands.

"OK," the judge went on, "let's talk about that." Then, one by one, she began to speak with each juror who raised a hand. "You, ma'am, on the end, what is your name?"

"Natalie," she said. "Natalie Bishop."

"You raised your hand," Judge Bruin said. "Who is this person that you know?"

"My uncle was an alcoholic, and my daughter also struggled with alcohol."

"Did either one of them go to treatment?"

The woman nodded. "They both did. I remember my uncle going to meetings, like Alcoholics Anonymous, and my daughter did an outpatient program. It was four days a week for a little over a month."

"Any treatment after that?"

"For my daughter, just individual therapy."

"And was it successful?" Judge Bruin asked. "Do you think treatment worked?"

The potential juror rocked back and forth, hesitant. "Sort of. I guess more so for my uncle. My daughter still drinks occasionally, but I think it's pretty much under control."

"This case is about addiction," Judge Bruin said. "Is there anything about the experiences of your uncle or your daughter that makes you either unsympathetic to people who are addicted to drugs or alcohol or overly sympathetic to people who are addicts?"

The woman looked around, a little embarrassed by the attention that she was getting from the judge. "I don't think so."

"If I were to instruct you to keep an open mind, and not *automatically* give more weight or less weight to a person who is an addict or is a chemical dependency treatment counselor on that fact alone, could you do that?"

"I could."

Soon Glade asked to approach the bench, and we both walked up to the judge. "I'm going to have to ask you to strike Ms. Bishop for cause," Glade said.

Judge Bruin leaned closer. "Why?"

"Because she obviously has strong feelings, and, with a daughter who is an addict and still drinking, it will be difficult for her to be fair to my client."

"Your Honor," I said, "I disagree. You rehabilitated the juror. Ms. Bishop stated that she will keep an open mind and follow your instructions. I don't see how anybody could interpret that as being hostile to pharmaceutical companies."

"I agree," Judge Bruin said. "Motion to strike is denied."

Jury selection went on like that for the rest of the morning and into the afternoon. It followed the same pattern: Judge Bruin would ask questions about relatives and friends who were addicted or abused drugs, then rehabilitate them just as she had with Natalie Bishop. And, over and over, Glade would object and move to strike the juror for cause. And, over and over, the motion to strike would be denied.

Each time Glade asked to approach the bench for a private conversation, I saw the jurors' annoyance grow. She was coming across as an obstructionist, somebody slowing down the process and wasting time. Glade already looked like a bully from the outset, and that was exactly what I wanted.

When the judge finished her individual questioning, she gave the jurors a fifteen-minute break. Once they'd left the room, she looked at us. "Anything that you'd like to put on the record before we take a bathroom break?"

Glade rose to her feet and repeated the exact same arguments she had made previously at the various conferences at the bench.

"And as I said every time this was raised," Judge Bruin snapped back, "your motions to strike for cause are denied." She tilted her head to the side, as if thinking carefully about her words. "If, Ms. Glade, you're searching for a jury comprising individuals with no family members, friends, or relatives that have ever abused drugs or alcohol, we're going to be here for an eternity. We want jurors who are real people, Ms. Glade, with real-life experiences, who promise to keep a fair and open mind throughout this trial. I've had enough of this. Sit down, and I'll note that your objection is continuing. You don't have to raise it every time. I'll also note that your objection is overruled . . . every time."

Jury selection continued for two more days. Shirley Glade asked the potential jurors about their community involvement, the medications they took, their experiences with doctors. When a juror hedged an answer, Glade never let it go. She continued to push. Several of them rolled their eyes every time she paused, reviewed her notes, and started a new series of questions.

I never paused to review my notes, because I didn't have any—they were in a binder locked in a room at Cahokia College of Law. So my questions were short and sweet, and I think that jurors appreciated that.

Ultimately, twelve jurors were selected, including six that Sherman and I had in our top ten. In Missouri, jurors did not need to be unanimous in reaching a verdict in civil cases like our lawsuit against NexBeaux—only in criminal cases did jurors need to all agree. So I just needed nine to prevail, and starting with six sympathetic jurors was a good start.

CHAPTER THIRTY-TWO

We all gathered at the new office after court adjourned. While we waited for pizza to arrive, we each went around the circle and talked about what happened.

"I know that Judge Bruin jacked us on the continuance," Cynthia said. "But she's been great on jury selection. I don't think Glade the Blade prevailed on any of her objections or motions to strike."

"I agree," Sherman said. "It looks like we have a very favorable jury, but how are your parents holding up?"

"OK," I said. "I think my dad is getting antsy to get back to work, and I think my mom is getting nervous about her testimony. Part of me wants to keep her sober, but I'm afraid if we do that she'll be an even bigger mess."

Once the pizza arrived, we talked about opening arguments between bites. The preliminaries were done, and the trial was about to begin. "Our plan is good," I said. "And our themes are good." I looked at the boxes stacked all over the room, most of which we'd never opened. "I wish we had our 'hot documents,' and I wish we knew what new documents Shirley Glade sneaked into her final disclosure."

"Speaking of that . . ." Screw stood up and exchanged looks with Jackson. "I have a hypothetical question. If, by weird circumstance, someone were to break into Cahokia and remove certain preparation materials or documents, what do you think these criminals should take? Hypothetically."

I put my hands over my face and bent over. "Am I hearing this?" I rocked back and forth. "I don't think I should be hearing this."

"Come on, brother, it's a hypothetical," Jackson said. "That's it."

I was reluctant to play along, because I knew what they were going to do when the meeting was over. Part of me wanted to go with them, and the other part didn't want to know.

"If Matt isn't going to answer, then I'll tell you what I would take in this completely hypothetical situation," Sherman said. "I'd take the trial binder. That's got the direct examination and cross-examination outlines and notes for almost every witness. Then, hypothetically, I'd take one of these big white boxes and I'd fill it with as many 'hot document' folders as I could hypothetically carry."

"Good answer," Jackson said. "And so now I think Screw and me gotta go, if you know what I mean, hypothetically."

"That doesn't even make any sense," I said. "You are actually going, so it's not a hypothetical. When something is hypothetical, it isn't real. It's just a theory."

◆ ◆ ◆

After everyone else went home for the evening, I began gathering the pizza boxes and generally cleaning up. While I filled a bag with garbage, I debated with myself about whether to go home to my parents' basement or sleep at the office. That's when I noticed a small stack of mail near the door. I didn't think I'd been renting the space long enough for junk mail and marketing companies to know that I existed, but perhaps the secret was out.

I walked over to the door and picked up the stack. I sifted through a solicitation for life insurance, an advertisement for a local vocational program, and a few office supply catalogs. There was nothing surprising or noteworthy. At the bottom of the stack, however, there was something different.

It was a small white envelope.

I opened it. Immediately, I recognized the smell: Gypsy Water. Tess loved that perfume. It would catch you when you least expected it, never overpowering. She bought multiple bottles at a time, afraid the small Stockholm company would go out of business or stop making it. The smell flooded me with memories of lying down next to Tess in our little Chinatown apartment and holding her close on the night I had proposed.

Inside the envelope was a card. Nothing was handwritten. It was printed, presumably using a laser printer—untraceable. On the front it read:

Been thinking about what you told me.
You are right.
I am a good person.
I'm better than that.

On the back was a series of Bates numbers—NBX000001, NBX000002, NBX000003, and so on. Alphanumeric codes attorneys used to identify and track discovery documents.

I turned and looked at the stacks of boxes surrounding me. *Did she really do this?* I ran over to the closest stack of boxes lining the edge of the room. I pulled one off the top, flipped open the lid, and grabbed a stack of paper. I thumbed through—finding nothing special—the same stuff we had seen hundreds of times. I put that stack of paper on the floor, then I grabbed another. I was specifically looking for a document that matched one of the numbers on the card that Tess had sent.

It took me about five minutes to find the first one, then about twenty minutes to find the second one. Each was a document that Shirley Glade had withheld until the last possible moment. They may have even been documents that Glade didn't want disclosed at all, but Tess got them to me anyway. I couldn't believe what I was holding in my hands. They were perfect, helping me establish causation, linking the acts to the injury. Tess had given me my ace.

CHAPTER THIRTY-THREE

"Counsel for the plaintiff," Judge Bruin said, "you may proceed with your opening statement."

I rose and put my hand on my father's shoulder, showing solidarity. "Thank you, Your Honor." I walked to an open space in front of the jury box. I didn't have a fancy slideshow or large pictures of my sister like I had originally planned. My introduction was going to be simple. The jurors would have only one choice: they had to focus on me.

"Ladies and gentlemen of the jury, my name is Matthew Daley. I am a licensed attorney, and I am also the victim's brother. This lawsuit is brought on my sister's behalf, because she's not here to do it herself." I paused. "Allison died of a heroin overdose. At trial, you will hear experts in the fields of addiction and treatment. They will tell you that my sister's death was not a surprise. Too many people, like my sister, die after being prescribed Bentrax, a product manufactured and sold by the defendant, NexBeaux Pharmaceuticals. Why is it so common to get hooked on heroin after taking Bentrax and eventually die of an overdose?"

I allowed the question to hang in the air.

"Because Bentrax and heroin are essentially the same thing. Despite its fancy name and clever marketing, Bentrax is, when broken down to its most basic elements, just another form of heroin. Morphine, heroin, and Bentrax are all in the opioid family of narcotics. So it's no surprise that people who take Bentrax get hooked. The brain gets hooked on Bentrax the same way a person gets hooked on heroin. The prescription for Bentrax eventually runs out, or a doctor won't allow another refill, and then, to the surprise of nobody, the person who can no longer get Bentrax seeks out and buys heroin off the street. That's what happened to my sister, Allison. She got hooked on Bentrax, because nobody ever told her or anybody else about the risks. In fact, the defendant, NexBeaux Pharmaceuticals, did just the opposite. The defendant marketed to doctors and told doctors how safe Bentrax was to take. The defendant ran television advertisements and took out full-page ads in all sorts of magazines."

I pictured Allison in my mind, thinking about her in the hospital with tubes in her arms and machines pumping oxygen into her body. "This case is about accountability. I don't know about you, but it seems like our world is changing and it has become increasingly rare for people to be held accountable—truly accountable—for their words and actions. My favorite is when somebody says something offensive, and then, when they are criticized, they say, 'I am sorry if you were offended by my words.'"

I stepped closer to the jury box and lowered my voice to a loud whisper. "Did you hear what happened there? The person who was supposedly apologizing just shifted the blame. The person didn't say, 'I'm sorry I misspoke.' The person didn't say, 'I'm taking responsibility for the words that I used and I will not say those things again.' Instead it's all on you. The message given is: 'I'm sorry you were offended, but maybe you should have a little thicker skin or maybe you shouldn't be so sensitive.'" I held out my hands. "'It's not my fault you're so stupid that you got offended by me.'"

I stepped back. "This case is about accountability. The defendant, NexBeaux, created a very dangerous product called Bentrax, but they said that it wasn't all that dangerous. The defendant, NexBeaux, said that Bentrax worked better than other pain medications, when it didn't.

NexBeaux said that Bentrax was less addictive than other pain medications, which it wasn't. NexBeaux lavished gifts on doctors who prescribed the most pills to the most people. And NexBeaux created an environment of addiction and ultimately death. Eighty percent of the people who use heroin were first exposed to opioids, not by a dealer at a party or on a street corner, but rather by a doctor in a white coat who prescribed them painkillers."

I paced a little, then started again, quieter this time. "This case is about accountability, and, throughout this trial, NexBeaux is going to try to shift the blame. They're going to talk about parts of my sister's life that are embarrassing and highlight choices that she made that perhaps you would not have made. But, at the end of the day, Allison didn't manufacture a highly addictive product. Allison did not misrepresent the truth in misleading and improper marketing campaigns. And she certainly didn't seek out a drug that isn't much more effective than extra-strength aspirin and a hundred times more dangerous. Allison certainly did not want to die."

I made eye contact with each juror. "When this case is done, I will have proven that NexBeaux breached its duty of care and was responsible for my sister's death." I stood still and silently counted to three. I wanted to force the jurors to think and absorb what I had just said, and when I had finished counting to three, I thanked the jurors for their time and sat down.

◆ ◆ ◆

Lawyers are often creatures of habit, finding comfort in routine. Rules, statute numbers, and case citations were memorized and recalled when needed. Rarely can a lawyer act and think nimbly. Spontaneity is a risk. As I sat, waiting for her to begin, I wondered how Shirley Glade would respond to my opening statement. Would she deviate? Great trial attorneys could improvise. I wondered whether she would address a statistic

I had cited or directly challenge a specific statement that I had made, or would she simply go forward with the opening argument that she had prepared and practiced? No doubt she was a good trial attorney, but if she couldn't adjust to changing circumstances, then she was not a *great* trial attorney and maybe I had a chance.

I sat a little straighter in my seat and listened. Glade the Blade approached the podium, a thin black binder in her hand. She placed it on the podium, opened it, and began to read. The delivery was warm and authoritative, but she never strayed. Instead she did exactly what I told the jurors that NexBeaux was going to do—blame Allison.

"I offer my condolences and sympathies to the Daley family. They have suffered a lot over the past few years, not just with Allison Daley's passing, but also with the stress and heartache that addiction often causes loved ones who struggle walking the fine line of loving and enabling."

She stepped closer to the jury box. "Here are the facts." She held out her hand, counting down each statement. "Number one, NexBeaux is a drug company. It manufactures many different types of medication, including pain medication." She took a step, still counting. "Number two, Allison Daley was prescribed by her doctor a painkiller called Bentrax after a car accident. We don't know whether she took the pills as prescribed. We don't know whether she sold the pills to buy other drugs. We just don't know."

Glade made her third and final point and it hit hard. "Finally, Allison Daley was an addict. I agree with that, but I fundamentally disagree with the idea that Bentrax *made* Allison become a heroin addict. Allison Daley grew up in a home where drug abuse was common. Her mother"—she looked over at our table at Mom—"is an alcoholic. She drinks a significant amount of vodka until she blacks out, multiple times a week. Allison's brother, Jackson, has multiple DWIs. Her father was abusive to her and her mother while Allison was growing up. Allison herself started drinking alcohol when she was twelve years old. She smoked marijuana regularly from age fifteen and certainly experimented with a variety of drugs, including heroin."

Now it was Glade's turn to hold out her hands and drive home her theme.

"Allison Daley was an addict long before she was prescribed Bentrax. Her family wants this to be simple. They want it to be cause and effect, but you'll hear testimony from experts and even some of the plaintiff's own witnesses that concede that addiction is not that simple. Allison Daley grew up in a high-risk environment. There was substance abuse in the home. There was physical abuse in the home. Money was tight, and there wasn't always a lot to eat in the refrigerator. She started experimenting with drugs at a young age and became sexually active at a young age." Glade nodded, as if she had it all figured it out. She pointed her nose in the air and gave a sideways glance at my parents. The suggestion was one of superiority. We were just running a con, and NexBeaux was our big payday.

"Any one of those things that I just mentioned," Glade said, "increases the likelihood of an individual developing a chemical addiction. Any one of those things increases the likelihood of an individual dying of a drug overdose." Glade looked back at me, patronizing as always. "I'm sorry for your loss, Mr. Daley, but we are simply not responsible for problems that started long before your sister was prescribed a pain medication and continued long after she stopped taking that pain medication."

◆ ◆ ◆

I expected Judge Bruin to take a break, then I'd call our first witness. Instead she did something different. "Members of the jury, thank you for your patience as well as your attention this morning. I know that the original plan was to begin testimony today and then continue tomorrow, Friday, before taking a weekend break and resuming the trial next week."

Judge Bruin looked at me, then back at the jurors. "Unfortunately I have another legal matter that I must attend to, which has nothing to do with this case. So I am going to release you now and ask that you return on Monday." Judge Bruin continued advising the jury not to begin deliberations, independently research issues implicated by the case, or talk about serving on the jury to friends, family, or the media.

Then Judge Bruin stood, and the bailiff pounded the gavel. "All stand for the jurors as they leave the courtroom." Judge Bruin waved her hand, granting permission for the jurors to leave, and we watched them file out of the courtroom. Then she looked at Glade and me. "I'd like to talk to both of you in my chambers."

A few minutes later, we were both sitting down across from Judge Bruin. Shirley Glade had brought Quinton Newhouse, and I had brought Sherman with me. The judge had taken off her black robe, which now hung on a hook in the corner near a wall filled with framed awards, certificates, and degrees.

"I want to apologize for delaying the first witness until Monday, but I do have a full caseload and there are going to be other matters that need my attention over the next three weeks. I'll try and keep such disruptions to a minimum, and I'll also try and give you more advance warning in the future. As I thought about this case last night, I decided that a little break at this point in the proceeding may do everybody some good."

Judge Bruin looked at me. "I had denied your continuance, but I figured you would not object to having a little more time to review the documents that Ms. Glade sent." She looked at Glade. "My law clerk tells me that they arrived later than expected, and so I'm sure you understand the position that Mr. Daley is in."

The message sent by the judge was clear. She wanted Shirley Glade to know that she was watching her, and she wasn't afraid to step in if needed.

"I also want to raise, once again, the possibility of settlement," Judge Bruin said. "We have a jury picked. You've heard one another's very polished and persuasive opening arguments. Perhaps it is time to reassess, because I certainly am not clear on how this trial is going to end."

"We have not made any new offers, Your Honor," I said.

"NexBeaux has also not made any new offers," Glade echoed.

Judge Bruin leaned in and smiled. "Well, maybe you two should talk." Then to Shirley Glade: "The last offer was a hundred fifty thousand dollars, correct?"

"I believe that is correct."

"Is that offer still open?" Judge Bruin asked. "If Mr. Daley says he'd be willing to settle this case for a hundred fifty thousand dollars, would your client accept it?"

"I'd have to discuss it with my client, Your Honor." Shirley Glade forced a smile. "Given the time and effort that has now been made as well as the strength of our case, I'm doubtful."

"You shouldn't be so sure of yourself," Judge Bruin said. "These are jurors, and jurors do all sorts of unpredictable things. This case is not just about Mr. Daley. This case is also about the thousands of people who, like his sister, have died. Lose this trial, and the floodgates are open. Your client should think about that."

Then to me: "And, Mr. Daley, it's nice to be on the side of angels, but wouldn't it also be nice to take care of your parents? A hundred and fifty thousand dollars could go a long way toward helping them retire with dignity and take care of health care costs down the line."

"I will discuss it with them."

The judge stood and shook our hands. "Glad we had this little talk."

◆ ◆ ◆

I went back into the courtroom to see if my parents or any of the students were waiting. The courtroom was empty, except for Jackson. "That was a good opener, brother," he said. "You did us proud."

"Thanks."

Jackson pointed at the plaintiff's table. "Looks like you left something."

I looked and saw a large black binder. My trial book. "You found it."

"I didn't find anything." Jackson did his best to sound innocent. "I came into the courtroom, and there it was on the table. Figured you must've left it here accidentally."

I walked over and picked it up. "You're right. Must've been what happened."

"You know," Jackson said, "Perry is still calling. He's still willing to deal. He even lowered his price a little bit, down to four thousand dollars."

"I told you we're not doing that."

"Hypothetically?"

"No." I began walking to the door. "I mean in reality. In real life, don't do it. Witness tampering is a crime. We all will end up in jail."

CHAPTER THIRTY-FOUR

Choosing our first witness was the subject of a lot of debate. Sherman wanted my mother to testify first. He thought the jury needed to understand that Allison was a real person and that her death was a tragedy. But I followed the rule of primacy in persuasion as posited by the psychologist Frederick Hansen Lund in 1925: the first argument or facts presented were the most persuasive and the best remembered. It was a theory that I first heard about in law school but was drilled into my head as a young associate at Baxter, Speller & Tuft. Tobias Tuft was a true believer. He structured all his arguments around the primacy principle, and he expected every attorney in the firm to do the same.

I wasn't sure what Mom was going to say, and therein was the problem. Our attempts to prepare her were not particularly effective. During Glade's deposition, she got nervous, and when she got nervous, my mom would comment on her own answers. She'd respond to a question, then call herself "stupid" or "dumb," or she'd say, "I never wanted to testify. Why are you making me?" Or "I just want this to be over." That was not the first thing that I wanted the jury to learn about my case and remember. I instead decided to start at the beginning. My first witness would be the doctor who first prescribed Bentrax to my sister.

On Monday morning, after a weekend of preparation, I stood and called the trial's first witness. "The plaintiff calls Dr. Christopher Hansen to the stand." I could see the jurors' excitement build. None of them had ever served on a jury before, so their only comparable experience was the testimony they'd seen on television or in the movies.

I couldn't disappoint them. I needed fireworks for every witness. Surprises were rare in civil trials, but Tess had at least given me a few opportunities for drama. No one at the defense table knew about my ex's subterfuge—she'd have been fired otherwise—and the needles in the haystack she had pointed out for me were going to sting.

Judge Bruin swore in Dr. Hansen and permitted me to begin.

"Dr. Hansen," I said, "thank you for taking time out of your busy schedule to be here with us today."

The doctor nodded, struggling to be polite. Doctors, as a general rule, hated lawyers and hated testifying. The only reason Dr. Hansen sat in that chair was because I had subpoenaed him.

"Do you recall a patient named Allison Daley?"

"I do not."

"Where do you work?"

"I work at Central City Hospital on the southside of Saint Louis."

"And how long have you worked there?"

"Fifteen years."

Done with the preliminaries, it was time to get to work. "You just stated that you have no memory of Allison Daley, but if medical records indicated that you treated her after a car accident, would you have any reason to dispute that?"

"No."

"Your Honor, may I approach?" She granted my request, and I walked from my table up to the doctor. "I'm holding in my hand what has previously been marked as Exhibit 75. It is an excerpt of Allison Daley's medical record." I showed the witness the exhibit, and Dr. Hansen agreed that it was Allison Daley's medical record and that he had indeed treated her.

Once the exhibit was entered into evidence, I circled back to him. "Did you prescribe Allison Daley a pain medication marketed under the name Bentrax?"

"I don't know." The doctor looked at the jurors and made a face. It was a smirk combined with rolling his eyes. He may have been trying to belittle me, but it was clear that he thought testifying was a joke.

"If Exhibit 75 indicates that you prescribed her fifty pills of Bentrax, would you disagree with that?"

"I would not. What's in the file is what happened."

"Good." I paused long enough for the courtroom to settle and draw the whole room's attention to me. This was going to be the first firework. "In January, the month you prescribed Allison Daley the drug Bentrax, were you the NexBeaux Doctor of the Month?"

The question caught him by surprise. He looked over at Glade the Blade for some help, but none came. "I'm not sure whether I know what that is."

"You don't?" I feigned shock. "The NexBeaux Doctor of the Month is awarded to the doctor who prescribed the greatest number of Bentrax."

Dr. Hansen shook his head, becoming visibly nervous. His face blushed as he messed with his collar and then loosened his tie, only to tighten it again. "I'm not sure about that."

"It's like a fun competition, right? It's not about medicine or what drug is appropriate pursuant to FDA guidelines. It's about numbers. Whoever prescribes the most pills wins, right?"

"I really don't know."

"Are you sticking with that answer?"

Glade stood. "Objection, Your Honor."

I preemptively withdrew the question and came back harder. "May I approach the witness again, Your Honor?"

"You may."

"I'm holding Exhibit 195 in my hand. Do you recognize this document?"

Dr. Hansen looked at the sheet of paper. "It's an email."

"Yes," I said, "and who is that email from?"

"NexBeaux."

"And what is the subject matter of this email?"

"The Doctor of the Month."

"Who was . . ."

"Me."

I offered the exhibit and asked for it to be published. Judge Bruin was about to grant the request, but Glade requested to approach. Judge Bruin looked at the jurors. "As we talk, you all may stand and stretch. This should only take a few minutes."

"May I see the exhibit?" Glade asked me at the bench.

"Sure." I handed her a copy of the email.

Her eyes squinted as she examined it, skeptical. "I don't believe that there's proper foundation for this email, Your Honor. This may be a fabrication."

"Fabricated?" I shook my head and took a step away from Glade, feigning that I had taken great offense and hoping the jurors were watching the exchange. "Do you see this number on the bottom? That's a Bates number, and it was a document that you disclosed to me as a response to my discovery request. I shouldn't have to authenticate documents the defendant gave to me."

"The objection is overruled," Judge Bruin said. "Mr. Daley is right. I don't want to hear those objections to your own documents. It's a waste of time."

The judge's law clerk lowered a screen near the witness stand, and I projected the email onto it and pointed. "Doctor Hansen, is that a picture of you?"

"It is." His face flushed, embarrassed.

"And what are you wearing on your head?"

"A hat."

"But what kind of hat?"

"I think you can see what it is," he said.

"No," I said. "This doesn't work like that, Dr. Hansen. What kind of hat is it? Answer my question."

"It's a hat in the shape of a pill."

"And that pill is Bentrax, correct?"

"Yes."

"Your Honor, may I have permission to read this email to the jury?"

The judge granted permission.

"'Your friends at NexBeaux proudly bestow upon you the honor of being its Doctor of the Month,'" I read aloud. "'Out of all the doctors in the Saint Louis region, you prescribed seventy-five hundred Bentrax pills in just thirty days, which was the highest of any other doctor. In addition to prescriptions, you participated in our Gas Talk promotion three times and attended five of our Free Lunch, Free Advice seminars. Congratulations, Dr. Hansen, you have won a two-hundred-fifty-dollar gift card to a restaurant or store of your choice.'"

I took my time formulating my next question. "Dr. Hansen, what is a Gas Talk?"

"It's when you go to a gas station near the hospital, and a NexBeaux salesperson is there . . . and they fill up your car with gas for free and, in exchange, you stand there while they are pumping the gas and listen to their sales pitch and take some free samples."

"And you did this three times in a month?"

"Correct."

"And what is the Free Lunch, Free Advice series?"

"It's when NexBeaux caters a lunch for hospital staff, particularly nurses and doctors, and you get to eat for free in exchange for listening to a sales pitch and taking some free samples."

"Thank you, Dr. Hansen," I said. "One more question: Did you attend a NexBeaux conference in Hawaii a few months before you prescribed my sister, Allison Daley, Bentrax?"

"Probably."

"And did you pay anything for that trip, like flight or hotel?"

"No, I did not."

"Let me guess: you didn't pay anything for the trip in exchange for listening to a sales pitch about Bentrax and taking free samples, correct?"

"Correct."

"And, finally, you weren't alone, were you? Other doctors were doing this, too, right?"

"Everybody was doing it," Dr. Hansen said. "NexBeaux made it a game, and I got sucked in. I was young and foolish. I wouldn't do that stuff today."

I sensed an opening, and I decided to risk asking a question without knowing how the witness would answer. "Dr. Hansen," I said, "not only was it foolish, it was also unethical, correct?"

He didn't answer right away, and I didn't push him. It was a powerful moment that he was creating all by himself. "Yes," he said. "I think it was unethical. I'm not proud of it."

"And when you prescribed my sister Bentrax, did you disclose the free lunches, free gas, and free trip to Hawaii to her?"

"I don't remember," he said. "I see hundreds of patients, and I don't remember specific conversations unless it was very unusual."

"OK," I said. "I'll try asking that question in a different way." I took a breath and came at him again. "Did you ever disclose that information to any patient that you ever prescribed Bentrax?"

He looked at Judge Bruin, a pleading look in his eyes.

"Please answer the question," she said.

"No," he said. "I don't believe I ever told a patient about how I learn about new products."

"And did you disclose that Bentrax is highly addictive and that it was and is, in essence, a close cousin of heroin?"

He lowered his head. His shoulders slumped, defeated. "I did not."

CHAPTER THIRTY-FIVE

The witnesses did not get better for NexBeaux, and Shirley Glade could do little about it. My focus, in the beginning, was entirely on NexBeaux's decision to market and sell Bentrax in the Saint Louis region.

NexBeaux's senior vice president of sales was confronted with an internal memo identifying Saint Louis as a top three region in the country to "market Bentrax and gain overall market share among opioid pain medications." As a result, NexBeaux tripled its Saint Louis salesforce and specifically targeted residents on the southside of Saint Louis, where Allison lived. A quarterly sales report stated:

> The higher than average per capita rate of residents with less than a college education as well as those suffering from arthritis or work-related injury makes the southern half of Saint Louis a particularly target-rich environment for the sale of Bentrax.

I loved NexBeaux's use of the term "target-rich environment." It was a military term and often referred to areas filled with enemy combatants. It suggested a certain level of callousness, cold and calculating.

I called expert witnesses in the field of addiction and from the pharmaceutical industry. Each time, I tied the witness testimony back to when my sister was first prescribed Bentrax and the deceptive marketing materials that were being used. I wound down with the testimony of Director Glasby from the Arch Treatment Center, who talked about Allison's final days before her overdose.

Then I called my mother to the stand.

"Mrs. Daley, or Mom, I know you're nervous."

She nodded. "I am. I'm a private person."

"You struggle with alcohol, right?"

She looked around the room at all the people and bowed her head. "I drink more than I should."

"How has Allison's death affected you?"

"Terrible. I blame myself. I think about what I shoulda done different. I think about stuff I know now, that I should've knowed back then, about treatment and such. Maybe if we caught it earlier. I don't know."

"What do you think of Bentrax?"

"It's like a trick. Nobody told her that it was that strong or that she should be careful, then once she got hooked, it was all over."

For my final witness, I called the president and CEO of NexBeaux, Chandler Hawkes. I wouldn't question him for very long—I didn't want him to talk about the benefits of pain medication or about all the clinical trials Bentrax went through before FDA approval. I just wanted to get him on the stand so that I could get the jury to see two documents: the final document that Tess had identified for me and one that I got myself when all of this was started.

"Mr. Hawkes, how long have you been CEO and president of NexBeaux Pharmaceuticals?"

He looked at Glade, then back at me. "Fifteen years."

"That's a long time," I said. "Did you know Allison Daley?"

"Personally, no, I did not, but I did learn of her."

"That's correct," I said. "In fact, shortly after this lawsuit was filed, you were sent a copy of her obituary, is that right?"

"I don't remember."

"You don't remember an email from your chief financial officer, Bashar Kadri?"

"I do not."

Judge Bruin allowed me to approach the witness, and I offered and entered the email into evidence. "This email contains a copy of Allison Daley's obituary, correct?"

He looked at it, and I could tell he realized what was coming the moment he saw it. His voice quivered. "That is correct."

"And you can clearly see that it is from CFO Kadri to you, up in this subject line. Correct?"

"I see it."

"Now, did you respond to this email?"

If I had a copy of the email from Kadri, Hawkes knew that I probably had a copy of his response. You could almost see the wheels turning in his head as he calculated whether it was better to admit it or be caught lying. He chose to admit.

"I responded," he said.

"And what did you say?"

He looked at Shirley Glade and the cadre of Nelson Rockler attorneys that he was paying enormous amounts of money to protect him and his company. Yet, at that moment, they did nothing. He looked down at his hands and took a deep breath. "I said, 'Another loyal customer bites the dust.'"

One of the jurors actually gasped.

I posted a copy of Hawkes's email up on the big screen, then stood back and admired it, making sure everyone could take it in and think about the ramifications of a big pharma CEO mocking a person who died of an overdose, mocking my sister.

"You meant it as a joke, correct?"

"Not that it's an excuse," he stammered, "but we have stressful jobs, and sometimes our humor is inappropriate. I regret my response, and I apologize."

"Do you joke a lot with your senior management team?"

"I don't know." He shrugged. "My leadership style is to try and keep people happy. Happy people work harder."

"Do you remember exchanging jokes with Mr. Kadri about people who were addicted to heroin?"

Hawkes shifted in his seat, looking just as uncomfortable as Allison's doctor had looked when I displayed the picture of him wearing a giant pill hat. "Perhaps."

"Do you remember forwarding a joke that asked, and I'm paraphrasing here, 'How are hockey players and women who use Bentrax the same?'"

Hawkes was silent. He hated me.

"'Answer: They only change their clothes after three periods.' Do you remember exchanging that joke?" I went back to my table and picked up the printout. "Here, I can show it to you."

More silence. The mood in the courtroom had grown cold. The women on the jury all had their arms crossed. Their lips were pursed, and daggers shot out from their eyes.

I walked toward the witness stand with the email his CFO had sent me at the Yankees game. Halfway there, Hawkes raised his hand.

"I don't need to see it," he said. "I remember the joke, and I thought it was funny."

"I bet you did." I stared at Hawkes. My face turned down in disgust, then I looked away. To Judge Bruin I said, "I have no further questions, Your Honor."

◆ ◆ ◆

When we adjourned for the day, the courtroom cleared fairly quickly. The law students dropped off their notes and thoughts about the testimony that they'd just heard. I said goodbye to Sherman and told him that I would call later in the evening, then I gave my mother and father a hug. I couldn't believe how patient they had been, sitting quietly as every aspect of our lives and family were discussed in front of a growing crowd of strangers.

The trial made the front page of the *Riverfront Times*, the city's alternative weekly that mostly focused on music and sex advice from Dan Savage. The *St. Louis Post-Dispatch* had also run a few articles about the trial, and somebody going by the name of "The Dutchtown Hawk" had started a blog. The Hawk posted a summary of the previous day's proceedings for his readers, including snarky comments mostly directed at NexBeaux and Shirley Glade. This combination, I think, was stirring up a lot of curiosity and courthouse gossip. Lines had started to form to get into the courtroom each morning, and people would line up again after the midday lunch break.

Alone, I sat back down at the plaintiff's table. I flipped through my trial notebook, updated my log of the specific exhibits that had been entered into evidence, and jotted down any objections or evidentiary rulings that may be important. I thought about whether I should rest. The CEO of NexBeaux came across as such an awful person that I questioned whether I could do anything more. It seemed like any further witness would dilute the impact.

I don't know how long I remained in the courtroom, but the bailiff eventually came in and asked how much longer I'd be. "Just a minute or two." I took the hint and gathered my things. As I walked out of the courtroom and into the hallway, a man was waiting for me.

He was tall, probably Jackson's height. His hair was slicked back, and he was wearing an expensive suit. "Mr. Daley," he said. "I know you must be exhausted, because I've been there." He took out a business card and handed it to me. "I'm Mack Hunter."

The name rang a bell. He made his fortune suing tobacco companies, and now he ran a pretty big class action law firm involved in everything from defective toys to contaminated water to malfunctioning medical devices.

"The trial attorney," I said.

He nodded. "One of my associates has been watching the trial, and she told me that I had to come see it for myself." His face brightened. "I flew in late last night, and I have to tell you, Mr. Daley, you are kicking their ass."

"Thank you." I checked my watch and took a few steps toward the elevator. Although I certainly liked the flattery, I was ready to go. I just wanted to meet Laura for dinner and collapse into bed. "Maybe when this is all over we can talk."

"I would love that," Hunter said. "I've got a deposition in California tomorrow, but I'm gonna try and make it back here before it's over." He held out his hand. "I got a few cases like this myself, and I was hoping that I could buy you a nice dinner and pick your brain."

"I'm not sure I'll have much of a brain to pick when this is done."

Hunter held out his hand, and we shook. "You're too modest," he said. "You've got a great touch in there, and if you're at all interested, I could use somebody like you. We've got some great cases going right now, and you could take your pick."

"You're offering me a job?"

Hunter shrugged. "Why wouldn't I?"

Our conversation wrapped up. I went to the elevators, and Hunter went in the other direction. It looked like a few of his associates were waiting for him at the end of the hall. I walked a few blocks from the courthouse to meet Laura at Charlie Gitto's for dinner.

We sat in the far back corner of the candlelit dining room. She drank wine and told me about her day, and I gave her the highlights and lowlights from the trial. I had started to relax and feel a little more energy when I told her about my encounter with Mack Hunter.

"*The* Mack Hunter?"

"The one and only," I said. "He wants to come back when the trial is over, says he wants to offer me a job."

"A job?" Laura nodded and forced a tiny smile, but I could tell something didn't sit right. She looked away and suddenly got quiet.

"What is it? I thought that was pretty exciting."

She took a drink of her wine, then dabbed the edges of her mouth with her napkin. "It is exciting." She put down the napkin and put her hand on top of mine. "I think it's probably time to go," she said. "I've got work tomorrow, and you've got another big day."

"That's true." I tried to get her to focus on me, but she wouldn't make eye contact. "But what's going on here?"

Laura sighed and looked me straight in the eye. "You're going to do it again."

"Do what again?"

"Take a job and leave Saint Louis, leave me." She shook her head. "I should've figured. I'm so stupid to fall for this again."

"Laura, I'm not doing anything."

"Right." She pushed back from the table and stood up. She wasn't screaming or throwing things, just exuding quiet disappointment. "Good luck tomorrow." She leaned over, kissed the top of my head, and left.

CHAPTER THIRTY-SIX

"The plaintiff rests." I sat down as planned. The heavy lifting was done. I got my evidence in and scored my points. Now it was time to watch what cycled back.

Judge Bruin turned to Shirley Glade. "Does the defense seek to call any witnesses?"

"Yes, Your Honor." Glade stood. "The defense calls Perry deCristo to the stand."

I turned and looked at Jackson, sitting a few rows back, as Perry came forward. He'd gotten a haircut, and he was wearing dress pants, loafers, and a button-down shirt. I wondered how much Nelson Rockler paid a consultant to help Perry pick out a new outfit.

"Mr. deCristo," Glade began. "Did you know Allison Daley?"

"I did," Perry said. "I loved her, and we lived together for a few years before she passed away."

"Do you use heroin, Mr. deCristo?"

Perry nodded.

"You need to say yes or no out loud, Mr. deCristo."

"OK." Perry started fidgeting with his hands, nervous, flicking his thumb off one finger and then the next. "Yes, I did."

"But not any longer?"

"I'm in treatment now." Perry's eyes darted from one side to the other. "Started a few weeks ago."

"Did you use heroin with Allison Daley?"

"I did," Perry said. "She was the one who introduced me to the stuff."

It took everything in my power not to spring out of my seat and charge him.

"Let me get this straight," Glade said. "*She* introduced *you* to heroin? You never used it before?"

"Nope, never," Perry lied. "It was totally new to me." It was clear he was becoming more comfortable, which was good. It would be his undoing. "She was dealing a little, too, not like big time, but a little." Once he got going, Perry couldn't help himself. He was going to continue, but Glade held out her hand. She knew he was off-script, ad-libbing, and that rightfully made her nervous.

She got him back on track, guiding him through a rehearsed history of Allison's substance use—from alcohol in her early teens to marijuana, then to harder drugs. Perry testified about all of this, even though he didn't know Allison when she was young. I thought about objecting, but I didn't want to be overruled. Perry would just say that Allison told him about it, and, under the law, that statement was admissible. Fighting about it would only highlight the information for the jury, which I didn't want to risk either.

"Long before she ever had Bentrax, Allison was drinking every day, correct?"

"Absolutely." Perry looked at me, smug. "Just like her mother. But heroin was her true love."

"To your knowledge, did Allison ever steal Bentrax or buy it from somebody on the street?"

"No, ma'am," he said. "It was the other way around. She took the Bentrax prescriptions she got and sold it, and she used the money to buy heroin. She used to say, 'Why use the imitation when you can have the real thing?'"

"Allison Daley said that to you?"

"She did."

"And when she sought treatment," Glade continued, "she sought treatment for her heroin addiction, not an addiction to prescription drugs, true?"

"Yes."

"In fact, Allison was already using heroin *before* her car accident and *before* any doctor had ever prescribed her Bentrax for back and neck pain, is that correct?"

"That is correct," Perry said. "The family should be suing her drug dealer, not you guys. This is all about the money." He smiled, revealing a new gold insert along his bottom teeth.

I was on my feet. "Objection."

Judge Bruin sustained the objection and tried to get Perry to stop talking, but he kept going. "The family is looking for a payday," he said. "The parents just happen to have a kid that's got a law degree. That's what this is about—"

"Mr. deCristo! One more word and you will be held in contempt of court." That shut him up. The judge looked at the jurors. "The objection by Mr. Daley was sustained, and I instruct you to disregard Mr. deCristo's statements as speculation and nonresponsive. They are not evidence and you shall not consider his statements during your deliberation of this matter." She gestured for Glade to resume.

"Do you think Bentrax had any role in Allison's overdose?"

I was on my feet again before Glade finished the question. "Objection, Your Honor."

Judge Bruin thought about it. "Sustained."

"Then no further questions, Your Honor."

I looked at my watch. "Your Honor, I need to prepare a few items for my cross-examination of Mr. deCristo." My heart was beating too quickly, and I needed to calm down if I was going to be effective. I needed to be in control. "May we take a break?"

Judge Bruin granted my request, and I sent my parents to the vending machines in the basement to buy some candy bars and sodas while I met Jackson and Sherman in a small conference room just down the hall.

"What the hell was that?" Sherman's hands were balled into tight fists. He was furious. "Where did that come from?"

"He was paid," Jackson said, then looked at me. "I told you they were going to cheat." He took a large white envelope out of his bag. "I knew you didn't believe me, but I figured we'd need some proof." He opened the unsealed envelope and put a small thumb drive on the table along with two copies of a transcript.

Sherman and I each picked up a copy and began to read. I quickly realized what my brother had done. "You recorded him?"

Jackson smiled, satisfied with himself. "I sure did," he said. "Met with him last night."

"Glade is going to go nuts," Sherman said. "She'll ask for a mistrial, for sure."

"On what grounds?"

The question gave Sherman pause. "Tampering with a witness?" He wasn't sure.

"I'm not sure Jackson tampered with him," I said. "He talked to him, but he's allowed to do that. Perry isn't a party to this lawsuit, and he's not represented by an attorney." I tried to think through Glade's potential arguments, but nothing came to mind. "There's nothing in the rules that prevent us from talking to somebody, and there's nothing illegal about recording a conversation if you're a participant in the conversation."

"I thought you needed consent from both people," Sherman said.

"No." I shook my head. "Some states are two-party consent, but in Missouri you just need one."

"What do you think Judge Bruin is going to do?" Sherman asked. "Isn't this a discovery violation? Shouldn't we have disclosed that we had it this morning, first thing, before Perry testified?"

"You couldn't," Jackson chimed in. "You didn't know about it, because I'm a clever bastard."

"Are you kidding me?" Sherman put his copy of the transcript back down on the table. "She's going to freak out. You have evidence of a crime, and you didn't disclose it to the court in advance. You knew if Perry testified that he was going to lie, and you let Shirley Glade and NexBeaux continue without warning. The judge is going to declare a mistrial. We're going to have to do this whole thing all over again."

"Hold on." I wanted to bring calm to the room. "My brother isn't a lawyer, and we didn't know, for certain, that Glade was going to call Perry to the witness stand." I started to pace the room. "I think if we disclose it now, maybe I can dance around it. If I disclose it now, it might be OK, but if we wait, it's going to be trouble."

"Throw me under the bus, bro." Jackson smiled. "I'll tell Judge Bruin that I was going rogue. She doesn't want to redo this trial any more than we do."

◆　◆　◆

Shirley Glade and I sat in front of Judge Bruin in her chambers. Judge Bruin was slumped in her chair, exhausted and drinking from a gigantic mug of coffee. "Mr. Daley, I truly hope that you wanted to meet with me because you and Ms. Glade have finally come to your senses and reached a settlement in this matter."

"I think it was clear that Perry deCristo was lying on the witness stand," I said. "Hopefully the jurors saw that."

Glade laughed. "You called us in here for that," she said. "He was under oath, and you'll have your chance to cross-examine him. I don't see why we're wasting the court's time with this."

Judge Bruin tilted her head to the side and rubbed her eyes. "I have to say that Ms. Glade has a point. If I had a nickel for every person who claimed a witness for the opposing party was lying, I think I'd be a rich woman."

I stayed calm and professional. "I assure you that I am not wasting anyone's time," I said. "I know for a fact that certain things stated by Mr. deCristo were false. He claimed that he never used heroin before meeting my sister, and yet he has multiple convictions for drug possession that prove that isn't true. But that's not what I want to talk about."

Judge Bruin sat up a little straighter. "OK," she said, "you have my attention."

"Prior to trial, Mr. deCristo approached my brother, Jackson, with a wild proposition." I decided that the key to pulling this off was to make sure the judge understood why it hadn't been brought to the court immediately. "Mr. deCristo told us that NexBeaux was going to pay him five thousand dollars to testify and say bad things about my sister, but Perry told us that he'd testify in our favor if we paid him more." I looked at Glade, who had now moved to the edge of her seat, then I turned my attention back to the judge.

"I thought he was just a drug addict, hustling us for money. Nothing ever happened. Obviously we didn't give him any money, and I, frankly, doubted that Nelson Rockler would ever call him to testify. As you saw, he's a terrible witness. Nonetheless, they just called him."

Judge Bruin's eyes narrowed. "Where are you going with this, Mr. Daley?"

"If Mr. Daley is actually asking this court to impeach Mr. deCristo with this wild accusation, I object." Glade held her hand to her heart, as if such an allegation hurt her personally. Her eyes widened like those of a kid trying to explain why they couldn't have eaten all the cookies in the cookie jar. "This is highly prejudicial," she said. "And it's just one person's word against another. There's no proof."

"Well," I said, "that's not exactly accurate."

If Judge Bruin was tired when we had come into her chamber, she was now wide awake. "Tell me what's going on." She checked her watch. "Get to the point."

"Mr. deCristo contacted my brother again last night and tried to get us to pay for testimony more sympathetic to our case," I said. "I didn't know this until the break. My brother didn't tell me, because I was so dismissive of the whole thing when he first brought it to my attention." I omitted the part where Jackson advised me to pay Perry, because everyone cheats.

"This is ridiculous," Glade said. "Like I said, Mr. deCristo will deny it, and it'll be one person's word against another, and in the end it's just going to confuse the jury and disparage my client."

"That would ordinarily be true," I said. "But my brother recorded the conversation." I took the small thumb drive out of my pocket and put it on Judge Bruin's desk. "How about we play it and then decide?"

◆ ◆ ◆

The fifteen-minute break turned into a two-hour break, which eventually spilled over into the lunch hour, as official transcripts were prepared of the audio recording and the flash drive was converted into a format acceptable to the court. In the late afternoon, the bailiff finally gaveled the court back into session, and the jurors were seated back in the jury box.

"We are back on the record in Daley v. NexBeaux Pharmaceuticals." Judge Bruin's voice was calm and reassuring. She smiled at the jurors, pretending that everything was normal and that nothing unusual had just transpired. "I apologize for the delay," she said. "After I had called a recess, the attorneys and I met in my chambers to discuss evidentiary issues, and I'd now like to recall Mr. deCristo to the witness stand."

Perry walked down the center aisle and retook his seat next to the judge. "Mr. deCristo, you are still under oath. Do you understand?"

I noticed Perry glance in my direction, then he looked back at Judge Bruin. "Yes, Judge."

"Good." Judge Bruin turned to me. "Mr. Daley, you may now begin your cross-examination."

"Thank you, Your Honor," I said. "Mr. deCristo, I have to admit that your testimony surprised me. I'd never heard my sister described that way, and it's inconsistent with her treatment records as well as the testimony of her mother and other loved ones. Do you agree?"

Perry shrugged. "Sometimes families can't see things for what they is," he said. "My impression was that Allison was a little princess. It'd be hard to see your little princess as a dealer and a junkie."

"I suppose it would," I said. "Or maybe you're making the whole thing up."

"Your Honor," Glade objected, "will you please instruct Mr. Daley to ask a question rather than badger Mr. deCristo?"

Judge Bruin halfheartedly instructed me to move on, so I did.

"Sounds like the defendant wants some specific questions, so how about this: Mr. deCristo, you testified earlier that Allison Daley introduced you to heroin. You left the impression that you'd never used it before you met her, correct?"

"Yes."

"And you met Allison Daley just two and a half years ago, correct?"

"That's about right."

"But isn't it true that four years ago you were convicted of fifth-degree drug possession, a felony?"

"Maybe."

"Maybe?" I pulled a certified copy of the conviction out of my folder and showed it to Glade. "I offer this exhibit into evidence." I walked to the witness stand and put it in front of Perry. "Says here that you pled guilty to possessing heroin about a year and a half or two before you ever met Allison."

"OK."

"OK?" I went back to my table and sat down. "OK, meaning that you now admit that you had used heroin before meeting Allison Daley?"

He didn't want to admit anything. From the bench, Judge Bruin looked down at him. "Answer the question, Mr. deCristo." Her face tightened.

"I was mistaken," Perry said. "It wasn't my drug of choice."

"You have a drug of choice? And what is that?"

"Meth," Perry said. "Methamphetamine."

"You also stated that Allison Daley was a drug dealer, but isn't it true that she has absolutely no convictions for either possessing a large amount of drugs or dealing drugs?"

"I don't know," Perry said. "I'm sure you do."

"You're right, I do know," I said. "And I also know that you, on the other hand, have been convicted multiple times for drug dealing, isn't that right?"

"That's true."

"And all this testimony about the things that Allison said about Bentrax and prescription drugs—you made those up, didn't you?"

"I did not."

"You fabricated those statements, just like you lied about Allison introducing you to heroin and Allison being a drug dealer, correct?"

"Objection, Your Honor. Asked and answered."

"Overruled." The judge instructed Perry deCristo to answer my question.

"Please answer my question, truthfully this time, Mr. deCristo."

He looked at Glade, but she couldn't help him. He was having difficulty staying afloat, and in a few seconds I was going to sink him to the bottom.

"You're wrong," he said. "All that was true."

"How much were you paid to testify here today?" I asked. "How much did NexBeaux bribe you to testify here today?"

"Nobody paid me nothing," he said. "I'm telling the truth."

"Mr. deCristo, isn't it true that you've contacted my brother and made a proposal to sell your testimony at this trial?"

"Wrong," Perry said. "That's fake news." He laughed at his joke, and a few of the jurors laughed as well.

"You are telling this court that you never spoke to my brother, Jackson Daley, and you never proposed to him that he pay you to testify in a certain way, is that right?"

"Right," Perry said. "I don't know your brother, and I never asked him for any money."

"Your Honor, I would now like to offer the exhibit we discussed with defense counsel into evidence, and I'd like permission to distribute transcripts so that the jurors can read along as the recording is being played."

"I object, Your Honor, for the record," Glade said, "but I also acknowledge that you have already made the ruling and that my objection has been overruled."

With that out of the way, Judge Bruin allowed me to proceed. The transcripts were distributed, and soon Jackson's and Perry's voices were amplified through the courtroom's speaker system.

JACKSON: I guess I don't understand the deal.
PERRY: It's simple. You pay me the money, and I say whatever you want.
JACKSON: Why would I do that?
PERRY: Because if you don't, I'll say whatever the Bentrax people want me to say.
JACKSON: They're paying you?
PERRY: Five thousand dollars.
JACKSON: But I don't have five thousand dollars?
PERRY: Doesn't matter. You pay me four thousand and we'll call it good.

JACKSON: Why are you charging them five thousand and us only four?
PERRY: Because I like you guys better.

I stopped the recording. "Mr. deCristo, I'm going to ask you again, under oath, as well as advise you that lying under oath may constitute criminal perjury and you could be prosecuted." I waited a moment to make sure that I had everyone's full attention. "Mr. deCristo, were you paid by NexBeaux Pharmaceuticals to give your testimony here today?"

Perry deCristo cracked his neck, then looked at Judge Bruin. "Can't I, like, plead the Fifth or something?"

CHAPTER THIRTY-SEVEN

Shirley Glade didn't even bother with a redirect of Perry deCristo. She cut her losses and called a series of witnesses to refute and muddle the damaging testimony and exhibits that I had presented to the jury. After the third day of tedious and mind-numbing testimony, I decided that boring the jury was a deliberate strategy. She didn't want the trial to end with my case fresh in the jurors' minds. She wanted to create some distance, give them time to cool.

After both sides rested, Judge Bruin read the final instructions to the twelve jurors. The excitement that they had on the first day had changed. Jury duty had turned from novelty into a job. They filed into the packed courtroom focused, ready to make their decision and go back to their regular lives.

As the attorney representing the plaintiff, I went first. I didn't like the idea of Shirley Glade having the last word, but those were the rules. I walked to the same spot where I'd delivered my opening argument.

"Here I am again," I said. "And I think you saw and heard everything that I told you to expect when we started this trial. You heard evidence about a company that targeted people like my sister. You heard evidence about a company that encouraged doctors, like the doctor who treated Allison, to prescribe Bentrax needlessly and recklessly. And you heard about and experienced the callous attitude of NexBeaux."

I turned and pointed at Glade. "And you also heard testimony of NexBeaux shifting the blame. In fact, NexBeaux did not just call witnesses to tell us that it was all Allison's fault. The attorneys for NexBeaux called Mr. Perry deCristo." I turned back to the jury. "I'm sure you all remember Mr. deCristo." I paused so that everyone could get a clear picture of Perry in their heads. "He was the man who tried to say that my sister, Allison, was some sort of drug dealer who introduced him to heroin, something that his own criminal record disproved." I smiled and shook my head. If this were a movie, the square-jawed actor playing my part would pound his hand down on the table as the orchestral music swelled and scream, "Preposterous!" But I knew better than to do something over the top.

I kept it level.

"Then you heard the recording of Perry deCristo trying to sell his testimony to my brother and saying that he was going to sell his testimony to NexBeaux."

I took a step back, then I recalled Judge Bruin's jury instruction related to assessing credibility. "What weight should you give to the testimony of Mr. Perry deCristo? Based on his demeanor and what you heard, the answer to that question is none. Similarly, you should give little to no weight to the other experts that NexBeaux put on the witness stand. Not only was their testimony largely irrelevant, each one of those experts was paid quite well too."

I then guided the jurors, step by step, through the jury instruction and verdict forms. When I was done, I got to the part where they needed to write the amount of damages. A lot of attorneys didn't like telling jurors how much to award their clients, but repeated studies found that this was a critical step. Plaintiffs needed to anchor the damages amount.

"I think damages are hard, because there are 'actual' damages and then there are 'punitive' damages." I picked up a marker and walked over to a large piece of white poster board. "This is what I think the actual damages are." I wrote down a number. "But this is the hard part, what punitive damage amount would send NexBeaux a message." I waited for the jurors to struggle to come up with their own initial formula in their minds, then I provided them with one of my own.

"In the year that my sister was prescribed Bentrax, the company made extensive efforts to market Bentrax as a safe, nonaddictive pain medication. There were television ads, and they courted doctors with free lunches, gas, trips, and other prizes, and these marketing efforts worked. The four primary pharmaceutical companies selling opioid pain medication made one point one billion dollars in profits. NexBeaux had a sixty percent market share that year. Therefore, I believe that a suitable punishment is for NexBeaux to simply give that profit back. Not their costs in wages or other expenses. I'm talking just profit."

Using the marker, I wrote the calculation on the poster board: 60 percent of $1.1 billion = $660 million.

"Obviously NexBeaux made much more money than this selling Bentrax over multiple years, but giving up your profit for one year, six hundred sixty million dollars, is both reasonable and fair given the damage that these drugs have done."

I picked up a small remote control and pressed a button. An old photograph appeared on the screen at the front of the courtroom.

"This was us," I said, staring at the image that Jackson and I had found in our sister's motel room after she died. The image of the three Daley kids standing in front of our house on Pestalozzi with a bare Christmas tree. Snow all around, Jackson was standing tall. My sister next to me, her little brother, with her arm around me, holding me tight.

"This is my family." Tears began to form in my eyes. "We were flawed and dysfunctional just like everybody else, but this was us, together. That's me"—I pointed—"the kid with the missing teeth, and my sister."

Tears started to come a little more, but I couldn't stop. I just kept talking. "You know those pictures you see now of brothers and sisters recreating old family photographs—same poses and locations many years apart—and then they put the two together?" I took a breath and tried to compose myself. I wiped the tears away and looked at the ground. "I want to recreate that shot with my sister. This Christmas I want to go chop down a tree with her and my brother and my parents. I want to bring it back to our house, and I want to stand on those steps with her."

My voice got fuller, louder. In my head I was screaming, but I don't think I was. I don't really know. "I want to stand on those steps with Allison, and I want her to put her arm around me, just like she did when I was little, and I want her to protect me, just like she did when I was little." I took a breath, then I looked back at Shirley Glade and Quinton Newhouse and all the NexBeaux executives. "They took that away from me." I held my head a little higher, and I turned back to the jurors. Nearly all of them were in tears.

"Lawsuits are blunt instruments, and I know that nothing is going to bring Allison back," I said. "I know that I asked for a lot of money, and I gave you an explanation as to how I came up with that number, but, in the end, the question for you is: How much would you pay for that photograph? If you were me, how much would you be willing to pay to stand on those steps again with your sister and feel her arm around you, smiling and laughing, and just be a family?"

I nodded, looking at each of the jurors through red and puffy eyes. "What is that feeling worth?" I asked. "Because that's what NexBeaux took away."

I walked back to the plaintiff's table and sat down.

My dad leaned over and put his arm around me. "You done good, son."

I did everything in my power not to collapse. Judge Bruin gave some instructions to the jurors, which sounded to me like a garbled mess as my mind refused to track. The only thing I understood was the end. She called for a fifteen-minute recess before Shirley Glade would give her closing statement.

I stood, weak-kneed, as the jurors filed out. When they were gone, I turned and quickly left the courtroom, cutting through the crowd. I went down the hall to the bathroom. My stomach churned violently, and, when I saw an empty stall, I went inside and threw up.

It wasn't nerves. I was finished. There was nothing left for me to do. Shirley Glade would give her closing statement, then we'd just wait. I'd given it everything I had, and how it ended was out of my control.

Exhaustion rolled over me, followed by chills. Slumped against the wall, I concluded that my body's collapse was simply due to the realization of how fast and how far I'd fallen in such a short period of time. Every aspect of my life had changed: work, love, home, family. I rubbed the back of my neck, still clammy with sweat, then flushed the toilet in the hopes that the smell of my vomit would dissipate.

I sat on the worn tile of that sixth-floor bathroom for what seemed like a long time. In silence, I wondered what I was going to do next. I thought about work, love, home, and family; then I began to wonder whether I had really fallen. I lost everything, but did I really?

"Matt, are you in here?" It was Sherman.

"Down here."

He opened the door to the bathroom stall and looked down at me. His eyes narrowed, concerned. "Are you OK?"

"Sort of," I said. "Can you give me a hand?" I held up my hand, and Sherman helped pull me to my feet.

"You gotta get cleaned up, Matt." He guided me over to the sinks and turned on the cold water. "Everybody's been looking for you," he said. "The judge wants to get started."

Shirley Glade wasn't going to give up. She wasn't a quitter, and she was smart enough to know that she had to address the most damaging evidence first. Other defense lawyers would've probably ignored it, hoping the jury would forget. Glade knew that was a mistake. The jurors were not going to forget. She needed to systematically pick each piece of evidence apart or she would surely lose, and Glade the Blade never lost.

"Let's talk about Perry deCristo," Glade said. "The defense called Mr. deCristo to the witness stand because he was Allison Daley's boyfriend and likely the last person to see her. I hope that he is criminally charged with extortion and contempt, but let me be clear: NexBeaux never offered to pay Mr. deCristo, nor did they ever pay him to testify. They certainly never asked that he lie. My belief is that Mr. deCristo was running a scam. He knew we would never pay him, but he thought that maybe the other side would. It wouldn't be the first time that a plaintiff's attorney played fast and loose."

The final comment came as a surprise, and by the time I thought to object, Glade had moved on. "I do not doubt the authenticity of the recording that we all heard, and I was as disturbed as anyone. But there is absolutely no proof that Mr. deCristo ever received any money from my client or anyone affiliated with my client. Mr. deCristo's story was vague, and I never heard a date or time this payoff occurred. I never heard Mr. deCristo provide a name or even a description of who he met with. Like I said"—Shirley Glade put her hand on her hip and cast me a sideways glance—"there was no grand conspiracy. What we had was a drug dealer hustling somebody for money."

Glade then took aim at my attempt to cast all of NexBeaux's expert witnesses in with Perry deCristo. "To equate experts in biochemistry and doctors with the likes of Perry deCristo . . ." Glade shook her head. "That's ridiculous. Yes, our law firm paid these highly educated experts for their time, just as every law firm, whether it represents a defendant or a plaintiff, pays their experts for their time. There is nothing to be ashamed of." She pointed generally at the jurors. "You deserve to know the facts, and we're obligated to bring forth witnesses who will provide you with unbiased information. That's what we did, and what we heard was that addiction is complicated. Allison Daley comes from a family that has struggled with their chemical use, and she likely experienced trauma during her childhood. She was certainly prescribed Bentrax, but to say that Bentrax caused her to automatically become a heroin addict, then eventually overdose, is a step too far removed. Thousands of people who never took a prescription pain medication are addicted to heroin, and thousands of people who have taken prescription pain medications never became addicted to heroin."

Then Glade came at me hard. "Six hundred sixty million is crazy. In fact, a dollar is unwarranted in this case, but six hundred sixty million is insane. Making NexBeaux pay six hundred sixty million for an overdose that we had nothing to do with is simply not right."

Shirley Glade stepped away from the podium. "Here are the facts: Allison Daley did not overdose on Bentrax. She overdosed on heroin. NexBeaux doesn't make or distribute heroin. I'm not saying we should blame Allison. Instead I'm saying that the plaintiffs simply haven't met their burden to hold us liable. That is the only question before you, and the plaintiff has not provided enough real evidence to prove his case. Allison Daley died because she was addicted to heroin, and when she could've gotten treatment, she ran. Allison Daley was surrounded by people who loved her, as well as trained chemical health counselors who were there to help, but, instead, she ran away from the Arch Treatment Center. NexBeaux had no part in that decision.

"Finally, I want to address these so-called smoking-gun documents that the plaintiff is touting every chance he gets. These are nothing more than normal business documents that have been turned into something quite sinister. There is nothing wrong with educating doctors and marketing a product. NexBeaux is a business, after all. It takes millions of dollars to develop a new product, test it, and get it approved through the Food and Drug Administration. Once that is done, NexBeaux will obviously want to recoup their expenses."

Glade paused. "As for the jokes . . ." She shook her head. "Those were totally inappropriate, and I hope that the CEO and anyone else is held accountable. But that's something for NexBeaux's board of directors. A vulgar email doesn't mean that NexBeaux is liable for Allison Daley's overdose. It doesn't establish causation. It is what it is, an inappropriate email."

Glade continued to recap testimony and poke holes in our case against her client. She was fearless and persuasive. She walked right up to the line, but never crossed, and when she sat down, I honestly didn't know what the jurors were going to do.

CHAPTER THIRTY-EIGHT

The jury went back to deliberate, and Judge Bruin asked the attorneys to remain near the courthouse in case of a final verdict or an issue arose where she needed to talk to us. Sometimes jurors submitted questions, which required the presence of the parties as well.

I texted Laura that I was free, and we met at the front of the courthouse. She gave me a hug, then we began to walk down the grassy mall that ran through the middle of downtown Saint Louis from the Arch. I held Laura's hand as my body began to relax.

"How are you feeling?"

"Better than I was after my closing argument," I said. "I think I'm going to stay in bed for a couple weeks when this is really done."

"You deserve it." We kept walking past various abstract sculptures and a small café.

"I'm sorry how it ended," I said. "I'm not sure I really ever apologized, but I want you to know that it was one of the biggest mistakes of my life. If I could take it back, I would, and I know I still have a long way to go to rebuild all the trust that's been lost."

"I might've overreacted," Laura said. "It's that the whole thing gave me flashbacks. I'm thinking that we have something special, then you go run off with Mack Hunter in his private airplane to who knows where."

"I'm not going to do that," I said. "After what happened at Baxter, Speller & Tuft, I don't ever want to work for anyone again. If Mack Hunter wants my help, he'll need to pay me for it as a consultant or something like that, but I'm not going to be his employee."

"So you're going to keep your little office space?"

I considered it. "Maybe," I said. "I've got it for a few more months. Maybe Sherman will reconsider his declaration of never practicing law and work with me. I don't know." I stopped and took Laura's hand. "I just know that I want to be with you." I leaned in and kissed her. "Maybe I'll run one of those marathons."

"You want to go to Australia with me?"

"Sounds perfect."

◆ ◆ ◆

The jury didn't reach a verdict after the first day. As we were dismissed, Judge Bruin told us that we were all on call. We didn't have to come to the courthouse the next day to wait, but we needed to be close by. Since it only took about ten minutes to get downtown from my parents' house, I decided to stay home.

That morning my mother made a big breakfast. Sherman and Jackson came over, and we all ate an enormous amount of pancakes and scrambled eggs. When breakfast was over, Sherman began helping my mom with the dishes, and Jackson and I told my dad that we had a surprise for him.

"A surprise?" He bit his lower lip, skeptical, then grunted. It was something we'd seen him do a million times, but this was different. It was exaggerated, like my dad was parodying a version of himself.

Jackson and I laughed. "Come on, old man." Jackson pushed back from the table and gestured to the door. "Outside." Then we all went down the back steps, and I led my father to the garage.

"I think you're going to like this," I told him.

I pressed a button, and the forty-year-old garage door sprang to life. The chain screeched and the machine growled as the garage door was pulled open. It was likely the first time the inside of the garage had been exposed to sunlight in thirty years.

"Today is the day that the Mustang gets a heart."

"A heart?" My father looked at me, puzzled. "What are you talking about?"

"I just got a text message, and the mechanic is on his way." I took the phone out of my pocket and held in the air as proof. "They're going to tow it to the shop and put an engine in it."

"And brakes and tires," Jackson added. "We want it street legal."

My dad didn't say a word, too stunned to speak.

"We'll get the paint job later," I said. "That's a project for a different day."

My dad put his hand on the car. "That's too expensive," he said. "You shouldn't waste your money."

"It's not a waste of money, Dad," I said, not caring that the last little bit of money remaining after selling the engagement ring was gone. "It's for Allison."

◆ ◆ ◆

On the afternoon of the third day of deliberation, Judge Bruin's law clerk sent messages to all the attorneys that we needed to return to court. The confidence that I had felt in the middle of trial had waned, and now I began second-guessing myself. I wondered whether I overplayed the Perry deCristo testimony or asked for too much money. I wondered whether the jury would punish me for being too greedy.

We rose as the jury entered the courtroom. None of them looked me in the eye, and that spooked me. I had always been taught that no eye contact was a clear sign that the jury did not rule in your favor.

Judge Bruin gave permission for everyone to be seated before addressing the jury. The courtroom was so full, however, that there weren't seats for everyone. A half dozen people stood against the back wall. One of the people standing was Mack Hunter.

When everything had settled down, Judge Bruin began. "Members of the jury, have you selected a foreperson?"

The jurors looked at an older gentleman in the back row. He was wearing khakis and a light-blue golf shirt. He slowly pulled himself out of his seat and stood.

"Mr. Foreman," Judge Bruin said, "has the jury reached a verdict?"

The older gentleman nodded. "We have, Your Honor. As it relates to Count I, false advertising, the jury finds the defendant liable." There was low buzz in the courtroom as everyone exhaled at the same time, adjusted in their seats, and texted the news to people on the outside. "As it relates to Count II, a breach of due care, the jury finds the defendant liable, and as it relates to Count III, public nuisance, we the jury find the defendant liable and award the plaintiff one point one billion dollars."

An entire year's profit on all the opioids sold in America. I sneaked a look at the defense table. Shirley Glade's head was down, and she was furiously scribbling notes. I heard cheers and some clapping from the crowd. Sherman leaned over and squeezed my arm so hard it left a mark, and I felt hands on my back—congratulations—as Judge Bruin tried to restore order.

◆ ◆ ◆

An impromptu party soon erupted at my parents' house. Once again, mostaccioli, gooey butter cake, and toasted ravioli materialized out of thin air. Everybody was there, and spirits were high. I worked my way around the backyard, greeting family members and neighbors. When I got to the cluster of law students, we got a group hug and took a selfie with Sherman.

"I don't know how exactly I'm going to repay you," I said. "But I will repay you."

"How about some jobs when we make it through law school," Cynthia said.

"You're back in school?" I looked at Sherman for confirmation, and he smiled and nodded.

"Somebody needs to tell Matt what happened," Sherman said.

Screw, her hair now bleached white, stepped up. "We got into Saint Louis University," she said. "They're taking our credits, and they cut us a reduced rate to finish up."

"Super reduced," Jeff said. "Just a couple hundred dollars a credit."

"Because of you." Cynthia poked me playfully in the chest. "Professor Friedman told them what we had been doing, what we had been working on and the research that we've done for your case. They were really impressed, and now we're back on track."

"That's wonderful," I said. "Just wonderful." I wanted to let them know that I intended to pay off all their student loans, but I didn't want to get their hopes up. I could only do it when NexBeaux paid, and I'd already heard that Shirley Glade was appealing the decision. It might be years before anything got resolved.

"Enjoy the food and drink," I said as I moved on to Uncle Walt and Aunt Connie. They were sitting in lawn chairs. When Uncle Walt saw me, he sprang to his feet and slapped me on the back. "Nice job, little Matty. Unbelievable." We talked a little more, then I went over to the picnic table and stood on top.

There was more clapping and cheers. "This feels great," I said. "It really does." I looked down at my parents. "I want to take a moment and thank a few people, but the ones I want to thank the most are my mom and dad and my brother, Jackson. They trusted me. They put faith in me, because we knew what happened to Allison was wrong. I am not the perfect son, and I never will be. But I learned so much about myself during this case's ups and downs, and I learned to love this family more than I ever have."

I looked at my mom. "You are a tough woman who nobody can mess with."

I looked at my dad. "I know you are a tough SOB, but underneath you care a lot about us kids. You love us, and I think I know you better today than before."

"And Jackson"—I looked at my brother—"you are insane. You are an example that all redneck socialists should admire and emulate. I love you. I don't want to go back to sharing a bedroom with you, but I love you." I continued, thanking Laura, Sherman, and the law students, then I got to the most important part.

"With everything that has happened, I want to lift up my sister, Allison. She was my big sister and protector. I was her little brother and her tormentor." I took a breath, trying to maintain my composure. "And I love her and I miss her. I threw many years of my life away in New York City, chasing a fantasy that was never going to feed my soul. I wish that I'd been here, and I wish that she could've been in that courtroom today and seen us fight not just for her, but for all the people out there struggling . . ." I paused and looked up at the Saint Louis sky before finishing. "Maybe I stand corrected. Maybe she was in that courtroom all along."

I held my glass high. "To Allison."

The assembled crowd shouted back. "To Allison!"

As the party wound down, Mack Hunter and a small entourage arrived. Nobody invited him, but he had somehow figured out where we were going to be. It didn't take long for him to find me and pull me to the side. "Great work today," he said. "Really great work all around. I'm sorry to crash your party, but I wanted to connect before I head out of town."

"The more the merrier." I really didn't want to talk to Hunter, but I wasn't going to be rude. "I'm taking a break," I said. "but I promise we'll talk."

"I hope so." Hunter leaned in. "You're going to need some help with this appeal. It really isn't surprising, but it's disappointing. I've been there many times. I get a big award from a jury, then the corporate bastards spend years trying to take it away."

"Is that how long you think it will take, years?"

"Might be a little quicker," he said. "You're in state court, not federal court. State appellate courts tend to move faster. State court judges don't have lifetime appointments." He could read my disappointment. "Listen," he said. "Investment banks and hedge funds are buying these things now. If you want to sell the verdict for cash, I know some people who I can put you in touch with."

"A hedge fund?"

"Pennies on the dollar," Hunter said. "But they take on all the risk. That money is yours, and if these other people lose on appeal, that isn't your problem. For some cases, it isn't worth it, but ten cents on one billion dollars is ten million. That ain't a bad place to start."

Ten million. Not a bad way to start at all.

CHAPTER THIRTY-NINE

The day after the verdict, I slept until one in the afternoon. When I woke up, my stomach was queasy. I had a headache, and all my muscles were sore. I felt hung over, even though I had only drunk a few beers at the party. I'd been running on pure adrenaline for a long time, and now, I guess, I had to pay the price.

I got out of bed, showered, and found a little something to eat. Then I went out back and got my bike out of the garage. It was a sunny day, but the heat and humidity of July and August were gone. There was a cool breeze coming from the west, which carried most of the smells from the brewery away from our house.

I biked down Lemp, and by the time I hit Cherokee Street, I was feeling better. It was an easy five-mile ride to Saint Matthews Cemetery. When I arrived, all my aches and pains had been worked out. The fresh air and some moderate exercise were just what I needed.

I got off my bike and set it down on the grass. Then I walked over to Allison's grave, sat down, and just let myself be there, in the moment. I wasn't there to think or to do anything in particular. I just wanted to be present.

I leaned back and absorbed the peace. It was the first time in a very long time that I didn't have a long list of things that I needed to do. I traced the letters of Allison's name on the gravestone. Then I reached into my pocket and removed a copy of the old photograph of Allison,

Jackson, and me on our front step with the Christmas tree. It was the image that I had used in my closing argument.

I stared at the photograph before placing it on her gravestone.

"It's a good picture."

Although I didn't hear him arrive, I turned and saw Jackson standing behind me. "It's the best." Then I chuckled. "Those darn Daley kids again, always causing trouble."

"Exactly," Jackson said as he helped me up. We walked over to my bike, then I rolled it over to Jackson's truck. He lifted it over the side and into the back. "You ready to try fishing again?"

"Beautiful day, and I don't have anything better to do."

An hour or so later we were back on Lake Lincoln trying to find a place where the fish would bite. Jackson, of course, had already pulled out a couple of bass, but I was having a harder time.

"No bobbers," Jackson said before I could even ask.

"Then hand me a beer instead." I secured my fishing rod in a black holder so that, if a fish did take my bait, I wouldn't end up in the lake like last time or lose the rod. With my hands now free, I told Jackson I was ready. He leaned over, flipped open the top of a little cooler, and tossed me a beer.

I caught it and decided that I'd be just fine if I didn't catch a fish. Hanging out in a boat on a beautiful day was enough. I leaned back and closed my eyes. The journey had been wild. I thought about sitting at my parents' picnic table with my laptop and starting to write the lawsuit, the press conference at Cahokia College of Law, the start of trial, and the moment when the verdict was read.

Shirley Glade must still be mad.

I thought about her closing argument. It was as strong and as well done as any closing argument that I'd ever heard. She hit all the right notes, and maybe another jury would've decided the verdict differently.

I opened my eyes and took a sip of beer, then I looked at my brother. "Hey, Jackson," I said. "I've been thinking."

"That's usually what I try and avoid when I'm out here on this boat." Jackson reeled in his line, briefly examined the bait, and cast it out again.

"You know what Shirley Glade said about Perry? The stuff about how there was never any details about who offered to pay him or how this person got in contact with him? Was it, like, at a bar, or did the mystery man come to where he's living? And it was kind of unclear whether he got the money or was just promised the money. I mean, everything was really vague."

Jackson didn't respond. He just kept casting his line, slowly reeling it in, and repeating the gesture. His attention was focused on the water, so I kept going.

"So then, I wonder . . . maybe Shirley Glade was right. Maybe he was just hustling us. Maybe the whole thing about NexBeaux paying him was a lie."

Jackson threw out his line, then he glanced over at me. "Possible." Then he got back to fishing. I watched Jackson cast out his line while I drank my beer. Each movement was smooth and perfectly timed. He kept hitting a spot about three feet away from a fallen tree, near the edge of where the cattails and lily pads had taken over.

"But that doesn't make much sense either," I said. "Because, if it was all a lie in order to hustle us, and we didn't pay him and NexBeaux didn't pay him, why on earth would he lie for NexBeaux on the witness stand?" I finished my beer, crushed the can, and put it on the floor by my feet.

"Don't know." Jackson didn't look at me this time. "Need another beer?"

"Sure," I said, so Jackson held his rod with one hand and retrieved a beer for me with the other. I caught the toss, opened the can, and continued. "It doesn't make any sense. Why wouldn't he just tell the truth?"

"It's a real mystery." Jackson soon got back into the rhythm, casting and reeling in the line. "You're a total Hardy Boy."

I ignored the comment. "But then I think that maybe there's something more going on," I said. "Like, let's pretend that he just testified honestly. Maybe it helps NexBeaux or maybe it doesn't. At the end of the day, Perry is an addict." I took a drink. "But what if Perry really loved Allison? Like in his own messed-up way. What if he wanted to help us, and so when one of NexBeaux's investigators interviews him, he says all this bad stuff about Allison so that Shirley Glade calls him as a witness and then he messes with their case? And what better way of undermining NexBeaux's credibility than a story about how NexBeaux was paying him off?"

Jackson stopped. He reeled in his line, then he turned to me. "I think you're thinking too much."

"You're right," I said. "Plus, for something like that to work, Perry would need help. He'd need somebody really smart to pull it off." I took a drink of my beer. "Somebody on the inside who could feed me information and who is even clever enough to record a conversation, but protect me by keeping me out of the loop if something went wrong."

Jackson cocked his head to the side. "Hypothetically," he said, "that sounds about right."

"Hypothetically." I smiled. "Of course, everything is hypothetical."

ACKNOWLEDGMENTS

I want to thank all the people at Thomas & Mercer for continuing to support me and creating a space for this book to grow. I especially want to thank Megha Parekh and Matthew Patin for their good ideas, thoughts, and critical feedback. I also want to acknowledge all the people out there who live life one day at a time, waking up with the question: What do I need to do today to stay sober? The path is not always straight, but the destination is certainly worthy.

ABOUT THE AUTHOR

Photo © 2016 Gwen Kosiak

J. D. Trafford, the award-winning author of *Good Intentions*, has topped numerous Amazon bestseller lists, including reaching #1 on the Legal Thrillers list. IndieReader selected his debut novel, *No Time to Run*, as a bestselling pick, and *Little Boy Lost* was an Amazon Charts bestseller. Trafford graduated with honors from a top-twenty law school and has worked as a civil and criminal prosecutor; as an associate at a large national law firm; and as a nonprofit attorney handling issues related to housing, education, and poverty in communities of color. He lives with his wife and children in the Midwest and bikes whenever possible. For more information on the author, visit www.jdtrafford.com.